J.B. had five seconds to get clear

He sprinted from the barn, arms pumping, five seconds to get to cover, five seconds to do the impossible. The howls and taunts of the bikers cut the air to his left, the growl of their engines generating a terrible drone.

J.B. was across the road in an instant, dislodged dirt skipping away beneath his boots. Up ahead, the tall stalks of corn waited like a fence, impossibly thin struts. Thirty feet away, the stalks were on fire, dark smoke wafting across the road as J.B. raced into the brush.

He dived to the ground, arms outstretched, holding the mini-Uzi far from his body. The bikes were close now, roaring past the barn in a cacophony of straining engines.

Then the building went up like a rocket, the interior expanding in a series of massive explosions that reached out to engulf the bikers, giving the companions a chance.

Other titles in the
Deathlands saga:

JAMES AXLER

DEATH LANDS®

End Program

A GOLD EAGLE BOOK FROM

W✇RLDWIDE®

TORONTO • NEW YORK • LONDON
AMSTERDAM • PARIS • SYDNEY • HAMBURG
STOCKHOLM • ATHENS • TOKYO • MILAN
MADRID • WARSAW • BUDAPEST • AUCKLAND

**Recycling programs
for this product may
not exist in your area.**

First edition May 2014

ISBN-13: 978-0-373-62626-7

END PROGRAM

"The black curtain is the instant when the eyes shut."
—Koji Suzuki,
Ring, 1991

THE DEATHLANDS SAGA

This world is their legacy, a world born in the violent nuclear spasm of 2001 that was the bitter outcome of a struggle for global dominance.

There is no real escape from this shockscape where life always hangs in the balance, vulnerable to newly demonic nature, barbarism, lawlessness.

But they are the warrior survivalists, and they endure—in the way of the lion, the hawk and the tiger, true to nature's heart despite its ruination.

Ryan Cawdor: The privileged son of an East Coast baron. Acquainted with betrayal from a tender age, he is a master of the hard realities.

Krysty Wroth: Harmony ville's own Titian-haired beauty, a woman with the strength of tempered steel. Her premonitions and Gaia powers have been fostered by her Mother Sonja.

J. B. Dix, the Armorer: Weapons master and Ryan's close ally, he, too, honed his skills traversing the Deathlands with the legendary Trader.

Doctor Theophilus Tanner: Torn from his family and a gentler life in 1896, Doc has been thrown into a future he couldn't have imagined.

Dr. Mildred Wyeth: Her father was killed by the Ku Klux Klan, but her fate is not much lighter. Restored from pre-dark cryogenic suspension, she brings twentieth-century healing skills to a nightmare.

Jak Lauren: A true child of the wastelands, reared on adversity, loss and danger, the albino teenager is a fierce fighter and loyal friend.

Dean Cawdor: Ryan's young son by Sharona accepts the only world he knows, and yet he is the seedling bearing the promise of tomorrow.

In a world where all was lost, they are humanity's last hope....

Chapter One

Ryan lay flat on his back, naked, cold. He stared up into black, nothingness all around him. He raised his head, struck something just an inch above his forehead and felt pain run through his face. The pain made his nose twitch, as if he needed to sneeze, and a flash of brightness seemed to lance across his eyes in a firework burst.

He moved more cautiously the second time, arms first, feeling around him. There were walls to either side of where he lay, their cool hardness running the length of his body. Ryan estimated that there was no more than an inch gap between the limits of his broad shoulders and those cool walls, as if he had been placed in a narrow tunnel.

He flexed his feet, noticing for the first time that he was not wearing his boots. Those boots had been with him for more miles of Deathlands road than he cared to remember. He would have removed them to sleep, but he could not recall where or when that had been. But now he was naked, his body cold.

When he stretched his toes, he felt another wall, pressing close enough that he could not stretch his feet to their fullest extension. Above too, a wall or roof pressed at his feet, and he could not bend his knees without meeting it.

Where was he?

His face still hurt. It was more than just the sudden

shock of striking the panel above him, he knew. There was a rawness there, running down the left side of his face, where he had lost an eye to his deranged brother, Harvey, who had made a power grab to rule the barony of Front Royal. That had been a long time ago, before Trader, before J.B. and the others, before the long roads of the Deathlands.

Something nagged at Ryan as he thought that, and he reached up to his face and probed gently, tracing the cicatrix scar and continuing to the eye patch that should cover his missing eye. The patch was gone.

Ryan closed his eyelids and touched at the depression of flesh all around his left eye, reaching for the alien thing he could sense was there. When his fingers touched the surface of the eyelid, he could feel something hard pressing back: An eye? He had an eye where he not had an eye in more than twenty years.

"An eye," Ryan whispered, barely believing it. The words hissed out and were gone, but saying them somehow made it more real in the darkness.

He ran the tips of his fingers across the surface of the closed eyelid, brought up his other hand and did the same with his right eye. They felt similar but different. The right eye gave under a little pressure, sprung, like a lump of jelly quivering on a plate. The left eye was harder with no give, more like a rock that had been planed off and worked into the empty socket.

He had been cycloptic for so long that he had almost forgotten what it had felt like to have two eyes, the way it changed how one saw dimensions and distance. In darkness, Ryan could tell nothing about the new orb that resided within his left socket. It could be dead, unworkable.

Ryan drew his fingers away and opened his eyes,

staring into the darkness once more. He could see nothing, just blackness, the way the countryside got at night when the moon was in hiding and the stars had been painted over by clouds. And yet, he could see something, the way that even in complete darkness a person could still see something—edges, shapes.

"Where am I?" Ryan muttered, reaching up again for that panel that rested above him. "And how the nuking hell did I get here?"

His mind drifted back, recalling the last hours that he could remember.

Chapter Two

It had been raining right outside the mat-trans chamber. Ryan and his six companions had materialized inside the familiar hexagonal chamber, whose armaglass walls were tinted the color of grass at the height of summer, when it had not seen water for a month.

Ryan had led the way out, opening the chamber door, his blaster—a SIG Sauer P226—held ready in his right hand: mat-trans jumping was dangerous.

The mat-trans was a matter-transfer system used by the U.S. military, with sender-receiver units located in hidden redoubts dotted across what had once been the United States of America and several other countries. The United States was no longer what it once was, ruined by the nuclear exchange of 2001 that had seen the U.S. and its ideological counterpart, the Soviet Union, engage in a push-button conflict that had lasted little more than a few hours. Afterward, North America and other parts of the world had been left in scarred ruins.

After the nukecaust came the radiation, warping what survived into something that at times was barely endurable. A hundred years later, Ryan and his companions trekked the lost roads of what was now known as the Deathlands, hoping to find something better, searching for a promise of a better tomorrow.

The companions used the mat-trans to travel the Deathlands, but their method of transportation was unreliable. A CD containing destination codes had been lost, so when they entered the chamber and initiated a jump, they never knew where they'd end up.

However, the mat-trans had one advantage over conventional travel—it was by and large secret, and utilized by few others.

"All clear here," Ryan announced as he stepped from the mat-trans doorway, crossed the anteroom and scanned the control room immediately beyond.

The one-eyed man stood in an area that resembled a predark greenhouse, with rain pouring through a large gap in the roof. That meant that this part of the redoubt was aboveground. Plants were everywhere, corded creepers twisting down the walls and across the surfaces of the ancient comp desks that ran in twin lines through the control room. Reeds and ferns spread across the room in spearheads, one group driving into the other like some alien game of chess. Flowers were dotted here and there, spotting the room with flourishes of color, as if a deranged artist had dropped paint on the swath of green.

Ancient lights flickered to life, automatically engaged by the movement sensors that detected that the mat-trans had been operated. The lights flickered for a few seconds before finally dying. Ryan peered at the ceiling. The fluorescent lights had been overwhelmed by creeping vines. Luckily, the hole in the roof provided enough illumination.

The floor was soft, and when Ryan looked down he saw a thick green carpet of moss stretched across the whole room beneath the plants. It smelled of life and of decay.

Ryan was a tall man with broad shoulders and a curly mane of black hair. His face, considered by some to be handsome, was hard and lean, bearing the scars of that life-or-death struggle with his brother, Harvey. He wore a black leather eye patch over his missing left eye, the tied knot hidden within his thick hair.

Ryan was followed from the mat-trans by his second-in-command, a shorter man called John Barrymore—or J.B.—Dix. He wore a battered brown fedora and a pair round-framed spectacles was propped on his nose. An expert in blasters, explosives and booby traps, J.B. was also known as "the Armorer." He was the companions' weaponsmith.

He stepped from the mat-trans door with a mini-Uzi in his hands, while other weaponry was hidden in various pockets and pouches. J.B. also carried a satchel on a leather strap crosswise over his chest, within which were detonators, explosives and a variety of ammunition and spare parts.

Jak Lauren, the third member of the group and a unique presence in any environment, sniffed the air as he crept from the mat-trans chamber.

"Smell wrong," Jak said, shaking his head.

A few inches over five feet tall, Jak was a slim man with the physique of an adolescent.. He was an albino, with chalk-white skin and bone-white hair, and eyes the color of blood. He moved fluidly like a stalking cat, his .357 Magnum Colt Python blaster raised and ready in his hands. Jak was a master of the blade, and had several throwing knives secreted about his clothing.

Behind Jak, the remaining members of Ryan's team were passing through the chamber doorway and anteroom, then into the redoubt's control room.

First came Krysty Wroth, a tall, curvaceous woman of stunning beauty whose vivid emerald eyes were mesmerizing. But it was always her long, bright red hair that people noticed first because it seemed to be almost alive. In fact, Krysty's hair was very much alive—she was a mutie, and her hair responded to her circumstances and moods, twisting or uncurling depending on her state of mind.

"It smells okay to me," Krysty said with a smile.

The next member of the group laughed at Krysty's comment. "Jak always thinks something's wrong," he said. He was a handsome youth named Ricky Morales, sixteen years old with shiny black hair and dark brown eyes. He held his Webley Mk VI revolver so casually in one hand that it gave the impression that he had been carrying the weapon since birth. Ricky hailed from a small seaport on an island once known as Puerto Rico but was now called Monster Island. An even-tempered youth with a happy-go-lucky attitude, Ricky had traveled with the companions only a short time, but he fit in well. He looked up to Ryan and the others, especially J.B., who reminded him of his uncle, Benito, who had been a weaponsmith too.

Striding behind Ricky, Doc Tanner thrust his ebony sword stick in front of his younger companion to draw his attention. Doc was dressed in a long black frock coat with a dirt-stained white shirt and dark pants beneath. "Watch your tongue, lad," Doc said. "Jak hass never steered us wrong."

Ricky began to argue but stopped himself. Doc was right, he knew. These people had worked together without him for a long time, and the fact that they had survived all that time was a testament to their effectiveness as a unit. Gently mocking Jak's pessimism was one thing; questioning the albino was quite something else.

"Sorry," Ricky said, turning his head from Doc to Jak. "I was just kidding around."

"No harm done," Doc said, lowering his sword stick. He was a tall man, almost scarecrowlike in appearance, with long silver-white hair. Doc looked old but that appearance belied a far more complicated life story. A man of great learning, Doc had been born in the year 1868 and for the first thirty-odd years had enjoyed a relatively ordinary life. However, in 1896, Doc had been the unwilling subject of time trawling technology and had found himself scooped out of his own time period and taken to the twentieth century to be studied by the white-coated scientists of Project Chronos.

However, Doc proved a rather less pacific subject than the whitecoats had hoped, and so in a second twist of cruel fate, he had been flung another hundred into the future, into the Deathlands. The shock of such time travel had left Doc artificially aged, so while his features and body were that of a man of some sixty or more years, his mind still clung to the memory of being far younger. To further compound his difficulties, the time journeys had left Doc's mind addled, and while he suffered fewer bouts of madness these days, his early days with Ryan's crew had been marred by heightened stress levels, panic attacks and the general sense of not really knowing who or where he was.

Despite all that, Doc was a valuable asset to the group, not only for his knowledge of the predark world, but also on the far more practical level of his ability with a blaster. Doc's weapon of choice was a replica LeMat pistol.

The final member of the group was a stocky, African-American woman named Mildred Wyeth, who, like Doc, was born in another era, but who had traveled through time in a rather more conventional manner. She had been born in 1964, and eventually became a physician, specializing in cryogenic research.

While in her mid-thirties, Mildred suffered complications during abdominal surgery. In an attempt to save her life, the decision had been made to cryogenically preserve her—just a few days before the nuclear conflict erupted. She had been freed from her frozen capsule by Ryan's crew. She had remained with them ever since, forming a romantic bond with J.B. and providing the ongoing field medicine necessary to the group.

"Don't tease the kid, Doc," Mildred warned, an undercurrent to her tone. She liked Ricky—in some ways he reminded her of her brother, Josh, when he had been that age.

"I am not teasing," Doc replied. "I am just setting the lad straight lest he ignore the warnings of his elders."

Mildred shook her head. "'Elders.' I never did like that term."

Mildred and Doc's bickering was a constant, but it was good-natured. On this occasion, Doc let the point go—they needed to be alert right now, ready at the drop of a hat to face potential dangers in this new environment.

The companions made their way through the knee-deep foliage that had all but overtaken the interior of the control room.

It was unusual to see a redoubt this close to the surface. Most of them were located deep underground, and all had been designed to repel direct bombardment by weaponry up to and including a nuclear bomb. Whether they could survive a nuke was not certain, but anything short of that would struggle to make a dent. However, what the redoubts had not been built to withstand were the vast tectonic and environmental shifts that had racked the Earth since the nukecaust. What weapons had failed to do, Mother Nature had done with aplomb, mashing the plates of the earth together beneath the redoubt and opening up a great fissure in the foundations. It was this shift that had caused chunks of the redoubt to break open, creating the vast hole in the redoubt's ceiling.

Doc followed the group past the channel of pouring rain, passing his sword stick through it and taking a moment to examine the results. The sword stick was jet-black with a silver lion's head handle. Few knew that a sword was hidden within the walking cane.

The rain clung to the sword stick, glistening there with a wisp of vapor. "The lad is correct," Doc agreed as he sniffed at the rain. "There is a definite tang to this downpour. We must be careful."

"We always are," Ryan responded, pushing his way through the room to a sliding door of vanadium steel that would grant them access to the corridor outside. A keypad, stained brown where its metal casing had rusted, was located beside the door set in the concrete wall to the right. Ryan punched in the usual 3-5-2 code which would open the door. He detected a hiss coming from his left, but the metal door refused to move aside.

Standing at Ryan's side, J.B. eyed the door and sucked thoughtfully at his teeth.

"Jammed tight," Ryan confirmed. While doors, like the lighting in the redoubt, would have been automatically reengaged with the activation of the mat-trans the dense vegetation or the humidity had obviously infiltrated and corrupted the mechanics.

"Want me to blast it open?" J.B. asked. The Armorer was adept with explosives as well as firearms—it would be little effort for him to obliterate the door.

"No," Ryan said after a few seconds' consideration. "We'll go up instead," he said, indicating the hole in the ceiling. "It's the path of least resistance."

J.B. nodded, and the two men joined the other companions in contemplating the easiest route to the opening above them.

"Jak? Do you reckon you can get up there and drop a line to us?"

Jak grinned, looking somehow sinister in the ghostly light that ebbed through the gap above, and holstered his blaster.

"Just watch out for the acid rain. If it gets worse, you could get burned," J.B. reminded as Jak scrambled up the sturdy-looking trunk of a creeper and worked his way farther into the canopy.

In a few seconds, Jak was balancing upright as he made his way along a length of thick branch to the hole above. The albino was catlike in his movements, displaying a sense of balance that bordered on superhuman. As he reached the gap in the roof, Jak shrugged the sleeves of his jacket down his arms, using them to cover his hands as much as he could. The mild acid rain wouldn't chill him, but it would eat away at his skin if it the acid content became stronger. Once the companions were outside, they would have to rig some kind of temporary canopy or umbrella-type system to keep the worst of the downpour off until it abated.

Jak reached up and slipped through the hole in the roof and onto the ground outside the redoubt. Grayish sunlight pushed through the cloud cover from the masked white orb that sat low on the horizon.

Jak looked around, scenting the air. He was in a forest with plants of the tropical variety, lush and green, slick with droplets of rainwater on their waxy leaves.

The mild acid rain seemed not to bother them in any way. The ground was soft, sodden with water. The area smelled of soil mingled with the acidic tang of the polluted rainwater.

As Jak looked around, Ryan's voice echoed from twenty feet below him. "Everything okay up there, Jak?" Ryan asked.

"Look okay," Jak called, peering around at the thick foliage. As he did, he spotted a face nearly hidden in the tangled vines and other vegetation. It was a human face, dark-skinned and almost camouflaged amid the lush greenery, the top of the man's head rose about six feet from the ground. But there was something not quite right about it, Jak felt, even as he took a step closer.

He parted a web of overhanging fronds with his left hand, slipping his Colt Python from its holster at his hip with his right and seeing the man fully for the first time. Only it wasn't a man—not entirely. Beneath the head was a stub of neck that ended in a pair of lungs, caged not by ribs but by a clawlike arrangement branches that surrounded the spongy sacks as they inflated and deflated. There was no body, only branches of pallid green, as thick as a man's arm and dotted with spiny thorns their full lengths. Automatically, Jak did a swift count of the spiny-covered branches—eight in all—saw that three of them reached above the head, entwining with the taller cover of the looming trees.

This was new, Jak realized. He had seen muties before; the Deathlands was populated by a variety of abominations. But this thing, part man, part plant—it reminded him of a vine master.

Warily, the albino took another step closer, his eyes fixed on the monstrosity before him. He couldn't work out if the man was a part of the plant, or if he had been partially consumed by it. His skin was dark with a greenish hue, the veins showing thickly along the forehead and neck like fingers under the skin. His eyes were open but glazed, and Jak realized that he had not yet seen the man blink.

"Jak?" Ryan called from the redoubt. "Everything okay?"

Jak turned his head to call back, and as he did so the mutie plant started to writhe, spiny branches undulating as they rose from the ground.

"Am—" Jak began, then turned back as he spotted the thing reaching for him.

Instinctively, Jak ducked as the plant-man reached for him with a writhing tentacle-like branch. The branch struck Jak across his flank, hitting with such force that he tumbled to the ground. Then the writhing limb was dancing in the air above him like a snake. Jak blinked back his momentarily blurred vision, and he heard a popping noise like cracking ice as a fleet of three-inch-long, spiny thorns launched from the branch toward him, racing through the air like bullets.

Chapter Three

The cloud of thorns hurtled toward Jak. He saw them and rolled, moving faster than he could consciously think, pulling up the collar of his jacket even as the thorns thudded against his back. The garment held, the tough fabric repelling most of the spines, a handful embedding up and down its length. Around him, hunks of trees and bushes were obliterated, cut to ribbons by the deadly onslaught.

Jak scrambled forward like a predark sprinter at the starting blocks, launching from the ground back onto his feet. He sprinted back toward the hole in the ground where the redoubt was located.

Behind Jak, the mutie plant's limbs flailed through the air, sending a second volley of thorns at his retreating figure. Jak peered back over his shoulder just once, saw the way the plant was moving, long, snakelike roots pulling up from the soil and slivering across the ground, propelling itself after him. Amid the green leaves, the man-face was strained, mouth open, eyes wide, watching Jak angrily as the plant trailed across the ground. Jak whipped up his Colt Python pistol and fired a lone .357 Magnum bullet at the face looming in the heart of the monster. He had turned away by the time the bullet struck, but he heard the swish of leaves tearing as the projectile slapped against the plant's greenery.

DOWN BELOW, RYAN and his companions heard the shot and went on high alert.

"Triple red, people," Ryan ordered, bringing his blaster up to cover the hole in the ceiling through which Jak had exited the redoubt. "We don't know if that was Jak or someone else—"

"It was Jak," J.B. confirmed. "Sound of a Colt Python, can't mistake it."

"What if someone else has the same weapon, John Barrymore?" Doc asked without looking away from the hole, his LeMat trained on the tiny patch of sky that could be seen through it. "Or what if they took it."

"Point taken," J.B. said, "though it'd be a bastard coincidence if it was someone else's."

Before the companions could discuss the issue further, Jak leaped through the opening above them, moving with the agility of a monkey. Behind and above Jak, the companions saw the thick, trailing cords of the mutie plant as it reached into the hole. In a second, it launched another wave of razor-sharp thorns—straight into the redoubt.

"Gaia!" Krysty cried as Jak came into sight.

"Get back!" Jak screamed as he dropped through the gap in the ceiling.

His six companions stepped back without question, and the clutch of thorns thudded against leaves and the hard surfaces of the walls and floor, striking with rattling beats. Doc took two on his left sleeve, while three more struck J.B.'s fedora—but none of them penetrated its target.

"By the Three Kennedys!" Doc gasped, brushing the thorns from his coat before they scratched him.

"What the hell is that?" Ricky hissed, stepping forward and raising his Webley Mk VI to target the shadowy mutie plant as it reached through the hole.

"Get back, kid," J.B. cautioned, reaching forward and shoving Ricky back. The youth was adventurous and courageous, but he had an impetuous streak that could get them all into trouble, J.B. knew, if he didn't keep his eyes on him.

Jak stood on a branch twelve feet above the floor of the control room. He leaped, tucking and rolling as he landed amid the dense foliage, his blaster clutched close to his chest.

"Friend of yours?" Krysty asked as Jak recovered at her feet.

"Angry plant," Jak replied, turning to face the gap in the ceiling.

"So I see," Krysty stated.

Impossibly, the plant lunged into the redoubt, roots trailing behind it, branches flailing ahead like the limbs of an octopus. With the plant blocking the hole in the roof, the control room became suddenly darker, its details lost in shadow. Whatever the plant was, it had a hunting nature and a rudimentary instinct, chasing after the young man who had disturbed its resting place.

The human face in its center eyed the companions in the semidarkness, eyeballs swiveling. It spotted Mildred with her colourful beaded plaits and sent one of its snakelike limbs toward her. The limb was fifteen feet in length and lined with thorns and budding flowers the color of sour milk.

Mildred stepped back and blasted a shot from her ZKR 551 target pistol, the weapon booming in the underground chamber. The bullet struck the limb, carving a line along its surface before embedding halfway down its length. At the same moment, another cluster of thorns spit from its surface, striking her along the left side of her torso and both legs.

Mildred yelled in pain, dropping to the floor.

The limb flailed toward her face, but Doc stepped in to block it, slicing at it with his sword stick. Then he fired his LeMat directly into the crook of the joint where that limb met the trunk. There was no time to check on Mildred's condition.

Across the room, J.B. and Ryan were busy fencing with another limb.

"Ugly green son of a bitch," J.B. snarled as he fired a burst of 9 mm bullets at the flailing limb.

The narrow end of the spiny protrusion whipped around and around like a bolo before grabbing J.B.'s blaster arm and yanking him off his feet.

J.B. yelled in agony as he was lifted from the floor and felt the thorns digging into him. Ryan took careful aim, holding his SIG Sauer in a two-handed grip. The one-eyed man squeezed the trigger, sending a 9 mm slug into the limb that clutched his oldest friend. The Swiss bullet drilled into and through the limb, three inches in diameter, pulling a great gout of green bark and fibrous material with it as it emerged from the other side.

There was a sound like splitting wood and suddenly, the fractured plant limb struggled with J.B.'s weight, swaying to and fro as it tried to hang on to its victim. Still in its grip, J.B. brought around the muzzle of his mini-Uzi until it pointed at the core of the plant, where that human torso rested amid the green. Then he fired, holding down the trigger for a short burst as the limb tossed him left and right. The volley of 9 mm bullets punched into the main stem of the plant in a line of dark circles, moving upward toward the human lungs and face in its center. As the bullets reached for the man within, other parts of the plant seemed to lunge forward—thick, waxy leaves swishing across the path of the bullets like a gaudy slut doing an old-style fan dance, each fan shuttering into place.

"The man's the driver," J.B. hollered as he swayed six feet off the ground, still snagged in the plant's grip. "Chill him and we might get out of here with our asses inta—"

J.B.'s statement was cut short as he was slammed headfirst into a wall by the flailing limb, the brim of his fedora snapping back, his throat issuing a croak of pain.

Ryan took another shot, lining up carefully with the figure in the center of the mutie plant. Around him, Ricky, Jak and Krysty were doing the same while Doc thrust and parried a lively limb with his sword cane.

Thorns whizzed from the fast-moving limbs, hammering into the walls and striking the companions as they fought.

Ricky held his hand up to shield his eyes as a wave of thorns rattled against him, ripping threads from his clothes and embedding themselves into his flesh.

The mutie plant loomed through the gap in the ceiling, half in and half out of the control room, but it was large enough to crowd the room itself. A tendril lashed toward Ryan as he loosed another shot from the SIG Sauer, whipping him across the face and knocking him back.

"Fireblast!" Ryan yelled as he toppled backward, slamming against the overgrowth, the leaves and ferns forming a soft bed beneath him. He was momentarily disorientated, the hard impact of the floor cushioned only slightly by the springiness of the flattened leaves. Ryan heard a whisper of sound, felt fléchettes of thorns pepper his chest and face, digging in with vicious precision.

Across the room, Jak found himself tangled with one of the vines, one arm and both legs trapped in the whipcordlike tendril as it snaked around him. Jak grunted as the vine pressed against his chest and legs, lifting him up from the floor. His blaster hand was trapped, the Colt Python useless where it was pressed against his right leg as if he had been tied.

Jak struggled as the mutie plant dragged him over the undergrowth.

"Got me!" Jak shouted, trying to alert his companions. But even as he said it he could see that only Krysty and Doc remained standing and they were both busy with their own battles. The plant, it seemed, could multitask, combating multiple foes at once.

Jak was dragged up high into the room, and he dipped his head as the ceiling came racing toward him.

Crash!

Jak found himself slammed against the ceiling, gasping as pain erupted across his back and his right shoulder began to go numb. Then he felt something squeeze against him where the plant held him, like a boa constrictor ensnaring its prey. Jak felt the press of spines against him, pushing through the protective material of his clothes.

He twisted and turned in place, felt the rain patter against his skin as he was dragged through the hole in the roof. His blaster was useless where it was, but his left arm was still free. In a fraction of second, Jak flipped his wrist in a sharp movement and a throwing knife dropped into his hand from his sleeve. As he was drawn toward the human head amid the monstrous plant, Jak thrust the knife forward, stabbing the man's face right across the jaw. A gout of flesh and sap went sailing into the air, and the man made a kind of ticking noise from somewhere deep in his throat.

"Let. Go. Me," Jak snarled, forcing out the words as the pressure of the vines increased on his ribs and lungs.

Still inside the room, Krysty heard Jak's strained words and looked up. She was fencing with another of those tendrillike vines, this one thick as a person's leg. The tendril kept trying to cinch around Krysty's feet and she kept dancing out of its way, using the butt of her blaster to rain hammer blows against it rather than waste precious bullets.

At Jak's call, Krysty leaped over the swinging tendril as it made another pass for her, grabbing an overhanging branch and pulling herself up from the floor. As she clambered up the branch, she called to Doc, who had drawn his sword from its sheath and was hacking at the writhing tendrils of the plant.

"Doc! Jak needs our help!"

Surrounded by a cloud of debris he had hacked from the living plant, Doc looked up, his pale blue eyes sweeping past Krysty's hurrying figure and up to where Jak was being drawn toward the human face that waited at the plant's core.

Krysty began to chant quietly, calling on the goddess of the Earth, Gaia, who had gifted the women of Krysty's family with an incredible power. Krysty felt a surge of strength rush through her, like a jolt of electricity firing through her muscles, igniting every artery, every vein. With the surge of strength came speed and stamina, turning the titian-haired woman superhuman for just a brief period.

With the power channeling through her, Krysty skipped over a grasping tendril as a wave of thorns launched from its surface. The thorns punctured her jeans and she was spattered with sap, but she felt no pain from the impact, merely kept moving through the vegetation toward the squirming thing that loomed above. Her hair seemed to jut around her in lightning bolts now, great slashes of red encircling her face like blood held frozen in the air.

Behind Krysty, Doc raised his LeMat and rested his finger against the secondary trigger, the one that would unleash a blast from the shotgun barrel.

The mutie plant jabbed at Krysty with its tendrils, but she batted them aside, yanking one so hard that it snapped in a shower of gooey yellow sap. Jak was above her now, his feet dangling inches above Krysty's head.

Without slowing, Krysty leaped, grabbing the thick vine that had wrapped around her pale-skinned partner and pulling herself up. The vine struggled with the weight of two bodies, and as Krysty rocked it the vine sagged toward the floor, depositing Jak there with a thump. The tendril was still wrapped around the albino, thorns digging into his clothes and the flesh beneath. Krysty took a secure hold of the tendril midway between where it held Jak and where it emerged from the stalk. And then she pulled, yanking both sides apart, twisting and ripping until they split, vomiting a splurge of yellow gunk as they tore.

From across the room, Doc's voice carried with eminent clarity. "Krysty—get down!"

Krysty dropped, her red hair trailing behind her like a flame. Then Doc squeezed the trigger of the LeMat, sending a burst of buckshot at the heart of the predatory plant. The sound of the blaster was like the crack of thunder in the enclosed space. In the center of the plant, the man's face and neck exploded as the buckshot struck, chunks of flesh, leaf and branch sailing in all directions.

The plant wavered for a moment, unleashing the last of its projectile thorns in a cruel flinch that peppered the room with debris, rattling against the armaglass of the mat-trans chamber with a sound like rain on a tin roof. Then, finally, it was still.

Doc let out a breath he hadn't realized he had been holding, his blaster still pointing at the center of the sagging plant. "Is...is everyone all right?" he asked.

Jak lay on the floor gasping, like a man who had been drowning tasting air thought lost. The tendril was still cinched around him, but the pressure had eased. Krysty crouched beside him, using the last vestiges of her enhanced strength to untangle Jak from his attacker. The Gaia power's fury could be measured in heartbeats, long enough to save a companion's life but not enough to change the world. In its aftermath, Krysty began to weaken, feeling utterly drained. As she loosened the tangle from Jak, he pulled his right hand free and helped her, producing another of his knives from a hidden sheath and using that to hack at the last of the sickly green limb.

Across the room, Ryan lay in agony, spines from the plant embedded across his face and chest. Mildred had recovered and, though woozy, she made her way past overgrown comp consoles to assist Ryan. He clawed at his face, plucking the thorns away before they could sink any deeper. They were nasty things, barbed down their sides with little spiny hairs that felt like needles pulling at the skin when Ryan removed them. A big thorn had embedded in the leather patch that masked his missing left eye, and Mildred pulled the whole patch away. Ryan hissed as the thorn's point scratch at his flesh.

"You're okay now," Mildred soothed. "It's okay." Though she said that, she saw that Ryan's face was dotted with black spines.

J.B. emerged from the deep vegetation close to the door of the room, wiping blood from his split lip and brushing himself down. He was scratched all over and he walked heavily, as if he had hurt one of his legs, but he seemed mobile at least.

"People," he said, getting the attention of the others. "Our troubles aren't over yet."

"What do you mean, J.B.?" Ricky asked. He was still disentangling himself from a wreath of spiny briars, pulling them carefully away from the bare skin of his hands and arms.

"The mat-trans took a hit," J.B. said, nodding toward the armaglass walls of the chamber, which were now almost entirely hidden behind the creeping vines of the mutie plant. The little that could be seen of the tinted glass was pocked with hundreds of thorns, their dark spiny protrusions trailing across the surface. The walls creaked ominously.

"*¡Salir!*" Ricky cried. "How will we use—?"

"I'm thinking it might be now or never, kid," J.B. interrupted as he strode hurriedly toward the mat-trans. "These walls are supposed to be tough, but I have a feeling that they won't last more than a few minutes under that pressure."

"Can we remove the creepers?" Krysty asked weakly.

In reply J.B. merely shrugged before turning his attention to Jak.

"What did you see up there? Anything worth sticking around for?"

Sitting on the floor, plucking thorns from his jacket, Jak shook his head. "Leaves everywhere. Sun hidin', rain pissin'."

J.B. was the unofficial second-in-command of the group, and he accepted the leadership role when the situation demanded it. With Ryan wounded and the clock ticking, J.B. figured now was the right time to take charge.

"Any more of these muties?" the Armorer pressed, indicating the dying plant. It had taken all seven of them to take out just one of the strange hybrid plants—J.B. didn't relish taking on another, especially given the injuries they were now suffering as a result.

Jak looked thoughtful, shaking his head slowly. "Not sure. Not see."

With his mind racing, the Armorer looked around the overgrown control room, picking out the struggling forms of Ryan, Krysty and Jak, the scratches on the exposed skin of Ricky, Doc and Mildred. Acid rain. Deranged plants. Wounded among their ranks. A mattrans on the brink of dying. It all added up to one thing. "We should bolt, right now," J.B. announced. "Anyone disagree? Ryan?"

The one-eyed man looked up from his position among the vegetation where he and Mildred were removing thorns from his flesh. J.B. could see the hollow in his face where he no longer wore his eye patch.

Before Ryan could reply, he added, "If we don't leave now, that mat-trans won't be running when we need it." As if to emphasise the Armorer's point, the walls of the mat-trans let out a loud creak under the pressure of the creeping vines, a fracture appearing in the armaglass like a streak of black lightning.

Ryan nodded. "Lead the way then," he said, rising slowly from his sitting position with Mildred's assistance.

The rest of the team moved toward the mat-trans doors, with J.B. standing in the open doorway itself, hurrying them along. "Triple red, people," J.B. said. "We count this place's survival time in minutes, not hours."

Krysty stumbled through the doors with Jak's assistance, as weak as a kitten after using the Gaia power. Now she was barely able to stand even with Jak's help. Still, she stopped just inside the mat-trans chamber and waited, her arm propped against a glass wall, watching as Ryan and Mildred made their way inside. Ryan was Krysty's lover, and they cared deeply for each other in this unforgiving world.

She joined Ryan as he pushed through the doors. Though weak herself, she asked how he was before he could speak. "Were you hit bad, lover?"

Ryan wiped a hand across his face. It was dotted with red marks where blood surged to the surface. "I'll live."

The walls of the mat-trans seemed to bulge as the creepers pressed against them. J.B. saw one of the strange creepers move, whipping upward across the armaglass as if it was still alive. A multiheaded tendril crept around the edge of the open door, reaching inside. Through the few plant-free gaps that remained in the armaglass, J.B. spotted the shadow of something moving in the room beyond. Something green and fleshy.

"Time to go, people," J.B. said the moment Doc and Ricky were through the door, pulling it closed in an instant.

The armaglass cracked with a sound like thunder even as the mat-trans powered up, sending its human cargo on its way to their next destination.

Chapter Four

Laying in the darkness, Ryan rolled his head back and forth. All he could remember of the jump was the armaglass imploding, accompanied by a whole lot of hurt. Wherever they had jumped to, wherever they had materialized—that was something he didn't know. If he had ever had that knowledge, it was lost to him now.

Ryan reached up again, knocking his right elbow on the side of the confined space where he lay. His hand played across his face, feeling that uncanny intrusion to his empty eye socket, the eyeball that hadn't been there hours—days? weeks?—earlier, when he was last conscious.

"Fireblast," he muttered, the word barely louder than a breath.

He listened to the whisper echo around him, the way it was contained in the tiny space that he was sealed within. The close walls, the scant room for movement, the panel above his head—it all spoke of one thing: a coffin.

He was inside a coffin, trapped here by person or persons unknown.

Ryan took a deep breath, wondering in the back of his mind just how much air he had. The air smelled okay, fresh not stale, and he couldn't detect any hint that he was being poisoned by the carbon dioxide buildup from his own exhalations, or by anything else for that matter. So maybe he hadn't been here that long, or the box wasn't sealed as tightly as it might be.

Ryan raised his hands and pushed, shoving at the panel above him. It felt cool and slick, more like plastic molding than wood. He pushed once, then tried harder but it didn't move.

He tried with his legs, pulling them up as far as he could and kicking first forward, then straight below him where his feet had been resting. There was a panel below but that didn't give either.

"Dammit," Ryan growled. "Where the nuking hell am I? Let me out of here!"

There was silence for a moment, just the ringing echo of his own words racing around and around in his ears.

Then something happened.

A light came on, softly at first, illuminating the top panel of the coffinlike space. It faded up from a dark gray to a lighter one, then took on a soft, yellow tint that grew brighter and warmer as Ryan watched. He blinked, both eyes getting used to the brightness.

Both eyes. Well, that was new.

Ryan peered around his container. It had white walls with a glossy finish like plastic or painted metal, though it was warmer than metal, coated wood maybe. The ceiling was made from some translucent material, behind which an unknown illumination device had been set. The device showed no bulb, it merely seemed to make the whole panel glow, though Ryan noted that the edges were slightly dimmer, especially where the corners met. The whole unit appeared to be sealed closed, offering no obvious way out. As he looked, his hands automatically moved across his body, checking for his holster. It was gone; and so were his clothes.

"Who's there?" Ryan asked, pitching his voice loudly.

"I am," a male voice replied softly. The voice seemed to come from either side of Ryan, close to his ears.

"Where am I?" he demanded, agitated. As he spoke, his fingers curled, turning his hands into fists. He might have to fight his way out of this; it wasn't the first time he had awoken inside a prison.

"Remain calm," the soft male voice replied. It was emanating from the walls to either side of Ryan's head. He couldn't tell how; he turned but could not see any evidence of a speaker or a hole. "I'll be with you momentarily."

Ryan lay there under the illuminated panel, clenching his hands into fists, ready to take a swing at the face of his jailer.

Chapter Five

Ryan listened intently as he lay beneath the illuminated panel. He was trapped, at the mercy of the person behind the voice, and he didn't know who the voice belonged to or why he was being held.

There was silence for a minute, maybe less, it was hard to tell. Then Ryan heard the soft susurrus of machinery coming to life, and he felt something subtly moving beneath his back.

"Relax, Mr. Cawdor," the softly spoken male voice instructed from the hidden speakers in the coffin walls. "You're quite safe here."

Ryan clenched his fists tighter. He would get one chance at this, one chance to surprise whoever the hell was waiting outside this sealed box. Ryan was a survivor—he would take that chance.

Above him, the illuminated panel seemed to be receding, but Ryan realized that it wasn't the panel that was moving but him. Beneath him, the traylike floor of the coffin bed was drawing backward in the direction that Ryan's head pointed. He tilted his neck back, craned his head and peered up at the panel there as it swished back on some kind of hidden runners.

After that, the bed of the coffin, as he had come to think of it, slid out from its position, and a room came into view, painted white and lit with subtle sidelights that were still dazzling after so long in the box. A man

stood to the side of the retreating bed, dressed in white
and facing the wall, his head tilted down to look at some
kind of panel or screen that jutted there. The man was
bald and wore a tinted visorlike item hooked over his
ears that shielded his eyes. The man's hands were poised
on the panel as if he was playing a piano.

As the bed slid out from the wall, the man in white
turned to Ryan and smiled. "How are you feeling, Mr.
Cawdor?" he asked.

Ryan moved then, rolling off the bed before it could
fully retract from the wall, and powering his left fist at
the man's jaw. He moved fast, his feet slapping against
the cool floor tiles of the room. Ryan's fist met the
man's jaw with an audible crack, and the bald stranger
went crashing backward in a confusion of suddenly
awkward limbs.

Everything was different now. Ryan had two eyes
where he had become used to just one. Everything
seemed suddenly more vivid, the whiteness of the walls
brilliant, like lightning in the mist.

Naked, Ryan stepped forward and brought his right
fist around in a brutal cross, striking the stranger's face
high on the left cheek before the man had even finished
falling. Ryan felt light-headed, unsteady on his feet, but
he knew he had to survive, which meant getting out
of this trap—or whatever it was—as soon as possible.

"Mr. Cawdor, please—" the man cried, blood showing now between his teeth.

Ryan leaned down, his head still reeling, and
punched the man again, striking him dead center of
that weird visor he wore and snapping the plastic in
two. The right half went spinning across the white-
tiled floor while the left shattered, still clinging to the
bridge of the man's nose. A thin line of blood began to

ooze from the man's nose, following a slow path down the side of his tilted face.

"Where am I?" Ryan spit, crouched over the bald man, his face close to the stranger's.

The man's eyes rolled around in their sockets, struggling to keep focus. Ryan took that moment to look around him. He was in a small room, twelve-by-ten with plain white walls and a series of drawers running up the wall from which his bed or coffin had emerged. A single, plain door that looked like a flat panel was set in a recess in the wall opposite where the man had been standing. It had no handle and no control mechanism that Ryan could see. He waved one of his hands close to the door to see if he might activate a sensor, but nothing happened.

"Locked," Ryan muttered, shaking his head.

There were no windows in the room, but where the man had been standing was a pane of glass at roughly waist height, recessed and tilted at an angle so that a standing person could look down into it. With his left hand pressing firmly against the bald man's breastbone, Ryan raised himself and peered at the glass: it was smoked but otherwise appeared blank.

Beneath him, Ryan felt the man stirring, and heard him mutter something. "Not…going…to hurt you," the man said, blood washing across his teeth. "Please."

"Where are my blasters?" Ryan growled. "Where are my friends?"

The bald man's pink head swayed on his neck like a flower in the breeze, his eyes drifting in and out of focus. Then, as Ryan watched, his victim's eyes rolled back so that all he could see were the whites behind the flickering lids.

"Fireblast!" Ryan growled, clambering up from the

sprawled figure in the white overalls. The man was a weakling, glass jaw, no stamina. He wouldn't last five minutes outside his lab.

Ryan peered around the room, searching for his weapons. Without warning, the vision in his left eye— the new one—flickered and changed. Ryan started as he saw something appear to scramble across the surface of the eye, flicked his hand before his face without thinking to brush it aside. It was a kind of cross-shaped overlay, like looking through the crosshairs of his Steyr longblaster.

"What the hell?" Ryan muttered, looking through the crosshairs. Almost as soon as he noticed it, it disappeared, as if willed out of existence. Something wasn't right here, and the sooner he got the heck out of this lab the better, he thought.

Ryan went back to scanning the room, searching for his blasters and panga, wary this time of the strange effect that had popped up across his vision. There was no sign of the weapons, only the plain walls, the coffin drawers and a single, low table propped against one wall next to the door. Ryan pulled one of the drawers at random, but it appeared to be locked. His friends could be in there. Dammit, Ryan raged silently, where was he anyway?

He paced back across the room, standing before the unconscious figure. This place was clearly well appointed, which meant the odds were that this man was not working alone. Even now, Ryan realized, there could be an alarm going off, sec men being moved into position against him. He leaned over the man and checked his pockets, searching for a weapon or something to use as one. There was a tubelike metal thing with a pointed end of the approximate size of a ball-point pen or a small screwdriver. Ryan took it, figuring he could use it like a knife if he had to. The rest of the man's pockets contained only papers and something that looked like a small circuit board, open with resistors and capacitors soldered to its surface. Ryan tossed it aside, checked the man's pulse. He was still alive, but his pulse was slow—he would be out of it for a few minutes yet.

Ryan straightened, and as he did so the white door slid open on hidden tracks. As the door slid aside, he saw the edge of a figure who was standing there, a white padded shoulder of a jacket of some kind. Ryan leaped, shoving the door open with one hand while his other—holding the implement like a knife—slammed into the newcomer's face. The man, dressed in a white topcoat and pants with a cloudburst of black curly hair around his head, staggered back under Ryan's assault, slamming into the corridor wall behind him. "What th—?" the man stuttered as he went sailing into the wall.

"My friends. My weapons. Where are they?" Ryan growled, driving his left fist into the man's gut to punctuate his statement.

The white-clad figure doubled over with the impact, hands reaching around to clutch his aching belly. "I—"

The Deathlands warrior pressed his hand against the man's throat, drew back the metal tube. "Where?"

"Ryan, back off." The voice was familiar, but it took a moment for him to register it. "Back off," the voice said again, calling from the end of the corridor.

He turned in that direction and saw J.B. hurrying toward him, shouting for him to stop fighting. His old friend looked different—his clothes were cleaner, the arms on his glasses no longer slightly bent from wear.

"Stand down, he wasn't going to hurt you," the Armorer stated.

"J.B.?" Ryan asked, bewildered.

Behind J.B., more familiar figures appeared in the white-walled corridor, along with several strangers, all of whom were wearing white clothing like the bald man. Mildred and Ricky hurried to join J.B., while Jak was somewhere behind the others but moving quickly to meet with Ryan. Mildred had a white, sleeveless jerkin over her olive-drab T-shirt, and Ricky was in his usual clothes but they had been cleaned. Jak, too, looked the same but different, his usually unruly long hair washed and smoothed. Besides those familiar faces, a man and two women—all of them looking to be under thirty— were striding up the corridor, looking surprised.

The corridor walls and ceiling were painted a clean white, while the floor had been finished in matching white tiles. Fluorescent lights ran the full length of the corridor without a break, set neatly in a recess that ran in the corners where walls met ceiling.

"What's going on here?" Ryan asked. "Where are we?"

"We're safe, we're among friends. It's okay," J.B. said reassuringly, pressing a hand against his friend's bare shoulder to calm him.

Ryan watched J.B., looking for that telltale flinch that would tell him that the Armorer was being pressured somehow, or that it was a trick. There was nothing, just J.B., clean-shaven, glasses polished, old brown fedora looking a little smarter where the dents had been knocked out of it for once.

"We're safe, Ryan," J.B. repeated. "We're safe."

Warily, Ryan drew the hand that held the metal tube away from the man he had attacked, pulled his other hand back from the man's throat. The figure sagged against the wall, breathing with an agonized, choking gasp, blood on his face, a hole in his cheek.

"Where are we?" Ryan asked J.B..

Chapter Six

"They call this place Progress," J.B. explained.

Ryan sat with the Armorer in a vast lounge area with panoramic windows that looked out over a ville of towering dwellings and predark factories. Jak, Mildred and Ricky were with them, and they all sat around a low table furnished with drinking glasses. The factories pumped smoke into the air, clouding the skies with trails of gray. Ryan had been given clothes to wear, a dressing gown with a simple tie that he had knotted at his waist. He had been assured that his own clothes would be returned shortly. They were being held in storage after being cleaned.

One of the locals, a young woman with flawless skin and blond hair tied back in a braid, had asked Ryan if he needed anything, and when he told her he was thirsty she hurried away and returned a half minute later with bottle of clear water. The bottle didn't smell of pollutants or of poison, so Ryan sipped at its contents warily as he took in everything J.B. was telling him. The blonde stood on the far side of the room, ostensibly admiring the view through the windows but actually keeping an eye on Ryan in case he went on another rampage. Other people from the ville had been sent to deal with the wounded that Ryan had left in his wake.

"Progress," Ryan repeated, skepticism clear in his tone.

"Stupe name, I guess," J.B. admitted, "but you get

used to it. The ville was built around an old military base—redoubt, mat-trans, the whole enchilada. When we jumped out of that redoubt greenhouse from hell… you remember that?"

Ryan nodded, taking another sip of water.

"When we jumped, we wound up here," J.B. continued. "We were all pretty beat-up when we arrived—"

"I remember the armaglass wall imploding," Ryan confirmed.

"Yeah, you got a face-full of that," J.B. told him regretfully, "and we all got cut up pretty bad. Some of the glass came with us too, and really did a number on us."

"Where's Krysty?" Ryan asked. "Is she okay?"

"She's fine," Mildred told him, leaning closer. "Doc too."

"Well, mebbe a bit more ornery," J.B. added, "if you want my opinion."

Mildred shot a look at J.B. "Everyone made it, Ryan," she said. "We're all okay. The people here in Progress went above and beyond to patch us up."

Ryan nodded, reaching up with one hand to feel at the alien eye that had been placed in the empty socket. "So I see," he said, the irony of the phrase lost on him. "What is this thing, Mildred? What did they do to me?"

"We've been here two weeks, Ryan," J.B. replied before Mildred could speak. "Some of us were badly wounded by the armaglass. We'd all lost a lot of blood."

"The locals treated us," Mildred stated. "They saw the damage to your face, and they plucked out all the debris you'd got showered with. When they saw your missing eye, well, they improvised."

"So, I can see again?" Ryan asked. He knew that he could, but he wanted to know how.

"The locals will explain it to you more fully," Mildred told him, "but basically they've fused a computerized camera to your optic nerve, allowing you to use both eyes once more."

"It has crosshairs," Ryan said, glancing across the room to where the blonde stood. Jak was watching her too, he noticed; as usual, the albino was alert, suspicious of anyone he didn't know.

"Your new eye has a lot of things," Mildred replied. "From what they told me, that's a pretty serious piece of hardware they've put inside your skull."

"And they did this for nothing?" Ryan asked, knowing that everything had a price. He gazed out the window behind Mildred, focusing his vision, changing the depth. The artificial eye responded seamlessly, and when he drew a close bead on something in the distance those faint crosshairs reappeared over his left field of vision.

"As far as we can tell," Mildred replied. "They have a philosophy here in Progress about changing the world and making things better again. They want to fix the mess that the nukecaust left us. They want to repair the Deathlands so people can live here and prosper."

Ryan looked at Mildred, then turned to J.B. before addressing them both. "Where is this place?" he asked.

"California," J.B. answered. "Some part of it that survived the San Andreas problem."

Ryan looked out at the blue sky, wondering what they had walked into this time; wondering if they could survive in a place where survival didn't seem to be a struggle.

SHORTLY AFTER THAT, two of the locals joined Ryan's group in the lounge, carrying his clothes—repaired and freshly laundered—as well as his combat boots and his familiar weapons.

The locals were a man and a woman, the man was quite young while the woman looked to be approaching middle age, slivers of iron gray in her hair, wrinkles clawed around her eyes. They seemed pleasant enough, albeit subservient in their attitude. They reminded Ryan of his childhood, growing up as a baron's son in Front Royal, where his every need was attended to by servants.

Ryan began to disrobe there in the lounge, but the woman held her hand up before her and suggested he follow her to a separate room, where he might dress in privacy. He followed her out of the lounge, into a white-walled hallway to a door. It slid aside at the woman's touch, and Ryan looked at her confused.

"How'd you do that?" he asked.

The woman held up her left hand, and Ryan noticed the unobtrusive band of silver she wore on her middle finger like a wedding ring. "The doors are programmed to respond to this," she said.

Ryan nodded, not really sure what to say. He had seen technology before; of course he had—the redoubts he and his companions used to travel the secret roads of the Deathlands were graced with working technology that dated back over a hundred years, and seemed far in advance of anything humankind was capable of these day. He had also fought with mechanical devices before now, robotic things that walked like norms but chilled with the coldheartedness of machines. Even so, this was new—this vile with its hidden locks and uncluttered, almost sterile environment.

The room's walls were painted white like the other parts of the complex that he had seen, with illumination gradually manifesting from a low dimness. The room had a small window at one end, and it featured a single bed, walk-in wardrobe and a small basin for washing.

"Let me know if you need anything," the woman told him as she placed his weapons on the bed. "I'll be just outside. My name's Roma, by the way."

"Good to meet you, Roma-by-the-way," Ryan said with a self-deprecating smile.

Roma left and the door to the room sealed behind her. Alone, Ryan paced, deep in thought. There was a mirror located on the wall beside the basin, set at a height to shave by, and when Ryan paused before it a hidden light tucked into a fold in the mirror's frame glowed brighter, lighting his face for the reflection. He looked at himself, assessing his appearance as if for the first time. Black curly hair, a little disheveled where he had been sleeping in the coffin-drawer. Chin, clean shaved for the first time in weeks.

Eyes—two.

The right one was an intense shade of blue, the left a little duller perhaps, but a close enough match. He looked at it in the mirror, the way it rested in his socket as if it had been there forever. As he looked, staring more and more intensely at the workmanship that had gone into that artificial orb, the crosshairs reappeared over his vision, like a faint blurring in the air, forming a central point that had been left open to view.

As Ryan continued looking, the vision in his left eye magnified—x2, x5, x10—running through the magnifications in rapid succession, so quick it made him feel nauseous. Ryan's right eye, his real eye, remained at normal focus, unable to magnify, leaving him with the disorienting double image of distant and close-up at the same time.

He closed his eyes, brought his hands up to his face, breathing fast.

"What did they do to me?" Ryan muttered, trying to keep from being sick.

Behind him, there came a light tapping at the door followed by Roma's voice. "Mr. Cawdor, are you decent?"

"Decent?" Ryan asked the air.

"Are you dressed? There's someone here who wants to talk to you."

Raising his head tentatively, Ryan opened his eyes and reached for the SIG Sauer blaster that rested on the bedcover beside his piled clothes. "Yeah, I'm decent," he said, flipping off the safety.

The door slid back on near-silent runners and Krysty stepped into the room, while Roma waited obediently outside. Krysty looked beautiful—more beautiful than Ryan had remembered, he would swear. Her vivid red hair swirled around her pale face like a flame, her eyes the green of sunlight through emerald. She was dressed in a version of her usual clothes—blouse, jeans—but they were white. Only her familiar blue cowboy boots remained as Ryan remembered, and even they had been reheeled and polished to remove the scuffs from walking thousands miles of the Deathlands. The boots looked almost new. Ryan held his breath as he saw her, his heart pounding.

"Ryan, I'm so happy to finally see you!" Krysty ran the last few steps and flew into Ryan's arms, hugging him fiercely. She pressed her face into his neck, as if she could not get close enough. "You're okay," she sobbed, "you're okay."

"I'm okay," Ryan assured her, stroking her red hair

with his free hand. She smelled of soap and cleanser, fresh like mountain air.

With his other hand, Ryan slipped the safety back on the SIG Sauer and dropped the blaster back onto the bed before bringing his arm back around to hold Krysty to him. "I'm all right," he told her again. "What about you? Are you okay?"

Krysty nodded her reply; Ryan felt the movement against his neck.

"What did I miss?" Ryan asked, his eyes locked on the door to the room to check it had closed, and that they were alone.

"Two weeks," Krysty said, the words coming out like a sigh. "You were two weeks in that bath, Ryan—"

"Bath?" Ryan asked, confused.

"Nutrient bath," Krysty said, pulling herself reluctantly from Ryan's strong arms. "When we got here, you'd been hit by the imploding wall of the mat-trans—did they tell you that?"

"J.B. and Mildred said something about it," Ryan confirmed, reaching for his pants. They had been freshly laundered and smelled—well, they smelled clean, which was nothing short of remarkable, considering how long he'd been wearing these particular duds.

"You were badly injured," Krysty explained. "We all were. A great chunk of that glass had jumped with us when the mat-trans activated, and we brought it with us in the jump. When we materialized, the glass was still moving. You got the worst of it, but Doc and Jak got a couple of nasty cuts too."

"And you?" Ryan prompted.

Krysty shook her head. "A few cuts and grazes," she said, pushing her right sleeve up and showing him the skin there. It was unmarked. "Had a few scabs here a week ago, but they've healed."

"Sore?"

"No."

Ryan nodded, slipping out of the dressing gown and reaching for his shirt. As he did, Krysty pressed her hand against his chest, running her fingers through his chest hair.

"I've missed you," she whispered.

Ryan was a pragmatist. He desired Krysty in that moment, but he wanted to stay alive too. He knew that staying alive sometimes meant foregoing the things he wanted. Right now, he needed to know all the facts, before someone put a bullet in the back of his head or dumped him back in that coffin where he had woken up.

"You said about a nutrient bath," Ryan said thoughtfully, pushing Krysty gently away.

"After you were hit by the glass, you fell unconscious," Krysty said, picking up her story. "You'd lost a lot of blood—were still losing it. We were all in a mess."

"What happened?"

"Someone outside the chamber somehow opened the mat-trans door. Doc figured they did it with a comp," Krysty said. "It was the people here, a team of them, and they came to help us. They took us away, nursed everyone's injuries. Mildred said they did a commendable job."

"What about me?" Ryan pressed.

"You'd suffered the worst of us," Krysty told him, and he saw worry in her face as she thought back. "There was a whole pool of your blood on the mat-trans floor. They took you away on a gurney, rushed you over to their medical center—"

"And you let them?" Ryan bit off the rest of his comment. It wasn't an accusation or criticism; he was merely surprised to hear his companions would have been so trusting.

"Like I said, we were pretty messed up after the jump," Krysty explained. "J.B. questioned them, tried to stop them, I think, but none of us was in a state to put up much of a fight. We didn't need to, thank goodness.

"They took care of you, lover. They took you straight to surgery and removed the glass, then they started patching you up. They have advanced techniques here—that's according to Mildred. She understands more about it than I do. She says they used nanobots to repair your body, dunked you in a nutrient bath full of them to give you time to recover."

"How long?" Ryan asked.

"Eight days," Krysty said, fixing him with her stare. She was looking at his new eye, Ryan could tell, trying to get used to seeing it in his face.

"Eight days," he muttered, shaking his head.

"I waited, but I wasn't allowed to see you in all that time," Krysty told him. "They were worried about contamination, because you were in such a fragile state."

Ryan pulled on his shirt, buttoning it from the bottom up. "What about the eye?" he said.

"I didn't know about that until you came out of the bath," Krysty told him. "None of us did. The surgeons thought you'd lost it in the mat-trans accident, I guess, because your patch was missing. They replaced it while they were working on you, fixed it the way they fixed everything else."

Krysty looked at Ryan, examining his face, his eye. "How is it?" she asked.

"It's…" Ryan stopped even as he began to reply. How did he feel about missing an eye for the better part of his life and waking up one day to find it had been put back? How could he react to that? How could he even process it?

"The eye has capabilities," Ryan told her. "It'll take some getting used to."

"There are counselors here in Progress," Krysty said. "One of them will tell you how it functions, show you how best to use it."

Ryan nodded uncertainly as he finished buttoning his shirt.

Krysty looked at him and smiled that dazzling, beautiful smile that would make any man's heart melt. "It looks good, Ryan. If I wasn't spoken for, I'd fall for you all over again right now."

Chapter Seven

"The eye has many properties that you will find useful," the gray-haired woman told Ryan.

Once he had dressed, Ryan and Krysty had been escorted to another room by Roma. Mildred and J.B. tagged along.

The new room was wide-open with white walls, a raised bed and a desk-type arrangement that pulled out from a recess in one of the walls, smoothly folding out in sections. A long window dominated the opposite wall of the room, looking out over the industrial center with its towering chimneys. Ryan could see that a river flowed fast and furious along the edge of the ville.

The woman stood before the desk. She was dressed in a long white robe with a high collar, and gloves molded into the sleeves. Her iron-gray hair was tied back in a neat ponytail. She acknowledged Ryan with a warm smile, introducing herself as Betty. Ryan's companions had met Betty before, and she knew them all by name.

J.B. took one look at the examination room and stepped back through the door. "It's going to get mighty cramped with all of us in there," he said. "Krysty, why don't you and me go to the lounge while the healer checks Ryan over?"

Krysty checked with Ryan before agreeing, and he assured her he would be fine. "Mildred's here with me," he said. "Finest shot in the Deathlands—she'll look out for me." He said that last statement as something of a couched warning, uncertain whether he should trust the whitecoat.

Roma led J.B. and Krysty from the room, the door whispering closed behind her. Once they were gone, Betty adjusted something on the desk and the long window assumed a tinted aspect, cutting the bright sunlight like sunglasses and casting the room in a grayish shadow. There was a machine in the room too, Ryan saw now—cylindrical and almost as tall as he was, the thing moved on hidden wheels, a bank of lights running across its metallic skin.

"You're looking well, Mr. Cawdor," Betty said, smiling. "Your recovery has been excellent."

"He's strong," Mildred said, taking up a position to one side of the room so that Betty could examine Ryan.

"Now, you're not going to start punching me, are you, Mr. Cawdor?" the woman in the white robe asked.

Ryan shook his head. "You heard about that, huh? I was a little disoriented when I woke up and I wasn't getting answers."

Betty nodded. "You were in recovery for a long time," she said. "It's understandable."

Then she indicated the bed and Ryan lay down, unbuttoning his shirt. Betty checked him over with detached professionalism, assuring him—and herself—that his scars had almost healed. The cylindrical thing waited silently beside Betty, scanning Ryan with its emotionless camera eye.

"Krysty said I'd been placed in a bath of nutrients," Ryan said. "Can you explain what happened?"

Betty nodded. "Yes, you must have a lot of questions. The nutrient bath that your companion spoke of was to assist in your healing. While there, nano-machinery—which performs surgery on a molecular level—was used to repair your wounds, including those sustained in surgery when glass and other material was removed from your body."

"What other material?" Ryan asked.

Betty stepped over to the desk and brought up a report on the embedded screen. "Some plant matter, much of it toxic. Similar material was found in almost all of your colleagues when you arrived, but we successfully removed all of it."

"We fought a plant," Ryan said. "I remember."

"Tough bitch of thing, too," Mildred added grimly.

"The nutrient bath assisted in your body's natural repair," Betty continued, "after which you were placed in a regulated environment where your body temperature could be kept at the optimum for recovery and could be fed proteins to maximize your healing."

"The coffin," Ryan stated.

"What's that?" Betty asked, turning her attention back from the comp.

"I woke up inside a sealed box," Ryan said. "I figured someone was trying to bury me."

"Quite the opposite," Betty told him, flashing her teeth in an awkward smile. The teeth were good, strong-looking but yellowed with age. Ryan saw a sliver of metal there behind the upper right canine where a tooth had been removed and replaced. "Would you sit up for me?"

Nodding, Ryan shifted himself until he was sitting upright once more. Then, while he sat on the bed, Betty asked him to do a few tests with his new eye, reading the characters on a distant chart that was projected in the air by the cylindrical machine, identifying colors and observing movement through a spinning device in its trunk. Once she had confirmed the eye was functioning correctly, Betty told Ryan that the eye had extra properties.

"I think I stumbled on one," Ryan admitted. "I focused my vision and a crosshairs target appeared."

"Yes," Betty confirmed. "You can also magnify the image in the left eye, like a longblaster scope. Are you right- or left-handed, Mr. Cawdor?"

"Right," Ryan said, holding up his right hand.

"Tsk, that's a shame." Betty sighed "But it is not a huge loss. Obviously, the targeting facility would have been better in the same eye as your blaster hand but that can't be helped now."

"I'll try to keep that in mind the next time I lose an eye," Ryan told her sarcastically.

The clinician acknowledged this with a snort before going back to her explanation. "The eye has other properties that feed directly into your optic nerve to be processed by your brain. You now have night vision, including an infrared functionality—which will also allow you to track the heat given off by a subject. You may access the former by blinking twice in quick succession while in darkness or semidarkness."

Since the room was shaded, Ryan first tried the night vision, blinking rapidly twice. The feed from his left eye switched to a gray-green hue. The feed from the night vision was confused because Ryan also had his real eye open, creating a double image, one normal and one cast in gray-green.

"Whoa," Ryan said, feeling a wave of nausea run through him.

"You may find it easier to process if you close your other eye," Betty said.

Ryan did just that. Then he gazed around the room, saw the figures and details of the room picked out vividly in what seemed to be a murky gray fog. He saw Mildred smiling as he experimented, her eyes and teeth a brilliant white lined in neon green, while the bank of lights on the surface of the cylindrical machine seemed brilliant in the gloom. "That's...working," Ryan said, blinking again until the feed switched back to normal.

"The infrared requires pressure here." Betty showed Ryan by touching the bottom left corner of her own eye.

He mimicked the woman's gesture and, after a moment's trial and error finding the pressure plate, he activated the infrared function. This time, he had the foresight to close his other eye, ensuring he saw only the feed. Suddenly, the room was cast in a dull gray through Ryan's left eye, with the two human forms burning a brilliant red-orange as they watched him. The cylindrical machine glowed a faint orange, cold and lifeless despite its ability to move independently. Ryan moved his head, looking around the room at the spots of heat at the desk and, more dully, across the bank of windows.

"Seems dandy," Ryan said.

When he drew his hand up to touch the pressure plate again, Ryan saw his own body recast in a brilliant swirl of red, yellow and white, as if he were made of fire. He pressed the hidden plate, toggling back to normal vision.

"What else can it do?" Ryan asked.

"You can hold an image for review at a later period," Betty said. "To do this, focus on the subject for five seconds and squint your eye like so. You may then recall this image at a later date, where it may be shown as its own image or as an overlay to whatever you are looking at for means of comparison."

"How many images can it store like that?" Ryan checked. "And how do I recall them?"

"Look to your left while holding down the pressure pad to retrieve an image," Betty told him. "Do the same once the image is visible and hold your eye closed for five seconds to delete."

"Delete?" Ryan asked, uncertain what the term meant in this context.

"Permanently remove the image from the eye," Betty elaborated. "You may hold up to twelve images, but that number will be less should you take images while in night-mode or infrared."

Ryan nodded. "Got it."

Mildred spoke up from where she was standing close to the now-tinted windows. "Is there anything else Ryan or I need to know, such as how to maintain or service the artificial eye?"

"The eye is self-servicing," Betty said. "You may detect some deterioration over the very long term—by which I mean decades rather than years—but should that be the case you may return here and we would be able to adjust the eye or replace it."

"Just one more question," Ryan said. "How did you find us?"

"This is Progress, California," Betty said. "The site grew out of the military redoubt you accessed via your mat-trans jump, which is how we found you."

"You found us?"

Betty smiled. "Not me personally, no. A patrol was sent to investigate when the mat-trans activated. I don't know how much you know about the mat-trans system, but it's largely automated, and that automation includes an alert sent to a number of linked monitoring stations when the system powers up to receive someone."

Ryan said nothing, merely accepting the information without reacting. The mat-trans was his little secret, one kept by himself and his companions. They did not know much about the functionality of the devices, only that they transported them across the continent—and occasionally off the continent—via some kind of hidden pathways and that there was apparently no way to predetermine where a jump would lead. Ryan was hesitant of sharing any information with the locals, even ones who had saved his life. Save your life today, shoot you in the back tomorrow—that's what Trader used to tell him.

"It's lucky we did," Betty continued. "You and your friends were in a terrible state on arrival. I don't know what you'd been putting yourself through, but it had left you all seriously wounded."

"The imploding wall of the mat-trans during the jump didn't help," Mildred said, deadpan.

"No, I don't imagine it would have," Betty agreed. She touched something on the inset screen at her desk and the shaded tint to the window glass seemed to recede as Ryan watched. Nothing moved there that he could see. The opacity merely altered in a gradual manner until the windows were clear once more. He flicked momentarily to magnification mode, staring at the window frame.

"You have some mighty advanced tech here," Ryan said. "Heck of a lucky find."

"Oh, we didn't find it, Mr. Cawdor," Betty told him, "we built it."

Chapter Eight

Once the examination with Betty was completed, Ryan felt the need to stretch his legs. "From what I can tell, I've been cooped up in a box for two weeks," he told Krysty as he met her and J.B. outside the examination room. "I need to feel some fresh air, get the wind in my hair."

"It's a large ville, Ryan," Krysty told him. "You'll be impressed."

"Yeah, I could see that through the windows," Ryan agreed.

Krysty led him to an elevator that spiraled through the building. The elevator was cylindrical with a door that slid silently back on a curved tread. Stepping into it was like stepping into an upright pipe. A single overhead light source was obscured by a screen that diffused the illumination into a subtle effect, preventing any glare. Ryan eyed it for a moment as he stepped inside, flicking through the different options with his new cybernetic eye.

Crosshairs.

Magnification.

Night vision.

Infrared.

"Hey, Ryan," Mildred called as he stood with Krysty in the elevator. "You be careful. You only just woke up—don't overdo it, okay?"

"Sure," Ryan agreed, still flicking through his visual options.

"And, Krysty," Mildred added, "I'm trusting you to keep an eye on the patient."

Krysty agreed and a moment later the door slid closed and the elevator began its smooth descent to ground level.

Ryan moved close to Krysty, kissing her mouth and then her cheek. As his lips came close to her ear, he whispered, "This place safe? Don't answer out loud."

Krysty nodded very definitely against Ryan's head, moaning once as if in delight at his kisses.

"Will I need my blasters?" Ryan asked, still whispering.

"Oh, lover," Krysty groaned. As she did so, she shook her head slightly: *No*.

Ryan kissed her again as the elevator stopped its silent descent and the door drew back. They were in a vast lobby now, its proportions dwarfing anything Ryan could think of—it was like a predark aircraft hangar or a shipyard, ceilings so high they were almost four stories above him. There were a few people in the vast room—too few for its size, in Ryan's opinion, but he had witnessed chronic overcrowding in the Deathlands and the sickness it had brought. The people were dressed in white and pale colors, loose-fitting clothes that better suited the climate of the West Coast. Some moved on wheeled devices, standing atop them, maintaining their balance with arms gently out to their sides as they sped swiftly across the room.

A quick scan, automatic now after all these years, revealed that no one appeared to be armed.

The room's illumination came from an impressive wall of windows that looked out on to the ville. Ryan and Krysty strode across the room, fifty steps from the elevator to the nearest doorway, a twenty-foot-wide gap in the glass that opened straight out onto a veranda beyond. There was an awning up above to keep rain off, should there be any, and the veranda and its surrounds were designed in such a way that no wind could penetrate into the lobby itself.

Ryan stepped out into the sunlight, taking in a deep breath of air. Morning sunshine and clear skies gave a fresh feel to the day. The wide streets were paved and clean, birds occasionally fluttering past, landing for a moment to scout the area for food. Buildings towered all around, eight huge structures clad in bold white like the great marble temples of ancient Greece. The lowest of them was two stories, the tallest much higher than that. The buildings were linked, Ryan saw, with bridges running across the streets from their upper stories. The bridges were open to the elements. Few people were about, given all the space, but Ryan noticed that several of them were traveling via the same wheeled disklike platforms, flitting between the buildings like a ballerina figurine pirouetting out of a music box.

"This place is incredible," Ryan said as he tried to take it all in.

"They've been very hospitable," Krysty told him. "We've wanted for nothing."

Ryan checked the weapon at his hip, noticed Krysty was still wearing her Smith & Wesson on hers. "Not that hospitable, though," he said, indicating her blaster.

Krysty smiled. "Force of habit," she admitted. "I haven't had to draw my blaster in two weeks. The only time it's been out of its holster has been to oil it."

Ryan nodded. Oiling their weapons was a ritual the companions strictly followed. A well-maintained blaster could mean the difference between life and death in the Deathlands; it would never do to become complacent, no matter how tranquil the surroundings.

And they were very tranquil. There was noise here—the hiss and drone from the factories, the sound of the nearby river rushing past—but it was muffled by the buildings and the wide-open spaces.

Ryan and Krysty walked slowly down a wide thoroughfare. Outside, the building looked newly built and was a pale yellow that was almost white, better to reflect the fierce California sun. It ran over three hundred feet before Ryan and Krysty reached its edge, the same in the other direction. Ryan was impressed by its size.

"Is this place all dedicated to fixing people up?" he asked Krysty.

"They're very advanced here," Krysty replied. "Mildred said they're doing a lot of experimental work into cybernetics—like the unit they put in your eye."

"Robot stuff?" Ryan asked, glancing back at the building.

"From what I've seen, they use the building as a repair shop and medical center," Krysty said. "I'm not sure they see much difference between those things."

As Ryan focused on the building, the crosshairs reappeared across his left field of vision, a ghost overlay on the image. "Yeah, I guess."

They continued walking, taking it slowly as Ryan realized how exhausted he felt. He had been fed a steady drip of proteins while held in the drawerlike unit, and while he was fully nourished he had little energy—that had been used up by his body for repairs.

People flitted past on the wheeled disks, while another group traveled toward Ryan and Krysty in a group, riding aboard a wheeled transport roughly the size of a wag but entirely open to the elements. Ryan looked at the vehicle as it passed them and moved down the road. Its passage was almost silent and it had no driver, just a cylindrical box of lights up front a little like the thing that had assisted Betty during her examination.

Krysty watched Ryan, the smile never leaving her face. She was pleased to have him back—it had been a fraught two weeks waiting for the man she loved to wake up after all that he had been through. As they walked, Krysty brought him up to speed on what the companions had been doing in his absence—J.B. and Mildred had checked out every nook and cranny of the medical center, while Jak and Ricky had spent time scouting the ville and its immediate surrounds, coming and going as they pleased. Doc, she explained, had been disappointed in the food here and had taken it on himself to show the local "Progressians" how to cook, despite the lack of a variety of ingredients. Krysty didn't tell Ryan about her own recovery, nor how much time she had spent in a medically induced coma; she did not want to worry him.

"You weren't tempted to move on?" Ryan teased. "To leave me behind?"

"No one gets left behind," Krysty reminded him. "Especially you, lover."

It was true. No one would ever be left behind. Ryan had been with J.B., Krysty and Doc longer than anyone, and the others were just as much family to him now. But there had been an occasion—once—when someone had been left behind: Ryan's own son, Dean Cawdor, stolen by his mother, Sharona, and lost to him for the cruel eternity that only a grieving parent could know. Dean was alive, but changed, and his recent reacquaintance with his father had been brief and had not ended well. It was something Ryan couldn't fix, though he hoped that one day Dean would come back to him. It was something that Ryan didn't vocalize, but he thought of Dean just about every day.

Fifteen minutes' slow walk brought the couple to the edge of the ville, where a mighty river flowed. "J.B. calls the river the Klamath," Krysty said.

J.B. was the guardian of the maps for the group, and he employed a mini-sextant to get their bearings when they traveled. Without him, the group would be lost in Hell; as it was, they traveled the post-nukecaust roads with the knowledge of where they were, but they were still the roads of Hell.

"A lot of California was devastated when the quakes hit," Ryan observed, peering out at the raging waters. Whiteheads leaped and dissipated there, like horses in the sea.

Ryan was correct in what he said. California had been struck hard by the nukecaust and all that followed. Great chunks of the west coast of America had been sheared off when the San Andreas Fault broke open, and some of the state had been relegated to an archipelago of tiny islands dotted in the Pacific. J.B. couldn't know it, but the Klamath River had been widened in the past century as a result of the tectonic plate movement, and now ran at a faster speed than it had a hundred years earlier.

Ryan looked across the rushing river to where a great dam had been constructed. The dam was made from huge hunks of stone that had been carved and shaped with craftsmanlike precision, barricading the river. A grand walkway ran across the top, as wide as a two-lane blacktop, arching forty feet above the tumultuous surface of the fast-flowing water. The dam ended in a high protective wall on the far bank, while the near side was attached to a monitoring tower that rose another twenty above the high wall. It was an impressive feat of engineering, something seldom seen in the devastated Deathlands.

"What's that?" Ryan asked, his eye focusing on the details of the pale, curved wall of stone. "A dam. But I don't see a whole lot of farming going on." In fact there was none; the area surrounding the ville appeared to be devoid of life.

"J.B. says they use it to power the equipment here," Krysty told Ryan. "Some kind of hydropower arrangement, like a watermill only bigger."

"Much bigger," Ryan acknowledged as he eyed the watchtower. "Stands to reason. Lotta tech here—needs a lot of power."

"That tech saved your life," Krysty reminded him. Then she reached inside the back pocket of her pants and pulled something free. Coiled on itself, the thing looked like a handful of thick black cord. "I saved this," she told Ryan, handing it to him.

Ryan took the item, unraveled it and looked it over. It was his old eye patch, the one removed back in that redoubt where they had been attacked by the mutie plant. He held it up for a moment, tracing the stitching that held the leather to the cord, seeing the spots where it had frayed. "I don't need it anymore," he said, and he drew his hand back and threw the patch toward the rushing water below.

Krysty's hand darted out, grabbing the patch as it dropped. "I'll keep it," she told Ryan when she saw his confused expression. "A keepsake of what you were," she added, slipping the eye patch back inside her pants pocket.

"I make my own keepsakes now," Ryan said, stepping back from Krysty. "Stay there." He looked at her and held himself still, waiting for the camera eye to snap a picture of her. After five seconds it did, capturing Krysty's image for posterity. In his eye, she would always be beautiful, her hair catching in the wind, the river racing behind her. Now he could call upon that image whenever he wanted to—in his eye.

Chapter Nine

"The food here is so terribly bland, do you not agree?" Doc asked as he blew on a spoonful of soup to cool it.

Doc was sitting at a beech wood table in a large room whose panoramic windows overlooked the river and the hydroelectric dam stretching across it like a stone cutlass. Across from him, Mildred, J.B. and Ricky sat eating from their own bowls of soup while Jak sat a space down from Doc, mopping his bowl with a bread roll from the pile that dominated the center of the table. Tasty or not, Jak ate the meal with gusto.

Around the room, several other groups were eating. They were locals, dressed in plain overalls and coverings in muted colors, whites and pastels. They ate quietly in ones and twos, and mostly in silence.

"I haven't paid it much mind," J.B. admitted distractedly. He had heard the argument before; they all had. The old man was nothing if not consistent.

J.B. was gazing down at the dam and the two people who stood close to its edge on the raised river banks. Krysty was easily recognizable even from this distance with her vivid red hair, while Ryan's huge frame made him easy enough to spot if you knew what you were looking for.

"I have spoken to the chefs de cuisine about adding salt, spices and so on, but they seem ignorant of the whole concept of seasoning," Doc espoused. "Alas it seems that humankind's culinary knowledge has been forgotten along with so much else in these terrible times."

"Food is food, and free food tastes that much better," J.B. said, his eyes flicking up to the white-haired old man over the rims of his glasses. "At least we didn't have to hunt and chill anything to get this, and that's a definite appetizer in my book."

"Quite," Doc acknowledged, nodding.

Mildred tore a chunk from a bread roll and chewed on it thoughtfully. "I've had worse," she admitted. "Rat meat, leafy stew, boot—" She stopped abruptly, remembering the horrific moments when she had almost become a cannibal. Ryan had secretly promised to chill her then, if that's what was needed, and so she had trusted him with her life until she could be cured. "I've had worse," she finished lamely.

Laughing, Ricky reached for another roll. "It won't ever taste as good as my mama's cooking," he said, "but I'll take it if it's free." Then he took a second roll and a third, and began juggling them with casual dexterity. "Anyone else want a roll?" he asked.

Jak and J.B. told Ricky that they did, and both found themselves the recipients of juggled rolls that landed perfectly on their respective plates.

"With an arm like that, he should have played baseball," Mildred said, shaking her head.

"Mayhap one day," Doc told her, "when all of this horror is past."

J.B. chewed a corner of his roll thoughtfully and glanced back to the window. Ryan and Krysty could be seen there making their way gradually back up the paved street. "You think Ryan's going to be okay?" he asked Mildred.

"He's got a new eye," Mildred reasoned. "That's going to take some getting used to. But it can only be beneficial for him, and for us too."

"I don't know," the Armorer said. "Ryan's done pretty okay by us with just one eye. There hasn't been an occasion I can think of where I've regretted the loss of his eye. Can you?"

Doc and Jak shook their heads, while Mildred verbally agreed.

"I have not known Ryan very long," Ricky admitted, "but the man is a crack shot with his blasters. I never gave much thought to what it must be like for him, living with one eye."

"It messes with your depth perception," Mildred told Ricky and the others, "but Ryan compensates well. He's had a lot of time to get used to living like that. I just hope this new eye doesn't throw off his rhythms."

"Ryan Cawdor is a survivor," Doc reminded them all. "He will always win through. I suggest we accept the outcome of this visit—his new eye—as propitious and do not look the proverbial given horse in its mouth."

OUTSIDE, RYAN HAD expressed feeling tired and so Krysty walked with him slowly back to the medical facility.

"Any idea how many people live here?" Ryan asked, admiring the towers.

"A hundred, maybe more," Krysty told him.

As they walked, Ryan assessed their surroundings. Everything looked newly built, even the street looked freshly paved, its stones shining a brilliant white. But here and there, Ryan spotted evidence of another world, the world before the nukecaust—a road sign, triangular metal on a pole that had been bent to one side; hints of the blacktop of an ancient road that had run along the same pattern as the streets.

"I wonder what this place used to be?" Ryan said.

Krysty pointed to a low building that ran crosswise to the others, poised at the end of the broad thoroughfare. It looked dirtier than the rest and older, despite some obvious attempts at repair work. "See that? Old military redoubt. That's where we popped in via the mat-trans. It must have been built back before the nukecaust."

"Unusual seeing so much aboveground," Ryan observed. In his experience, most of the ancient army facilities were built underground, with just an entrance visible aboveground.

"Doc figures that when the plates started shifting around the whole redoubt popped out from under," Krysty said, "or that everything around it sunk."

"That sounds more likely," Ryan said. "Redoubts were built to last." He eyed the ancient building a few seconds longer, marveling at their luck in landing in a safe community. Usually it went the other way—if there were people living near a mat-trans, the first thing they would do would be to try to chill Ryan and his companions. And the second thing they would do, as the old Deathlands joke had it, was die. Heaven Falls came to mind.... Nothing was given away free.

RYAN AND KRYSTY joined the others just as they finished their meal.

"'Tis heartening to see you back on your feet," Doc said, standing to shake Ryan's hand.

"Thanks, Doc," Ryan said, grasping the old man's hand. "You too."

"You've had a look around?" Mildred asked. "Is

everything okay? Do you feel all right?" Mildred was a doctor and her question was strictly professional; if Ryan expressed any concerns she would have him checked over immediately.

"I'm okay, Mildred," Ryan answered, keeping his voice low, "and I think it's time we were going."

J.B. looked at Ryan quizzically. "Something bothering you?"

He shook his head. "Nothing particular," he said. "I just don't like staying in one place for too long. Remember Heaven Falls."

"I hear you," J.B. agreed.

"Jak? Did you look around?"

Leaning back in his chair, Jak nodded solemnly, picking at his teeth.

"We both did," Ricky explained. "Got about a mile out. No one was bothered much about it."

"What did you find?" Ryan asked the dark-haired teen.

"Nothing worth finding," Ricky told him. "We're a little way up in some mountains—"

"Here," J.B. said, showing Ryan their approximate position on a map he had produced from one of his capacious pockets.

Ryan looked over the map as Ricky continued.

"The immediate area is dead, nothing much out there other than birds and insects," Ricky said.

"Nothing worth eatin'," Jak elaborated tersely.

"Looked like mebbe some villes out to the east," Ricky picked up. "Small dwellings bunched together. Could be farm types, but we didn't get close enough to find out."

Ryan nodded. "That's okay. Gives us something to go on, anyhow.

"Now, unless anyone objects, I'm going to speak to our hosts and thank them for their hospitality, and for my hospitalization," Ryan continued, "and then we are going to do what we always do—walk. So, any objections?"

There was none. The companions had traveled the hell roads for a long time; they trusted Ryan's instincts, and when he said it was time to move on, then it was time to move on.

WHEN RYAN EXPRESSED his desire to leave, Roma escorted him to another building that lay close to the Klamath River. "I'd like to thank our hosts for everything they've done," he told her.

They traveled on the back of an automated vehicle, its driver a box of lights located at the front of its open frame. Ryan sat, his hands resting on the tops of his thighs, close to the holster on his right hip. He didn't like traveling around alone like this, but the others had gear to pack up, so there it was.

After two minutes of smooth, near-silent movement, the automated vehicle drew to a halt outside a towering circular structure overlooking the river. The tower rose three hundred feet into the air, housing over fifteen levels within.

Roma walked with Ryan, leading him inside. "The ville is ruled from in here," she explained, as they strode through an empty lobby.

The lobby was circular like the structure, empty with a vast column in its center that thrust up into the main body of the building itself. The lobby's walls were made from tinted glass, possibly even armaglass, like the walls of the mat-trans. The glass was smoky and behind it

Ryan could see electrical circuitry, tiny diodes flashing frequently amid the complex structure.

"Lot of tech here," Ryan observed, indicating the walls.

Roma merely smiled as she ran her hand over the hidden sensor plate that opened the doors to one of a bank of elevators located in the central hub of the lobby. They stepped inside and the elevator door swished closed before the car sent its passengers up into the body of the building. The elevator was silent, Ryan could only detect the movement by the way his stomach dropped— it was fast, then.

Five seconds passed, and then the door pulled back and Ryan saw a shadow-filled room beyond. The room was huge, with high ceilings, grand walls and no seating. The lights were recessed and obscured, casting only a little illumination into the room. It smelled of recycled air, grease and oil, mechanical things, fans dissipating heat.

As Ryan entered, he flicked his artificial eye to night vision, scanning the poorly lit room. Though the room was not fully circular, the walls were curved, and there appeared to be no exits other than the elevator bank located behind him. The room was large enough to comfortably house a dozen wags without anything getting scratched. There was glass along the walls, cabinet-type doors behind which more circuitry hummed, diodes twinkling with light like stars in the night sky; colored stars, reds and greens and yellows.

Up ahead, dominating the room, was something that looked like a high wall, and it was plated with circuitry, the copper lines of the circuit boards catching what little illumination was cast from the lighting to create a ghostly crisscross of shining metallic streaks. At the top of that wall, Ryan saw people waiting, standing twelve feet above him, pacing along the high balcony as they came to see who had arrived. There were seven of them in all, their faces hidden in shadow, even to Ryan's enhanced night vision. They wore long robes that trailed down to the floor, shapeless things that obscured their bodies entirely.

Roma waited by the elevator as Ryan entered the room, her hands held neatly behind her back.

"Mr. Cawdor has expressed his intention to leave," she announced, "along with his companions."

Ryan took up a position in the center of the room, scanning the shadowy figures above him. "I wanted to thank you for everything," he said. "My friends tell me you patched them up pretty good—me too—and you asked for nothing in return. Charity like that's rare in my experience, so I owe you my gratitude."

He stopped, and for a moment the only response was silence. He eyed the figures poised above him, watching for any signs of life.

"I don't like being in a man's debt," Ryan finally added, breaking the silence. As he spoke, he switched his vision to infrared, scanning the figures above. They were alive—he had seen them move when he had arrived with Roma. In infrared, their bodies gave off heat. "So, if there's anything my people can do—"

"There is no debt to pay, Ryan Cawdor," a male voice said, deep and resonant.

It took Ryan a moment to pinpoint who had spoken, and he turned to face the man, holding up one hand up as if to shield his eyes and better see in the darkness. "I'm grateful for that. Can I ask why?"

There was silence again, a long pause while Ryan waited. Finally, the resonant voice spoke again.

"Humankind destroyed itself in a nuclear exchange one hundred years ago," the voice said. "What little remains is barely enough to sustain the survivors. We in Progress plan to change that. We are working hard on a solution, or on multiple solutions, that will grant a reprieve for all that has been wrought on this once-great nation."

Memories of Judge Santee washed across Ryan's mind, but he let it pass.

"And the hardware in my eye?" Ryan asked. "Is that part of your solution?"

Ryan waited once more while the room fell silent. Then a narrow spotlight came on, focusing solely on another figure, who had been waiting in the darkness. The man wore a gray robe with a headpiece that covered the forehead and back of his skull like a hood. Ryan automatically commanded his left eye to magnify, focusing on the man's face. The headpiece looked to be made of plastic or metal, Ryan thought, while the man looked to be in middle age, with dark skin.

"My name is Emil," the man told Ryan. "I designed the hardware in your eye, along with my companions here—Una and Turing. What you are experiencing is an infinitesimal step toward the betterment of this world. Tiny steps are all we can expect at this moment, but that will change."

"You have an impressive setup here, Emil," Ryan said. "I saw the dam out there. Krysty said you get your power from it."

"It takes a lot to power the future," Emil told him. "We intend to make things perfect."

Ryan smiled. "Perfect's a tall order."

"Rest assured, Mr. Cawdor—all we need is time," Emil answered.

Then the spotlight dimmed and the room was cast in darkness once more, the seven figures returned to shadows watching Ryan from above.

"Thank you for your time," Ryan said, dipping his head once, respectfully, before stepping back and returning to the elevator, where Roma stood waiting. A moment later, they were back in the lobby, making their way toward the exit, where the automated transport waited.

Chapter Ten

They were back in Hell. Their pilgrimage through the hellscape began again, picking up where it had left off.

Ryan and his companions trekked across the ruined landscape, following a dirt road that was scored in the soil like a scab. The road nudged through overgrown fields of rapeseed and corn, an orchard full of skeletal trees—the apples withered and dead on their branches, poisoned by the toxins in the soil. Behind them, Progress soon became just a smear on the horizon, the smudge of white towers barely visible beside the winding silver snake of water. Ryan turned back occasionally, framing the ville in his sights and pulling up the magnification mode in his artificial eye. He would see the ville towers if he magnified the image, could make out the three-hundred-foot point where he had enjoyed an audience with the ruling cabal of the ville. How they had built such magnificent structures when all around them was devastated he could not imagine. It was a jewel amid the trash, a single diamond in the dirt.

Up ahead there was little evidence of human life. No settlements, no buildings. Occasionally they would pass the foundations of something that looked like a building, but it had been razed to the ground so long ago that what remained looked like a floor plan carved into the dirt, more like a game of pick-up-sticks than a place a human could ever have lived.

Ryan led the way, the SIG Sauer holstered back at his hip, the Steyr Scout Tactical longblaster held across his shoulders like an old days' milkmaid's rig. Beside him, Krysty walked along with a spring in her step, still dressed in the white clothes that she had acquired while in Progress, her old clothes folded neatly into a knapsack she had hooked over one shoulder along with her bearskin coat. She wouldn't need a fur coat out here, not with the sun beating down on what was left of California.

Doc and J.B. huddled along behind the couple, bickering about some point of geography until Mildred saw fit to pull them apart. Mildred was walking beside Ricky, swapping stories about his childhood on Monster Island, hers in twentieth-century Alabama, where her skin color was still an issue to some.

"I don't believe anyone would hate you because of that," Ricky said with wide-eyed innocence.

"Hate's too clever a word," Mildred mused. "It implies that the people who did it actually had the smarts to know what it was they were doing."

"Hate makes the world go 'round, Millie," J.B. opined, overhearing their conversation during a lull in his own.

Mildred shook her head. "I don't believe that. Humankind's meant for more than hate."

Doc turned back, his face an expression of sorrow. "Much as it pains me to admit," he said, "it seems that the more I see of this world, the more I am inclined to agree with J.B.'s outlook. Hate fuels so much of this world, it is hard to ever see a time past it."

"And what about Progress?" Mildred asked, indicating the distant towers of the ville behind them. "They helped us when they didn't have to, when they could have just left us all to die. You think hate is at the heart of their philosophy?"

"They exist because of the damage wrought by man on his own home," Doc said. "That ville grew up on a spot where man's hate and fear made him bury a military time bomb, the redoubt waiting to be accessed. We only arrived there because of that fear, that distrust that destroyed the world and almost everyone in it."

"But we arrived and we got help," Mildred argued. "I'd see that as a victory for humanity, wouldn't you?"

Behind the others, Jak tuned out the babble of debate and scanned the territory around them. He was a tracker by nature, attuned to changes in wind direction and intensity, to scents and sights and the mood of any environment he found himself in. He hadn't liked the ville so much—it had been too built-up for him, all those paving slabs, balconies and verandas, all that artificiality slung down amid the natural. When he hadn't been out scouting with Ricky, he had spent much of his time scouting on his own, or simply sitting down by the river where he could be closer to nature.

Jak didn't talk about those things. Heck, Jak didn't talk about much of anything if he could help it. When he did speak, it was in fractured sentences, broken syntax.

But Jak knew stuff; stuff that other people missed. He could focus his senses and get a feel for a place that other people wouldn't detect. It wasn't something he switched on and off, it simply was what Jak was. That's why he made such a good point man and scout.

Right now, he hung a little way back from the others, alert to his surroundings but also aware of the technological marvels that lay behind them back in Progress. A ville like that had weapons, Jak figured; that stood to reason. They might have shown kindness to the companions, but even a cannie showed kindness to a fella long enough to take a bite from him. Catching people unawares might just as well be the motto of the Deathlands, when it came down to it.

Jak looked around furtively, scanning the emaciated trees that lined the left-hand side of the trail, the overgrown tangle of crops that ran along the right. The crops changed now and again, here rapeseed, there maize, but they all looked pretty much untended to, their once-neat rows ramshackle, spilling out and vying for space. Insects buzzed around, birds too, pollinating and pecking at the seeds as was their wont. The birds were big predatory things that most likely preferred a diet of meat to seeds. That's why there weren't any smaller birds, Jak guessed—the big ones had eaten all the little ones long ago.

This place had a smell to it; a smell of burned crops, like farms in the fall. But it wasn't fall. Although the nukecaust had altered the Earth's environment dramatically, shifting seasons and rewriting their effects, it was still clear to Jak that this place, wherever they were, was experiencing the start of summer. The leaves on the trees and bushes were a healthy green, the grass at their feet the same. But that smell, that scent of burning vegetation—that was wrong. The sun wasn't intense enough to start fires yet, and Jak had spent the past two weeks in this place, he knew it was getting warmer not cooler.

"Ryan," Jak whispered. He was way back from the group now, thirty or forty paces at least, standing on his own on the dusty trail.

Ryan and the others halted, turning to face Jak. Ricky, youngest and most impetuous of their number, was already drawing his blaster, the Webley Mk VI, whipping it out from its holster in a flash.

"What is it, Jak?" Ryan asked.

"Smoke," Jak said, sniffing at the air. "That way."

Jak pointed and the companions looked in that direction, searching for a hint of the smoke he had detected. Ryan engaged the magnification in his artificial eye, scanning the horizon the way he used to do with his longblaster's scope.

"See anything?" J.B. asked from behind him. He had a pair of mini-binoculars up to his eyes now, retrieved from his satchel.

"No...wait...yes," Ryan said, watching the horizon. There was smoke there, dark wisps of it curling among the trees.

"Want to take a closer look-see," J.B. asked, "or should we get moving?"

Ryan weighed the options for a moment. Keeping a wide berth until they were well clear of whatever was burning was probably the smart choice, but it left them open to whatever had caused it coming up behind them. Better to go look, not get too close mebbe, and assess what had happened. "We'll take a look," Ryan said, then added, raising his voice, "Everyone on triple red. Let's not let anything sneak up on us from here on in."

Ricky began to argue. "We never let anyth—"

Mildred silenced him with a look as she pulled her Czech-made ZKR 551 target pistol from the holster at her hip. "Ryan says stay alert," she told him, "he means it. Got it?"

Ricky nodded, chastised. "Got it."

The group trudged through the lemon grove to their right and made their way toward the source of the smoke. They trekked across overgrown fields,

where crops had grown so tall they loomed well above
Ryan's head. The crops were some kind of cereal, narrow stalks a pleasing golden color, but they had grown
so thick that they had become tangled, and in places
the crops stood almost like a fence barring the companions' way. Ryan and J.B. used their knives to hack
their way through the densest parts, while Doc used his
sword stick to do likewise.

"Sure is a quick way to dull a knife," J.B. lamented
as he hacked through a plaited tangle of golden stalks.

"We'll sharpen them after," Ryan replied, sweat glistening on his arms and forehead. It was proving harder
going than he had anticipated.

As the others pushed on through the wall of crop,
Krysty halted, her head rotating slowly as if she was
scenting the air. Mildred turned back, realizing that
Krysty was already dropping behind them where she
stood.

"What is it?" Mildred asked.

Krysty's emerald eyes seemed almost to glow for a
moment, as if they had caught a shaft of moonlight in
darkness. Her hair had tensed around her head, coiling
in on itself like a pit of venomous snakes.

"Krysty?" Mildred prompted.

"Danger." Krysty uttered the word with a strain of
emotion. "The field… The plants are on fire."

Mildred stared at Krysty for a moment, and only then
did the full weight of her words sink in. "This field?"
Mildred asked, her voice barely a whisper.

Krysty nodded as her hair clung to her skull. "Yes.
If we don't do something, we're all going to burn."

Chapter Eleven

Krysty was a mutie, with an empathic connection to Gaia, goddess of the Earth. She could sense things that others couldn't, draw on the wellspring of energy given to her by the Earth Mother. She also knew about flowers and plants like no one Mildred had ever met, but she was no gardener—this was more than that, an ability to almost "tune in" to the plant life around her, the way a person might have tuned in the frequency on an old transistor radio back in the day.

By now, the others had stopped hacking at the tight-packed rows of corn, aware that the two women of the group were discussing something of import.

"Krysty?" Ryan asked.

"The field's on fire," Krysty said. "We have to move quickly or we'll be caught up in it."

"Where?"

Krysty pointed, ahead and to the left. "That way, small but building rapidly."

Doc licked his index finger and held it aloft. "The wind's coming from that direction," he stated after a moment's consideration. "If there is fire, it will be moving this way."

Ryan peered in the direction Krysty had indicated, cursing the thick growth of corn that blocked his vision. He switched his robotic eye to infrared vision, gazed for a moment into the distance hoping he might be able to peer through the crop—but it was no good, all he saw was the same image painted in eerie, luminescent streaks. The eye would take some getting used to—and now wasn't the time.

At the same time, Ricky crouched and made a stirrup of his hands, which Jak stepped into to be lifted into the air until he could see—just barely—over the tops of the yellow corn.

"Smoke," Jak confirmed. "Corn like candles. People too."

It wasn't much to go on—Jak's explanations rarely were, with his abbreviated patois—but it painted a clear picture of what was happening: the tops of the corn were on fire, and fire spread.

"They could be burning off the crops to clear the field of pests," Doc proposed. "It is not unheard of."

"We'd never be that lucky," J.B. griped, handing his binoculars up to Jak. "What do you see?"

Jak used the binocs to scan the area more carefully. There was a farmhouse about a hundred yards away and almost directly ahead of them, and a barn towered nearby over to the right, its high roof gleaming in the sunlight. Several motorbikes in good condition were parked outside the farmhouse, with two riders waiting. The riders held burning torches. Jak related what he had seen to the others.

"They don't sound like farmers clearing the fields," Mildred said ominously.

"We'll split up," Ryan stated, nodding.

"That barn would be a good spot to pick people off if you're setting up an ambush," J.B. proposed.

Ryan stared at him querulously. "Us or them?" he asked.

"Either," J.B. replied. "Me and Doc'll check it out."

"Carefully," Doc added.

With that, the two men moved off to the right, pushing their way through the overgrown stalks of corn. In a moment they had disappeared, the thick cornstalks closing behind them like a golden curtain.

Jak and Ricky moved in the opposite direction, pushing onward via a circuitous route toward the farmhouse, granting the approaching fire a wide berth.

That left Ryan with the two women. They would approach more cautiously, holding back a little and relying on Krysty's strong connection to the natural life around her to steer them away from the fire as it spread.

Ryan barged his way between the close-knit stalks, occasionally employing his panga to cut back the most tangled of the stalks. Krysty joined him, producing her own hunting knife from a sheath to hack at the tangled stalks.

Mildred had her blaster in her hand, scanning the field for signs of danger. The reality was that anyone could sneak up on the companions at any time while they were here in this field—the crop was so thick that they would not know they were being attacked until their assailants were almost upon them. Mildred was a crack shot. She trusted her wits and speed to at least give them a fighting chance if it happened.

CLOSE BY, J.B. and Doc made their own path toward the barn looming at the edge of the field. The barn was all but hidden by the thick curtain of gold, but its high roof could just be seen, a streak of red resting above the highest spokes of the crop. They found the easiest route they could, using their blades only occasionally to cut aside the most truculent of the golden crop. Dust flew all around, a haze of golden specks from the corn.

"By the Three Kennedys, 'tis hard work this. How far do we have to go?" Doc asked. He sounded breathless.

"Hundred fifty yards mebbe," J.B. told him, using his combat knife to hack at another tangled spike of corn.

"Slow going," Doc muttered, shaking his head.

"Tough terrain," J.B. replied, tying a rag around his neck and pulling it up over his mouth and nostrils to help filter out the flying corn dust.

Doc followed suit, wrapping his handkerchief over the lower part of his face.

It wasn't far now—they just had to keep ahead of the spreading flames.

JAK FOLLOWED A more circuitous route through the overgrown fields, with Ricky keeping up behind him. Jak was lithe and athletic, and his smaller frame was better suited to finding or creating gaps in the tangled, mutie crop.

"You have any idea what's ahead of us?" Ricky asked, keeping the volume of his voice down.

Jak sniffed the air, searching left and right for his next pathway. "Death," Jak replied grimly. One way or another, that's always what smoke meant.

THE SCENT OF the smoke changed as they got closer, turning from that dry smell of burning vegetation to something richer and headier, the smell of burning meat. Puffs of soot-gray smoke plumed into the sky, curling slowly above the field of corn, painting the nearest ears with smudges of black.

Jak and Ricky were the first to see the burning property as Jak parted the tall sheaves of golden corn. It was still in the distance, a little down slope with a ring of flames burning all around it. Something moved in those flames, a four-legged animal that could have been a horse or a mule, its back on fire.

People were walking among the flames, casually making their way from the lone farmhouse that burned in its center. The farmhouse was constructed of wood, and large enough to provide a home to three or four families, mebbe even give them each their own quarters, separate from one another. Jak guessed that perhaps twenty or thirty people had lived there in a commune— maybe not enough to tend to the fields that surrounded the place but at least enough to try. The whole place was on fire now, flames licking up its sides and dancing on its roof.

Six figures were striding away from the flames, not hurrying and not bothering to look back to the burning building behind them. They were mostly men, tall, broad-shouldered, strong-looking, and they wore denim, hard wearing but leaving tanned skin showing. Jak couldn't make out the holsters from here, but he knew they would have them—these were predators, coldhearts, chillers. There were vehicles parked a little way from the property, motorbikes and a quad bike, retrofitted engines and patched-up tires testaments to their endurance. The group was making its way toward them, leaving the farmhouse and the fields immediately around it to burn.

"What's going on?" Ricky asked, his eyes fixed on the distant farmhouse.

"Nothin' good," Jak replied without turning.

Waiting in the field, masked by the towering sheaves of corn, Jak and Ricky watched as a figure crashed through an upstairs window of the burning property. It was a woman, her dress on fire. She landed in a crumpled heap beyond the flaming porch, rolling over and over to put out the flames that licked at her clothes, screaming in fear.

One of the coldhearts who had been striding away from the property swiveled on his heel and shot from the hip without warning, driving a bullet through the burning woman's skull before she had even had time to put out the flames. The shooter turned back and strode away, not bothering to look as the fire took hold of his victim once more, consuming the tattered remains of her dress and blazing across her flesh.

Ricky was horrified. "We should do something," he hissed, grip tightening on his Webley, reaching for his other blaster with his other hand—a repro De Lisle carbine that hung on a sling across his back.

Jak held up one ghost-pale hand to halt him. "Stay," he said. "Go now, get chilled."

It was sound advice, but it didn't sit well with Ricky. The burning woman had put him in mind of his sister. Together, they watched as the six figures mounted the bikes, two of them sharing the quad bike, and tore away through the smoky field.

Chapter Twelve

You didn't have to go looking for trouble in the Deathlands for it to find you. It was a lawless state, with too many people vying for too little resources, and far too many of those people comfortable taking from those who could not defend themselves.

In the cornfield, Ricky and Jak watched as the bikers roared away, kicking up a wall of dirt as their beaten-up tires sought purchase, before tearing away from the burning building. The bikers bumped over the dirt track that encircled the farmhouse like a lasso, before following it through the field in an insect hum of powerful engines.

A woman passenger was clinging on the back of the quad bike, holding a flaming torch that Jak guessed had been used to ignite the farmhouse and its surroundings. She ran the torch over the crop as they passed, setting light to more stalks of corn. The tops of the corn flickered like a line of candles where the torch touched them with its red-gold tongue, sending winding trails of black smoke into the sky.

As soon as the bikes had passed the edge of the house, Jak and Ricky began to move, running toward the burning domicile. They exchanged no words, gave no cue; they simply knew when it was the moment act, the moment when it would be safe—or as safe as it was going to get, anyhow. Jak ran ahead, faster than Ricky,

his hands slicing the air like knives as he raced toward
the house. Blaster in hand, Ricky was slower. He gal-
loped sidewise, eyeing the building's edge where the
motorcycle gang had disappeared. His heart was drumming against his chest, adrenaline pumping and he was
ready to blast the strangers if he had to.

The intensity of heat could be felt even fifty feet
away, radiating from the raging inferno that had once
been a house. The horse or mule was lying outside the
circle of flames, still burning like a pyre, clouds of thick
black smoke billowing from its blackened form with an
awful stench of cooking flesh. Beyond that, the flames
themselves licked at the building, windows lost behind
curtains of flame, the open doorway a dark stain amid
the flickering wall.

The woman was lying close to the front door, body
aflame, her dress now barely more than a wisp of material where it had either burned away or been singed
to her body. Jak ignored her, skirting around the flames
issuing from her as he ran for the house.

This close to the building Jak could hear shouts and
screams over the crackling of the flames, a baby wail-
ing, people shouting in fear, children crying. There was
a smell too—burning wood plus burning flesh; death by
fire. Jak didn't think about that, he just ran for the dark
sliver of open door that was playing peekaboo through
the flames. As he raced through it, the lintel gave way,
crashing down two inches behind his retreating form.

Ricky watched in astonishment as Jak disappeared
inside the farmhouse, the doorway falling apart around
his retreating figure.

"Jak! Don't—" he shouted, but his warning was cut
short as he swallowed a mouthful of smoke and started

to cough. He stood outside the burning house, hacking over and over, his eyes streaming from the smoke.

JAK WAS INSIDE, sweat already running in rivers down his forehead, his cheeks, his chin.

He stood in the building's lobby, a wide space with a staircase running up into the upper levels. He could see the staircase even through the flames, the struts of its banister rail alight with fire, like a line of burning jail cell bars.

The air was thick with smoke, great clouds of blackness masking anything more than a couple of feet ahead. Moving quickly was his best chance for survival—track people by their screams, find anyone still alive.

People screamed upstairs.

Jak took a step toward the stairs, feeling the intense heat all around him like a blanket. The house creaked, and he heard something come crashing down on the floor above. Yes, he would have to move quickly if he was going to get out of there alive.

He eyed the stairs. The people were up there. The coldhearts, whoever they were, would have chased them up there to make sure they couldn't get out when they torched the place. That's why the woman had come crashing through the upstairs window, because that had been her egress.

Standing at the foot of the staircase Jak called out, hoping to get a better idea of where the survivors were. "Anyone?" he called. "Shout out."

As he spoke, the thick smoke assaulted his nostrils and a layer of ashy saliva seemed to carpet his tongue. He hunkered down into himself, pulled his shirt out of his pants, and raised the top of the shirt until he could hook it over his mouth and nose. That way he could breathe through the material, filter out the worst of the smoke. Even then, he wouldn't have long.

A shout echoed back from above, but whether it was meant for him or just a cry of fear, Jak couldn't tell.

Breathing through the makeshift mask of his shirt, Jak ran up the burning stairs. His feet skimmed across their surface as he sped deeper into the burning building, barely touching the stairs before he moved on to the next. Behind and all around him, the walls were burning as well as the banister as spots of flame began to take hold on the stairs themselves.

"SMOKE'S GETTING HEAVIER," Mildred said as she shoved back a tangled mass of stalks, holding them so that Ryan and Krysty could pass.

"Get ready," Ryan warned, drawing his SIG Sauer and brushing the last of the corn aside.

Behind him, Ryan's companions steeled themselves for what lay beyond the cornfield.

"MADRE DI DIABLO!" Ricky gritted as he bent double in the dirt.

He was in the yard of the burning house, still trying to catch his breath. The smoke had tickled his throat, and it was all he could do to stop the coughing. He rubbed his free hand across his eyes, swiping at the tears.

"Hello, pretty boy," a voice called from close by. A man's voice with an affected accent that made it sound almost as though he was singing the words.

When Ricky looked up, he saw the man poised there, still astride his motorcycle, and his eyes darted immediately to the metal glinting in the man's hand. The stranger had a patchy beard and long hair. He rested one hand atop the turned handlebars of his bike. He wore a denim vest and had tattoos across his bare chest and arms—but they weren't decorative, Ricky saw; the tats were lines, like markings for surgical incisions. The biker had similar markings across his forehead and around the left side of his jaw, and Ricky saw something metallic glinting behind them.

It had taken less than a second for Ricky to see all that, processing what he saw in his brain even as he raised the Webley Mk VI to take a shot at the stranger. The man shot quicker, a blast exploding from the handlebars and whizzing beside Ricky with a howl of splitting air.

Chapter Thirteen

Ricky dived, cursing himself for allowing someone to sneak up on him. He was around the far side of the burning building in an instant, even as a second shot from the biker kicked up dirt where he stepped. Still coughing, Ricky landed on the ground, rolled and pulled himself into a crouch, bringing the Webley around to train it on the building edge. He recognized the biker as one of the motley crew who had driven away a minute before. They had to have heard Ricky's coughing and sent one of their crew back to check.

"Why so shy, pretty boy?" the biker taunted in a loud, singsong voice. "Don't you want to play?" He laughed at that, the sound mingling with the crackling noise of the inferno at Ricky's back.

Ricky took a steadying breath, fighting back the urge to cough again, and peered out from the red-hot cover of the farmhouse. His head popped out for just a fraction of a second, taking in everything he could, confirming the bike man's position. To Ricky's left, the sounds of combustion engines grew louder. Damn! They were coming at him from all sides, hoping to surround him, trap him.

Ricky leaned out again, the Webley extended in his right hand. Out there, the bearded biker was laughing, and he looked surprised when he saw Ricky. Even so, he reacted well, sending another burst of fire from whatever weapon he had resting on the handlebars of his bike. Ricky stroked the Webley's trigger at the same time, sending a .45-caliber message to his laughing foe.

The biker's large bore blast missed Ricky by a foot, disappearing into the burning wall above his head and emerging in a trail of flames like a firefly. Ricky's shot was better placed, drilling into the biker's left cheek even as he dipped to avoid it. The biker's face erupted in an explosion of blood, a line of crimson-black spattering the ground like spilled paint.

Ricky ran in a weaving, zigzag path toward his would-be chiller, firing another bullet on the run.

"How pretty do you think I am now, huh?" he spit as he pulled the trigger.

The bullet struck the biker high in the chest, and he watched as the man sagged back in his seat, head lolling on his shoulders. Behind him, Ricky could hear more engines getting louder, closer.

As the biker was thrown back, his bike teetered and fell, striking the ground with a crash of metal like clashing cymbals. Ricky stood transfixed, eyeing the fallen biker where his leg was trapped beneath the weight of the fallen hog. He saw now that the man didn't have a blaster—not in his hand anyway. What he had was a pipe in place of his right arm, like an attachment on a predark vacuum cleaner. The pipe was made of ridged metal, wider than the man's muscular arm at the elbow, then tapering to a narrow opening at the end, as thick as two of Ricky's fingers. The youth tilted his head as he looked at it, trying to make sense of what he was looking at. The man had shot at him. But there was no blaster—just this thing. A tube, like the barrel of a blaster, but attached somehow to the man's limb. But it was too narrow at its extremity to be a glove. So, not attached to the arm then—but in place of it.

Behind Ricky, the roar of the motorbike engines grew louder, like the angry buzzing of a hornet's nest. He turned, broke open the Webley and used a moon clip to reload the revolver, spying the first of the gang as the tires of their bikes rounded the building's edge. They were coming at him from all sides, whooping and cheering, death on their minds.

THE SMOKE WAS SPREADING, painting the sky above the field with a thick smear of charcoal gray. Doc and J.B. pushed on through the cornfield, finally reaching its edge.

The Armorer parted the last line of golden stalks, warily eyeing what lay beyond. It was a road, just a dirt track really, lined with stones and ridged by the frequent passage of a cart or carts heavily laden with produce. The farmhouse was two hundred yards down the track, off to J.B.'s left, while the barn waited on the far side of road, a little way to his right.

Doc nudged against J.B.'s shoulder as he slipped the shining blade of his sword back into the sheath that made up his cane. "The fire is still a little ways off," Doc said, his voice muffled through the handkerchief he had tied over his mouth. "Shall we?" He pointed to the barn as if inviting J.B. to partner him in a grand old dance hall.

J.B. held his arm out before Doc like the safety barrier on a ride.

"Hold up, Doc," he said, the words spoken in hushed tones. As he spoke, J.B. slipped his combat knife back into its hidden sheath behind his hip with his left hand

and pulled his mini-Uzi out of its hiding place with his right.

Doc scanned the road, following where J.B. was watching. Black smoke billowed into the air from the burning field, whipping across road and fields like the tail of a kite. Glowing spots like fireflies danced in that black smoke, the stubs of the corn as they caught alight. Then Doc saw the movements through the dark smoke, vehicles moving along the track toward the farmhouse. "Who—?"

"Jak mentioned motorcycles," the Armorer reminded Doc. "They're circling the house, playing sentry...or worse."

"Worse?" Doc asked, alarmed.

J.B. nodded toward the barn. "Let's get to cover before we're seen. We can figure our next move"

Doc nodded his agreement and the two men darted across the dirt road, wisps of gray-black smoke trailing around them, the long tails of Doc's frock coat billowing behind him like a bird's tail.

JAK SCRAMBLED UPSTAIRS and weaved past a burning timber as it fell from the ceiling. Wherever the survivors were, he hoped that it was on this floor and not the one above—because there wouldn't be much left of that floor in a few minutes, not with the way the roof beams were dropping in firework streaks.

"Where?" Jak shouted, pulling the shirt down from his mouth long enough to expel the word. "Anyone here?"

He listened for a moment, trying to detect a human voice over the crackling of the flames. Smoke filled the hallway, doors burned along it like flaming sconces. He wouldn't have long.

"Help!" a voice cried back, sounding strained and fearful.

"Where?" Jak repeated the word twice more as he turned on the spot.

"We're here!" the voice replied. He figured it for a woman or mebbe an adolescent, but he couldn't be sure. It was high and strained, of that much he was certain. And it was coming from ahead and to his left.

Jak moved, hitching the shirt back over his mouth and nose as he ran across smoldering floorboards, past burning walls, the smoke thick all around him.

A door stood to his left, closed tight, the paintwork on the frame and door edges beginning to blister from the heat. Jak tried it once, pulling the cuff of his jacket over his hand to protect him from the heat. "You here?" he shouted as he tried the doorknob.

Locked, the door held.

"You here?" Jak repeated, louder this time.

A voice came back, too quiet, choking on something. "H-help us," the voice pleaded. It seemed to be coming from behind the door, a little way behind it but behind it all the same.

Jak stepped back, then kicked out at the doorknob, once, twice, with the heel of his boot. The knob shook in its frame, while the wood around the lock began to splinter. Jak kicked a third time, and the metal lock, knob and a five-inch hunk of door fell away with a crash.

Inside was a bathroom, tin bath in its center, the walls turning black with smoke. And there was a figure standing by the wall, a hole in its gut wide as a man's fist. The figure looked like a man, hairless but it was made of metal that shone with the rainbow colors of oil on water.

Unconsciously, Jak stepped back as he spotted the
metal man, his hand going automatically to his holstered blaster.

"In here!" a voice called from the far right of the
room. Jak tracked the voice, saw there was a second
door to the side of the metal man.

"What you?" Jak muttered, eyeing the metal man
more closely. The metal man stood silently before the
inner door like a suit of armor, its innards ripped out
and strewed across the floor like a person's guts. Something had damaged it, probably just a single shot from
a large bore weapon, ripping its middle out as it tried
to protect the door. It had succeeded, or its opponent
hadn't cared—either way, there were people behind that
door, Jak knew; people in trouble.

He moved past the metal man and tried the door
handle.

Locked.

No surprise there.

"Safe now," Jak said, pressing his face close to the
door so he could be heard.

The voice that came back was quiet, breathless.
"Help us."

"You lock in?" Jak asked, trying the handle again.
As he did, he glanced back over his shoulder, watching the way the flames were charring the walls of the
corridor just beyond the little bathroom.

"We can't...open..." The voice trailed off, weaker
with every syllable until it couldn't be heard at all.

The bikers had locked them in then, or something
like that. Maybe they had locked themselves here for
their own safety, but the lock had broken or the door
had warped with the heat.

Jak pushed his shoulder against the door, twisting

the handle and pressing his weight against it, feeling for movement. Yeah, it still had a little give, there at the top and the bottom, either side of the lock itself.

"Stay back," Jak called, shouting to be heard over the spit-hiss-crackle of the flames.

The reply was a whimper, that was all.

THE BIKES CAME FAST, blazing around both sides of the farmhouse and bearing down on Ricky as he crouched in the dirt.

Ricky fanned the trigger of his Webley three times, sending a stream of shots at the approaching bikers as they raced around the corner closest to him. He should conserve his bullets, he knew, but conserving bullets and staying alive sometimes didn't go together so well. Right now he was surrounded and outnumbered, with a burning building to his rear and a burning field as his only escape route.

Behind him, two bikes bumped over the ground, weaving past their fallen comrade as they raced toward Ricky. The youth spun, sending a .45 ACP blast at the woman riding the lead bike. She had long brown hair trailing down one half of her head while the other side was shaved almost bald. She laughed as Ricky's shot went wide, ducked low in the saddle as he loosed another blast in her direction.

Three bikes were emerging from the other side of the building, fanning out as they tore around the corner, blocking the space between the burning building and the blazing field. Two of the riders held flaming torches, one posted pillion behind the tattooed driver, the sound of engines cutting the air like a swarm of angry honeybees.

Ricky blasted again, sending another bullet at the trio

of bikers roaring toward him. He watched as it struck the central rider's cheek, and gasped as it pinged away with a flash of sparks.

IN THE BATHROOM with the metal man, Jak kicked out at the locked door, his booted foot slamming hard against it at the high point of the handle. The wood snapped with a splintering noise, creating a small round hole above the handle, two inches across.

"Back!" Jak instructed before moving forward and kicking out again.

Slam! His foot struck the door beside the handle.

Slam! Again, and this time a great chunk of the door fell away when he drew his foot back.

Jak gave it one more kick, watching dark lines appear in the wood like streaks from a painter's brush where it was cracking. Then he ran at it, shoulder first, colliding with the locked door like a runaway freight train.

The door tumbled forward, its lock shattering in a wrench of metal and splintering wood, hinges straining and ripping from the frame.

Then Jak was in the next room, recovering himself as the door sagged on its remaining hinge, caught at a forty degree angle to the floor.

It was a smaller room, less than half the size of the bathroom and it featured a chamber pot attached to a wooden seat. The room was filling with smoke, paint peeled down the wall that abutted the corridor and the tiny window was so black with smoke it was like looking out into the night. Three people crouched in the corner of the tiny room behind the commode, a straw-haired woman holding a baby and a youth in his teens, with long, dark hair that fell over his face. They looked up at Jak fearfully, their faces red with the heat.

"Go," Jak said, shoving the ruined door back on its single hinge.

The youth looked at Jak through the curtain of his long bangs. "Are they still here?"

Jak shrugged. That didn't matter; they would die if they stayed here, that's all he knew. "Go," he said again, this time more forcefully.

The youth stood, helping the woman unsteadily to her feet. She swayed as if she was drunk, and Jak guessed she was light-headed from the smoke.

"Do this." Jak showed the lad, pulling the top of his raised shirt down then hitching it back up until it covered his nose. "Go quick."

The youth copied Jak and so did the woman, traipsing out of the toilet area and into the bathroom. Once they reached the corridor, Jak heard them cry out in surprise.

"The whole place is on fire," the youth said. Jak figured he had been the voice he had heard through the door. "We can't—"

"Can," Jak said, pushing him onward with one hand until he staggered into the corridor. "Only death here."

The youth glared at him, then took the woman's hand—probably his mother—and pulled her out into the corridor as flames licked at the walls.

"Who else?" Jak asked, keeping pace with the threesome.

"Betsy," the youth replied, "my dad, Trev—he works the farm—"

"Not matter," Jak interrupted. "How many?"

Jak could see the teen doing the quick count in his head. "Twelve, plus the baby," he said.

"Eleven then," Jak said. "Nine now."

Jak didn't say anything else, as he moved down the

corridor, checking the doors. The youth and the woman watched him for a moment before darting down the burning staircase.

"Find them," the youth pleaded.

Jak nodded. "Not promise," he replied.

METAL ON METAL. That was the burst of sparks that Ricky had seen when his bullet hit the lead biker, he was sure of it. It had that same blue tint that he had seen in his uncle's workshop, when Tio Benito had struck the bent barrel of a useless blaster with his hammer to try to force it back into shape.

Then, just like the first biker, this one had metal in his face, behind the skin, there below the eyes. What the hell was he fighting here? Who were these people?

But there was no time to think about that now. Ricky was surrounded, hemmed in on all sides as the motorcycles roared toward him across the dirt patch behind the farmhouse. Ricky fumbled in his pocket for another moon clip, broke open his blaster and reloaded in scant seconds. He brought up his blaster for another shot, knowing full well he could not win—not against so many enemies, not on his own like this. He glanced at the farmhouse, hoping—wishing—that Jak would emerge—but he didn't.

Bike engines roared. Cruel laughter resounded through the air, coupled with the cackling taunts of the bikers and their women.

The lead bike's engine growled like an animal as it raced the final few feet toward Ricky, crouched in the lee of the burning building. He saw the biker's cruel sneer, saw the sadistic rage in the man's eyes, saw the silver streak of metal where his bullet had struck and achieved nothing. The two other bikes ran to either side, just a couple of feet behind the leader. Ricky pushed himself back, squeezed the Webley's trigger again, hoping against hope that somehow, some way, he could survive the impossible.

Chapter Fourteen

And then the lead bike exploded in a fireball, erupting into a ragged, orange-yellow sphere as the fuel tank blew, sending its madly grinning rider high into the air. Riding beside the exploding bike, the leader's two companions were caught in the shock wave—one went careening into the burning farmhouse, slamming into and through the wooden wall in a pillar of expanding flames; the other went racing off toward the field, front wheel bent, a blanket of thick black smoke enveloping bike and rider in an instant.

"Madre de Satanás!" Ricky cried, rolling out of the way as the inferno that had been the lead bike barreled toward him with the force of its momentum, burning pipes and red-hot slivers of rubber from the disintegrating tires preceding it in a deadly hailstorm of debris. Ricky rolled onto his chest, bringing his arms up over his head as the bike roared past in a flaming mass of skeletal struts.

As he rolled, Ricky saw the muzzle-flash from the edge of the cornfield, heard the familiar report of Ryan's Steyr Scout Tactical longblaster. Behind him, one of the bike riders toppled off his steed, his face erupting in a geyser of blood as he went crashing to the ground. His passenger clung on as the bike reared out of control, speeding past Ricky with a high-pitched roar of twin-stroke engine. Ricky turned and loosed a shot at the passenger. He watched in grim satisfaction as the biker's chest bloomed with an expanding stain of blood.

"Ricky! Stay sharp!" Ryan cried from the field's edge, where he was kneeling with the Steyr Scout in his hands. As he spoke, he squeezed the Steyr's trigger again, unleashing the bullet on the exhalation of his own breath, sending it on an arrow-straight path at the last biker's chest. The woman took the bullet full force, falling backward and yet crashing over her own handlebars. In an instant, her long hair had caught in the front wheel and she let out an agonized shriek as her face was pulled mercilessly into the spinning wheel.

Ricky turned away, heard the scream and the sound of snapping bone as the woman was dragged under her own bike. The bike sped on, wrenching its rider's hair from her scalp and disappearing into the cornfield where black smoke cast a cover like an umbrella.

A moment later, Krysty and Mildred emerged from the golden corn, blasters ready as they scoured the area. Ryan remained kneeling, his robotic eye lined up with the longblaster; he had not bothered to use the scope.

"Are there more of them, Ricky?" Mildred asked urgently.

Ricky shook his head. "I…I don't know. We saw six, including the four-wheeler—"

"Where's Jak?" Ryan interrupted, standing up but still holding the longblaster ready against his shoulder.

"In there," Ricky said, indicating the farmhouse. The building was a flaming inferno now, thick black smoke billowing above it like the swirl of the Grim Reaper's cloak.

"Fireblast!"

DOC AND J.B. turned at the explosion. They were standing at the doors to the barn—two joining doors, locked with a thick chain. Each door was twice the height of Doc's tall frame.

"That came from the house," Doc said, his brow furrowed with concern. "Do you think that Ryan—?"

"It was too big to just be from the fire," J.B. said. "There was an accelerant—mebbe a fuel tank of some kind."

"An engine, perhaps?" Doc proposed. "One of the bike gang?"

"I reckon," J.B. said, nodding grimly. "Which means, if they've got friends they'll have heard and they'll be on their way before we know it." He glanced up and down the bare dirt road. "Best we get inside."

Doc agreed, but they still hadn't solved the problem of the locked barn doors. People weren't very trusting in the Deathlands, locking something up went 90 percent toward owning it, even if you hadn't owned it to begin with.

"There may be another door," Doc suggested, pointing around the side of the building.

"No," J.B. muttered, reaching into his satchel. "We'll use this one." With that, J.B. produced a small charge from his bag. The charge looked like putty, and when the Armorer pressed it against the chain it molded there and stuck fast. He stuck a remote detonator into the plas ex.

"Get back," J.B. instructed, stepping away from the doors.

Doc did as he was told and after a moment the charge went off, creating a small explosion, as loud as a gull's call and just enough to break the links in the chain.

Broken, the chain clattered to the ground with a cymbal clash of metal on metal.

A moment later, J.B. reached for the doors and pulled one open before stepping inside. Doc followed.

"Black dust!" J.B. cursed as he saw what lay beyond the doors.

Standing at his side, just inside the doorway, Doc's hand tensed on the grip of his LeMat pistol. Before them, the barn was filled with metal struts and arms that seemed utterly incongruous to its worn wooden structure. Nothing moved, and there was an eerie silence to the whole, spacious room.

"What the Dickens have we walked into?" Doc asked, his voice barely above a whisper.

J.B. had no answer.

NINE TO FIND. That was the only thought running through Jak's brain as he scrambled up a second flight of stairs and into the final third story of the farmhouse.

He had checked everywhere he could on the floor below, zipping into whatever rooms he could open but finding no one. The three from the bathroom would be down the stairs by now, leaving Jak alone to find whoever was left.

The stairs creaked and hissed as Jak's booted feet skipped over them. There were sparks running up the sides of the stairs and the walls, tiny specks of white hotness as the rooms behind burned. The smoke was so thick that it was hard to see much other than the sparks, and Jak misjudged where the last stair was and slipped, treading down hard on a step that wasn't there.

At the landing, the smoke was like a curtain of fog, masking all but the closest of things. Jak could see he was in a corridor, saw two doors peeling off to left and right, the right-hand one wide-open with a flutter of flames dancing across the frame. Jak ducked his head through the open doorway and peered into the room beyond. He was in a child's bedroom, a wooden cot standing by the wall, simple toys lining the shelves, only visible now through gaps in the billowing smoke.

Jak rushed over to the cot, peered inside. There was a child there, wrapped in a blanket, not moving. Jak reached in, lifted the child out and realized he had been mistaken—it wasn't a child, just a doll. Lifelike when seen through the haze of smoke, but just a caricature up close.

Throwing the toy down, Jak stalked out of the room, calling out as he went. "Anyone here?" Jak shouted, speaking through the buffer of his shirt. Even through the material he could taste the smoke, a burnt taste that made his throat feel painfully dry. "Call out!"

Jak listened, hoping to hear someone call back. When no one did he tried again, then a third time, but no response came.

Jak hurried along the corridor, trying the door handles as he passed them. They were red-hot, too hot to touch without protection. He used the pulled-down sleeves of his shirt to protect his hands, but even with that he had to move quickly, checking each door with the swiftest of movements before the heat bled through the material and burned him.

The first three rooms were empty—two bedrooms and a simple restroom. The fourth door was locked and Jak knocked hard against it and called out, but he received no response.

There were no other rooms here. If the people were in the locked room, then they weren't responding, which meant they were either unconscious or dead, probably from asphyxiation.

Frustrated, Jak looked around again, his eyes stinging with the smoke. It was hard to see straight now, his eyes were burning with tears, aching in a way that made them feel as though they were too large for their sockets.

Then he saw the ladder, leaning at a seventy degree angle at the end of the hallway before a window, stretching up into the roof space. An attic or perhaps a loft; somewhere to hide, anyway.

Jak grabbed a rung of the ladder and called up. "Anyone there? Here help." As he spoke, he climbed up the ladder, his feet clattering on the rungs.

OUTSIDE THE FARMHOUSE, Ryan and Krysty surveyed the area while Mildred scrambled over to join Ricky, grabbing his head and turning it to check for wounds.

"You hurt?" she asked.

"Few scratches," Ricky admitted.

"No shots?"

"Nada."

The bikers were strewed around the burning building, their motorcycles scattered about them, one of which was nothing more now than a burning pile of red-hot scrap.

"Who are these people?" Krysty asked, eyeing the fallen bikers warily.

Ryan shook his head. "Would knowing that change anything?" he asked.

"Probably not," Krysty replied, accepting his point.

As she spoke, Ryan scanned the bike gang using his new eye. It flashed through infrared, focusing sharply on one of the crew where he lay facedown in the dirt, his beard thick with dust. There was something about the man. Ryan saw a metal plate where his cheek had been shot by Ricky, as if he had suffered reconstructive surgery. There was more metal in his hand, a replacement that turned it into a weapon. That wasn't so unusual—people lost limbs and healers did what they could with what tools they had to let people carry on. But it nagged at Ryan, seeing advanced tech like that welded to a man's arm.

The scan showed the man to be human, or warm-bodied anyway. Ryan couldn't tell more than that. He was no expert in what to look for, and he was not yet proficient with his remarkable new eye.

Mildred noticed Ryan staring as she looked up from checking over Ricky's cuts and abrasions. "Something caught your eye, Ryan?"

Ryan looked at her—scanned her—saw the way her body heat emanated from her central core. It was the same as the biker; so whatever that metal was, it was an implant in his skull, his hand. He was still human, more or less.

Before Ryan answered, there was a crashing sound at the burning doorway of the house and two people stumbled out—a teenager with long, dark bangs that brushed in front of his eyes assisting a straw-haired woman, who walked as if she was drunk or high on jolt or both. Looking more closely, Ryan saw that the woman had a baby cradled in her arms, wrapped in a blanket. He stepped across to them, got his arm behind the woman and the boy and pushed them, gently but firmly, away from the burning house and the blazing debris all around.

"You okay?" Ryan asked as Krysty and Mildred hurried over.

The dark-haired youth nodded and tried to speak, but he was caught in a spasm of coughing, and bent over as he tried to catch his breath. "Yeah," he finally gasped, his voice strained. "Got...trapped...inside."

"Is this your mother?" Ryan asked, indicating the woman with the child.

The teen shook his head. "Aunt," he said.

"Mildred, get a safe distance and check these people over," Ryan instructed.

"Will do," Mildred said, immediately leading the group away from the burning farmhouse, out into the charred circle of dirt that remained between flaming fields and burning building. She watched the area around as she went, scanning for more coldhearts.

Ryan looked around him at the fallen bikers, gazed up at the house that was now a black shell burning like a lighter.

"Jak's still in there," Ricky said, joining Ryan.

As they looked at the house, a great chunk of its wooden facade creaked and crashed to the ground. Ryan pulled Ricky and Krysty aside as smoke and a shower of sparks billowed outward.

"He won't last long in there," Ryan stated.

"Jak might not be able to get out either," Ricky said grimly.

"I'll go," Krysty told them, and before Ryan could argue she had slipped past the burning debris in the doorway and disappeared into the inferno.

"Ryan," Mildred said ominously as he watched Krysty disappear. "I think we have another problem."

Ryan turned at the warning, looking where Mildred was staring from her spot twenty feet away in the shadow of the farmhouse. There, amid the burning remains of a motorcycle, one of the bike gang was getting back onto his feet. His flesh was alight, stringy trails of skin and muscle tapering away in streaks of black smoke. Framed in a halo of fire, the biker's face grinned maniacally—a face more metal than flesh.

Chapter Fifteen

The silence inside the barn was eerie. It seemed unnatural somehow, with all that mechanical equipment laid out across the vast space. It wasn't stored here or "parked" here—J.B. could see that much, just by looking at it—at least not most of it. One item had caterpillar tracks at its base, with a kind of turret resting on a swivel point above them, able to rotate through 360 degrees. But the rest looked fixed, mounted along the walls, locked in place by rivets and counterweights to ensure it didn't overbalance.

A maze of metal struts seemed to dominate the barn, weaving through the air above their heads like the tentacles of an octopus. Each strut ran eight feet in length and was jointed at its midpoint, creating a kind of hinged arm effect. The ends of each strut featured a different tool, and J.B. and Doc recognized buzz saws, drills and threshing equipment among those utensils. Below those robot arms ran a conveyor belt, fixed in as a part of the machinery itself, molded into the base unit from which the metal arms sprouted. There were storage bins placed beside and at the ends of the belts, and more to the sides of the room. Some had lids, while others remained open to the air.

While the equipment took up a lot of the wall space, the arms themselves ran high over the barn, sitting at rest where the second story of the barn would be. This

arrangement left plenty of space within which Doc and
J.B. could walk, and they strode warily into that space,
trying to take everything in.

"What have we found?" Doc asked, bewildered.
"Some kind of manufactory?"

"Yeah, but not for blasters," J.B. said, drawing on his
own frame of reference. "This is all farming equipment,
designed to sift crops, chop and process." As he spoke,
he reached into one of the open bins—running his open
fingers through the dusty grain that resided within.

Doc looked at the octopus arms with new understand-
ing. "Robots to sort the wheat from the chaff. Incredible," he said.

"Tech like this takes time to install," J.B. said, hurrying through the poised robot arms toward a set of
wooden slatlike stairs that climbed up into the abbreviated second story. The upper level covered only one-
third of the barn, like a wide shelf sitting against the
rear wall of the structure. J.B. could see a small window there, a good vantage point to look out across the
farm grounds.

J.B. ran up the steps, the Uzi clutched in his right fist.
He sprinted across to the window—it had no glass—
and peered through. He could see the road leading up to
the farmhouse, wisps of smoke galloping across it now
like a stampede. The farmhouse itself was located off
to the far left, which meant that J.B. could see the edge
of it if he strained. Columns of flames ran up its walls,
and a thick plume of dark smoke billowed above. J.B.
leaned on the window frame, resting his blaster there
as he studied the road. Narrowing his eyes, he watched
the trails of dust spiraling up in the distance—someone was coming down the dirt road; a long way off but
getting closer.

"Doc," J.B. called, "we're going have company. Mebbe bad company."

"Such are our odds," Doc muttered from the level below J.B., checking his LeMat with habitual thoroughness. Once he had, Doc eyed the machinery around him warily. Nothing moved. Nothing made a sound. And yet, there was something unsettling about this place, something almost alive.

DROPPING THE STEYR, Ryan whipped out his SIG Sauer blaster in a single, fluid motion as he ran across the dirt toward the rising man-machine. The blaster barked one shot, two, three, sending a trio of 9 mm Parabellum bullets at the figure amid the flames.

The first shot struck the burning biker in the chest, drilling into his body with a screech of metal scraping against metal. The second and third shots followed, one striking higher in the man's chest, close to his breastbone.

The biker staggered back at the blows, his long beard whipping out to his side like a burning scarf.

Ryan had his distance now, and he approached more slowly, his left hand adopting a steadying grip below his right wrist, holding the SIG Sauer P226 level with the biker's flaming head.

The biker smiled, grinning amid the ruined flesh where the fire had singed it away, exposing a metal frame of pulleys and joints beneath. "Gonna enjoy chillin' you," the biker snarled. His voice sounded doubled and wheezy, as if he was speaking through a harmonica.

Ryan stood ready, waiting for the man to take another step. Behind him, Ricky brought his own weapon to bear, thrusting the Webley toward the standing figure.

KRYSTY RAN WITHOUT conscious thought, racing up the
burning stairs to the second story of the farmhouse,
calling Jak's name over and over. The walls had been
stripped back by the fire now, and several stairs had broken through, leaving nothing but their boxlike frames,
charred black where they sat exposed.

Jak didn't respond, so Krysty kept climbing, running through the thick curtain of smoke, past another
burning door, another burning wall. What furniture had
lined the hallways was trashed now, chair backs burned
away, an occasional table black with smoke and playing
host to the remains of a vase of flowers that had shattered with the heat. It was crippling hot, so stifling that
Krysty had to breathe through her clenched teeth. But
finding Jak was paramount.

Jak would be on the top floor, she sensed—he would
have searched each floor in turn, checked for survivors
and kept moving up higher into the building, away from
its burning first floor. Not that that would save him—
heat rose, fire moved upward and so did smoke. Trying
to outclimb a fire was like trying to outrun a bullet—it
simply couldn't be done.

"Jak?" Krysty called again. She had reached the loft
ladder now, pulled herself up it in a great sweep of her
long legs. "Are you up here?"

Jak's voice came back, but it was weak and breathless. "Krysty? That you?"

Krysty's head was above the sill of the gap now, peering into the roof space where the ladder led. Like the rest
of the house, it was thick with smoke, a dark, oppressive
grayness that swirled around like fog. The roof was low
here, creating a slanted ceiling that ran in a point down
the middle, just high enough to let a grown man stand.
Jak was huddling with a group of survivors—some of

them wrapped in blankets that they had drawn over their heads to try to filter the smoke.

"Quickly," Krysty told them. "We need to——" She felt something give below her, and suddenly the ladder was toppling away from the trapdoor that led into the roof, its lowest struts licked by rising flames. Automatically, Krysty reached out and grabbed the edges of the hole above her, clinging there as the burning ladder fell away.

With a supreme effort, Krysty pulled herself up and scrambled into the loft area. It was fiercely hot there, like standing in an oven.

A child looked up from among the gaggle of survivors. She was a girl of no more than five, with blond hair tied up in twin pigtails to either side of her head. "Are you an angel?" she asked, tears streaming down her face where the smoke was irritating her eyes.

Krysty shook her head. "We need to get out of here, right now."

"How?" a man asked. He had short-cropped hair and a ginger beard trimmed in a goatee style. "There's no way to——"

"Always a way," Krysty told him firmly. "Just got to find it—or make it."

"What do?" he asked, pulling the top of his shirt away to speak.

Krysty scanned the loft space, searching for a way out. She would have to come up with a plan quickly.

J.B. SAW THE motorcycles rushing down the road toward the farm from his vantage point at the barn window. There had to be thirty in total, alerted by the smoke and coming to scavenge what they could from the disaster. To scavenge and to chill.

Chapter Sixteen

Ryan's shots were having no effect. The biker kept coming, striding through the fire, his body aflame, metal glistening through the gaps in his burned flesh.

Beside Ryan, Ricky was reloading his Webley and taking aim once more, but Ryan ushered the lad back.

"Keep your distance," he advised. Ryan had faced machines and implausibly strong creatures before now, and one thing he knew was when they approached the best thing to do—sometimes the only thing to do—was to stay out of their reach.

The biker laughed—a terrible metallic sound like clashing gears—as he stepped out of the shell of the burning motorcycle and into the shadow of the flaming farmhouse.

Ryan heard the report of Mildred's ZKR target pistol, and he looked back automatically, a swift glance, taking in everything he could in a blink. His artificial eye held the image, displaying it directly down his optic nerve like a photograph sent to his brain. The other bikers were rising too, wounded and some of them burned like the leader. They stood unsteadily like mannequins on a stage, as if relearning how to walk after some terrible trauma. Mildred's blast had targeted the first to rise, but already the others were on their feet, and it was clear that Mildred's shot had had little effect.

"Ryan, I don't like this," Mildred said unnecessarily.

J.B. WATCHED THE thirty-strong bike gang approach. It was a veritable army, one neither he nor his companions were prepared to fight. He might be able to pick off a few from up here, mebbe more if he had a scoped longblaster like the one Ryan carried, but it would be a stalling tactic, nothing more.

"Doc," J.B. called down to his partner, "we're going to have to make a barricade, hold these coldhearts back long enough so we can beat feet."

"How many are there?" Doc asked. He stood close to the double doors of the barn, one of them propped open just enough that he, too, could spy the road—albeit only a tiny strip of it.

"I count thirty," J.B. said, "give or take. More than we can handle."

"How long would you say before they get here?"

"Long road," J.B. said. "Speed they're traveling, I'm guess mebbe three minutes."

"That doesn't leave us much time to construct your barricade, John Barrymore," Doc observed.

"You know what they say about creating," J.B. replied as he came hurrying back down the ladder, "first you got to clear your work surface." As he spoke, the bespectacled Armorer was reaching into his satchel and rooting around for the right tools for the task.

Doc recognized the look on J.B.'s face. It was the blissful look he wore whenever there was serious ordnance required. "It certainly does a man good to enjoy his work," Doc muttered as he hurried across the barn to assist J.B..

THE FARMHOUSE LOFT was sealed tighter than a drum. Krysty searched the edges and corners, but other than a few mouse holes and a couple of tiny gaps where the roof beams joined, there was no space to escape.

"Jak, I'm going to try something," Krysty said. She didn't say what. "Hold everyone back."

Jak just nodded, trusting the woman and backing her plan without question. He stretched his arms out wide, guiding the farmhouse survivors to remain behind him like a man ushering the queue at a carnival attraction.

Krysty began to chant a prayer to the Earth Mother, asking for strength in this hour of her need. As she whispered, she stepped across to the highest part of the room, where the two eaves of the roof met, and pressed her hands against the supporting strut. Then, with a grimace of effort, she pushed against the strut, leaning into it and shoving as hard as she could.

They all heard a creak like the opening of an old door in need of oiling, and then, without warning, the support beam bent outward, snapping along its midpoint and crashing through the exterior wall of the loft.

Around that support beam, the joining planks that held it in place snapped, the floorboards began to creak and break apart, and nails that had held the thing in place for years fell from the wood as it disintegrated.

Jak watched as Krysty shoved the support beam clear through the front of the house, flickers of flame dancing in the gap revealed beyond.

OUTSIDE, RYAN, RICKY and Mildred had congregated back-to-back-to-back, covering one another as the still-burning bikers surrounded them like jackals surrounding a wounded lion.

Everyone looked up at the sudden noise from the house, saw the thick support beam come bursting through the front of the building, bringing with it a great chunk of the roof and frame. The tangle of beams was burning when it fell, plummeting through the air like a comet.

Ryan shoved Ricky and Mildred back as what seemed like half the burning farmhouse crashed to the ground, slamming into the unsuspecting bikers, slapping them to the ground like the wrath of some terrible god.

The result saw a great cloud of dust and smoke kicked up, lances of fire whipping off in all directions like rockets. Ryan held his arm up to protect his face as the fireball kicked out in the aftermath of the roof collapse.

Four of the six bikers had sunk beneath the fallen roof, while another was caught by a flying chunk of debris that speared him straight through the chest. He sagged to the ground, cursing in a strained howl like a wounded dog, a spike of burning wood wedged through his back and emerging between his ribs. In a moment, he went up in flames, flesh parting into holes like burning tissue paper.

The female passenger whom Ricky had observed taking such delight in setting light to the crops remained clear of the falling material but could not avoid the shower of sparks that erupted from it once it slammed against the ground. Ricky, Ryan and Mildred watched as the woman went up in flames, her clothes and hair turned into a flickering curtain of red-and-orange fire.

Then a figure emerged from the gap in the building roof, her hair also like flame as she stepped out into nothingness. It was Krysty, walking out into the open air as if it could support her weight, falling in a windmill of whirring arms and legs. She landed with a "woof" of expelled air, rolled and turned to catch the next person who dropped.

Three more came out from the building eaves in quick succession, leaping out into the void, kicking out as far as they could to land clear of the flames that engulfed the scene. They looked beautiful in their way, like divers on the high board. The figures emerged one after the other, clinging to bundles of rags that held possessions and babies inside, screaming as they dropped to the ground.

The first landed with a yelp of pain, a snap of bone, but rolled clear to give the next room to land. Krysty caught the next, guiding the young woman to a sort of running landing, trotting across the bare ground as she tried to lose the momentum from her fall. The third fell against Krysty, and hit hard, knocking them both to the ground. But Krysty was okay, she cushioned the fall of the survivors, worried naught for her own safety. Ryan watched with concern, ran across to help, even as the next figure leaped from the burning building. Things were moving so fast, gravity ever relentless.

The adults were followed by two kids, maybe eight- or ten-years-old, holding hands as they dropped to the relative safety of the ground where the adults caught them. As Krysty recovered, Ryan stepped in and caught the next figure, a girl with blond pigtails, her face blackened with soot.

Jak came last, leaping with all the agility of a jungle cat and landing in a crouch, his muscles moving him smoothly to discharge the force with which he struck the ground, a baby in his arms.

Across the way, the last of the bikers was struggling free from the burning hunk of roof he had become entangled with. Mildred and Ricky watched, ready with their blasters to mow the man down if he tried anything. He finally recovered just as Jak landed, doing a kind of strange two-step to extricate himself from the flaming debris and round on whatever target was closest.

Denim vest alight, the biker's pawlike hand reached out for the first survivor, the one who had fallen badly and twisted or broken his ankle. Mildred and Ricky blasted without hesitation, sending a volley of shots at the shambling figure—but he came on, grabbing the fire survivor, who was still recovering.

Alert to everything, Krysty's gaze fixed on the biker like a laser sight, and she was pushing past one of the victims of the blaze before anyone saw her. Still charged with the power of the Earth Mother, Krysty sprinted the ten steps to where the biker was reaching for the survivor, flames licking up and down his arms, metal visible beneath. Krysty grabbed him by the short hairs at his nape, yanking him back with such swiftness that he fell off his feet and crashed to the ground.

Krysty's foot was on the man's throat in an instant, driving the heel of her cowboy boot into his windpipe with the force of a jackhammer. Flames burned all around, sparks spit across the dirt like scurrying insects, and the biker cried out just once. Then his neck snapped and he was just a burning corpse. The metal parts replacing sections of his body were now just lifeless metal once more.

Standing over the corpse, Krysty dipped her head heavily, as though she had run out of energy. The truth was—she had. The power ebbed away in a flash, disappearing as quickly as it had been called on, leaving Krysty as weak as a kitten and struggling to stay upright.

Ryan saw all that in a moment, and he ran across the

space between them and held his hands out for Krysty even as she began to sink to the ground. He caught her, swept her up in his arms and carried her away from the burning biker and the flames dotted all around.

"You can tell me what happened later," he told her in a whisper.

They had to keep moving before that fire spread any farther.

J.B. HAD GAINED the nickname of the Armorer because of his incredible knowledge of weapons. He lived up to that name by carrying an enviable wealth of ordnance and supplies in the pockets of his jacket and in his satchel. The satchel held various grades of ammunition, including some that would fit none of the companions' weapons but which the companions could still use for trade when they came upon a ville—bullets being one form of precious currency in the post-nukecaust world. J.B. also carried a cleaning kit suitable for most blaster types, and he took meticulous care in maintaining his mini arsenal as well as the weapons of his companions. "A healthy blaster will see you through longer than a healthy body," he once remarked when Ricky had asked if running wasn't a better option than standing and fighting.

Besides all of that, J.B. also carried explosives when he could find them—big, small, even tiny charges that were just barely powerful enough to blow a padlock— whatever he count get his hands on and carry away. Among those charges, he had a whole host of incendiaries that he had taken from a deep storage unit they had recently found.

J.B. was in the process of planting six of the incendiary devices on the machinery that lined the walls of the barn. He had handed Doc two more, which the old man was securing to the double doors that opened onto the road. He had asked J.B. about that, worried that they were about to blow up their only exit, but the Armorer had dismissed his concerns. "We'll be out of here long before these things go off," he assured him, but Doc saw that devilish twinkle in J.B.'s eye that meant he was pushing their luck as far as it would go.

It took two minutes to place the charges. The last two J.B. had simply tossed underhand high into the rafters, watching with grim satisfaction as they landed in the upper eaves of the building. That left twenty seconds to exit the hot zone before the charges ignited. Then, with Doc watching the bikers approach through the gap in the doors, J.B. gave the signal for the old man to start running.

Doc slipped out between the doors and began running, not bothering to look back. He ran up the road, past the burning crops in the direction of the farmhouse. Behind him, he could hear the drone of motorcycle engines, hear too the whoops and taunts of the bikers as they spotted him, their prey.

Fifteen seconds.

J.B. was still in the barn, hurrying across the open space between robot arms, making his way toward the doors. As he reached them, he saw the bikers bearing down on him, twenty yards away, closer than he had estimated. Their engines were loud and reeked of alcohol fuel, so rich that J.B. could smell it even this far away.

Ten seconds.

J.B. stood at the open doors and peppered the road with bullets from his mini-Uzi, sending a steady stream of 9 mm slugs up the road and cutting down the lead bikers as they roared toward the barn. He used the door for a shield, but in five seconds he knew that door would not be there—it would be nothing but dust as an explosion ripped through it.

Three of the five lead bikes went crashing to the ground, their riders caught by J.B.'s stream of bullets, their blood smearing the air in red clouds.

Five seconds.

J.B. sprinted from the barn doors, arms pumping as they cut the air. He had five seconds to get clear, five seconds to do the impossible. The howls and taunts of the bikers cut the air to his left, the growl of their engines forming a terrible drone like approaching thunder.

Three seconds.

J.B. was across the road in an instant, dislodged dirt skipping away beneath his toes. Up ahead, the tall stalks of corn waited like a fence, impossibly thin struts that somehow stood against whatever nature threw at them. Thirty feet away, the right-most ones were on fire, dark smoke wafting across the road as J.B. raced into the brush.

One second.

J.B. dived to the ground, arms outstretched, holding the mini-Uzi far from his body in his right hand. The bikes were close now, roaring past the barn building in a cacophony of straining engines.

Zero.

The barn went up like a rocket, the interior expanding in a series of massive explosions, one immediately after another, erupting and building in an instant until it looked like a miniature sun had been thrown down to Earth beside the dirt track by some tempestuous titan.

Doc half dropped, half fell as the explosion hit, crashing to the ground at the edge of the dirt road. Even facing away from the explosion, even with his back to it and his eyes closed, he saw that explosion like a sudden burst of sunlight rushing across his eyelids, the flare lighting the fields where even the fire had not.

The light was accompanied by sound that seemed for all the world like the cough of some vengeful god, casting final judgment on a world that had failed him.

The doors blew, blasting outward like missiles, lopping off the heads of two bikers as they roared past on their mechanical steeds. Hunks of metal flew through the air, the ruined parts of what had resided within the barn, great slices of metal rotating through the air in deadly arcs, cutting down crops and people without distinction. A half dozen riders were impaled or chopped by that flying debris, several lost limbs in less time than it took them to realize that something had exploded.

The rest of the crew was caught by the shock wave, a force like a tidal wave of air blasting through the fields, knocking down everything in its path.

Chapter Seventeen

There were nine survivors from the house fire, including three babies. It was too few. Everyone had suffered from smoke inhalation, and several now struggled to breathe without coughing.

Ryan gathered the group together, ordering his companions to stay alert. Close by, the angry growl of motorcycle engines buzzed in the air. Too close by.

"We can't stay here," Ryan said, scanning the nearby dirt track and beyond, toward the horizon. His artificial eye magnified whatever he looked at, bringing distant sights closer, breaking them down into identifiable components. "More bikers will come."

Ryan scanned the horizon. The barn was a burning tower of flame now, and the ground all around it had been scorched by the explosion and lay burning in its aftermath. There were bikes there, splayed across the ground like a child's discarded toys, but a few had evaded the explosion and they were rallying around to check on the survivors. Ryan turned his attention to a second track that wound through the burning fields. The air was curtained with smoke in the immediate space behind the farmhouse, but farther back he could see the crops swaying in the breeze, heat haze making them waver. There, amid the crops, nine figures were moving, just visible over the heads of the corn. Ryan focused his new eye, closing the other one to better concentrate. They were bikers, momentarily paused by the explosion across the farmlands, trying to see what had happened. As Ryan watched, they began to pick up their speed again, following the dirt track toward the farmhouse.

"How close?" Mildred asked, glancing up from the ground where she crouched beside Krysty, tending to the red-haired woman, who struggled to stay conscious.

"They're already on their way," Ryan replied, before switching off the magnified view and turning to face his allies and the other survivors of the farm inferno. "We need to move now. If any of you have any idea of which way we go, or know of a place to hide, get us there."

The survivors were hacking and coughing from smoke inhalation. Some looked up at Ryan, but their expressions showed fear mixed with hopelessness. "There ain't nowhere around here," one of them said regretfully. The man had ginger hair and beard, and his pale skin had turned red with the heat from the inferno. "Not left no more, anyway."

Ryan nodded, slipping his Steyr from his back. "I'll cover our retreat then," he stated.

"Jak? Ricky? Either of you think you're in a condition to find us a way out of here?"

Black with smoke, Jak was struggling to catch his breath, but Ricky spoke up. "I'll find somewhere," he said.

With that, Ricky parted a section of crop that had yet to catch light and urged the others to follow. A moment later they were gone.

Alone now, Ryan kneeled and adjusted the Steyr Scout against his right shoulder, pushing it there in a familiar move of muscles until it sat snug against him. Then, watching the dirt road through the sight, Ryan waited.

DOC'S EARS WERE RINGING. He woke up lying facedown in a field of tall maize, not really sure that he had been asleep, but disoriented enough to know something was up. He started as something rocketed nearby above him. It was uncomfortably close and brought with it a trail of heat he could feel through the material of his coat.

"By the Three Kennedys," Doc muttered as he rolled over on the ground. The rocketing thing was a great chunk of jagged metal, fifteen feet across and as sharp as a knife, and it spun through the sky above him leaving a flaming trail in its wake. Doc followed its passage for a moment until it disappeared behind the tall rows of cereal crops, landing with the impact of an earthquake, throwing up an expanding cloud of fire.

The barn was burning—the one where J.B. had set the ambush. It couldn't really even be called a barn now, it was just a shell, a few struts poking up in the air at crazy angles while everything around it burned.

"John Barrymore Dix," Doc said, shaking his head, "what did you do?"

Mention of the name was enough to bring Doc back to full alert. He scanned the nearby field, searching for J.B.. The crop here was tall, and it had escaped the fires that had begun around the farmhouse, though parts of the field were now aflame thanks to the barn explosion. It took Doc a few seconds to locate the Armorer, who had landed on the ground about a dozen steps away from the road. He was hidden by a wall of crops from the recovering bikers who had been caught up in the explosion. Doc scrambled toward him in a crouched run, keeping below the height of the maize, keeping his LeMat level and remaining alert.

"John Barrymore," he whispered urgently. "Get up."

J.B. didn't respond and he didn't move. Doc realized he had been so close to the explosion that his hearing had to have been effected. Maybe like Doc he had blacked out, too. But there was no time for that now—they had to get out of here before the bikers came looking for their fallen comrades, and found the source of their woes instead.

"John Barrymore," Doc said again, shaking the Armorer by his shoulders. "Come on, we must keep moving."

J.B. grumbled something nonsensical, then he stirred and after a moment he was looking up at Doc. His glasses had become dislodged, and he wore a bewildered expression. "Doc? That you?"

"It most assuredly is," Doc told him, looking around the immediate area until he spotted J.B.'s glasses. He picked them up and looked them over—one arm looked a little bent maybe, but they seemed to be okay. "We have to get out of here. Swiftly."

J.B. nodded, pulling himself up into a low crouch to ensure he would not be seen from the road. "What happened?" he asked, taking his glasses back from Doc.

"You blew up a barn," Doc explained. "You must have been caught up in the shock wave. Do you remember?"

J.B. put the heel of one hand to his ear and rubbed at it, wincing. "Can't hear shit," he told Doc.

With Doc's ears ringing and evidence that J.B. couldn't hear, it probably meant the bikers were suffering some degree of temporary deafness, too. That was something in their favor anyway, so long as they could move swiftly. Doc eyed the burning barn and its surrounds anxiously for a moment, peering through the tall stalks of maize to see if anyone was coming. Right now, no one was—the bikers he could see were still sprawled out on the ground like so much driftwood washed ashore.

"Let's move," Doc said, pointing to the field.

J.B. nodded, and together the two men made a path deeper into the tall crop.

RYAN KNELT BESIDE the corn, watching the dirt track through the scope of his longblaster and the magnification capacity of his new eye. The heat emanating from the burning farmhouse pressed against his side like a physical object, but he pushed it from his mind, concentrating on the view of the bikers through the scope. There were ten of them in total, not nine as he had first counted—one was riding low to the saddle, his head not high enough to crest the rows of corn. Two riders shared a bike, twin exhausts pointing high and billowing a snake of dark smoke into the air.

They were heading this way, passing some burned-out farm machinery that Ryan didn't recognize.

Ryan settled his breathing, waiting for the targets to reach the kill zone. The first of them—a dark-skinned man with a bare chest and some kind of military helmet on his head, came roaring around the corner, keeping his bike steady. As he did, Ryan squeezed the trigger. In the longblaster's sights, the biker dropped backward as his face exploded in a bloody burst of red.

Ryan shifted target immediately, popped off another shot that took out the driver of the coupled bike. He didn't wait to check what happened to the bike and its passenger. His third shot took a rider in the chest, and he slumped over the handlebars with a cry of pain.

Ryan shifted to his next target. In five seconds their numbers had been cut by a third and they were becoming more wary now, wise to the fact they were in a sniper's sights. Stroking the Steyr's trigger, Ryan sent another shot on its way, and he watched grimly as the passenger in a sidecar on one of the bikes slumped in his seat, dropping the automatic longblaster he had been wielding.

For a moment, the bikes disappeared behind a clutch of trees as they came around a shallow curve in the track. Ryan shifted his aim, anticipating where and when they would show. He commanded his artificial eye to focus in, studying the upcoming landscape for possible hiding places where the bike gang might fight back. As he did, something rushed across his vision, a blur of movement, dark redness like fresh blood.

"What th—?" Ryan muttered, pulling himself out of the crouch and checking around him. It had been something close, he was sure of that.

Ryan swung the longblaster around, bringing it lower to his body as he checked the immediate vicinity. A stupe position to hold a rifle, he knew, but he didn't have time to change weapons. But there was no one there— even his companions had gone now. It was just him.

Ryan turned his attention back to the road, using the magnification lens in the artificial eye once more to find his targets. In the scant few seconds he had been distracted, they had gotten much closer, goosing more speed from their engines, taking risks on the rough terrain as they tried to outpace the sniper.

"Fireblast!" Ryan growled. He pulled himself up, hefting the longblaster with him and slinging it over his shoulder on the strap. The bikers were too close to pick off now—he might get one or two but the others would reach him and he had no way to defend himself; not here.

He ran, scrambling into the fields where the corn grew high as a mutie-phant's eye, as the old poem had it, chasing after Ricky and the others, and hoping to outrun the trail of fire that was sweeping across the land.

Chapter Eighteen

Ricky and the others scrambled through the wheat field where the crop was at its thickest. Ricky ran ahead, encouraging the others to keep up. It was hard going. Krysty was propped up between Mildred and Jak, who was in not much better shape than she was after the struggle in the burning farmhouse. Jak pushed on without complaint though, adrenaline keeping him going.

Behind them, the roar of bike engines filled the air like a backbeat, getting gradually louder, gradually closer.

How many of these people are there? Ricky wondered. A whole army?

He dodged left and right, keeping one eye on the expanding fire that was sweeping through the fields around the farm. It wouldn't do to get too close to that. Fire was unpredictable and once you got caught in it there wasn't much you could do to get out again.

"Ricky?" Mildred called. "Where are we heading?"

"This way," Ricky said, trying to sound confident. He wished Ryan or J.B. were here. The companions all had their roles, and those guys were leaders. As for Ricky, he was just backup, the guy who held an extra blaster when they needed it, not the guy who made the decisions. But here he was, making decisions that might get people chilled.

They reached a clearing in the wheat field, like a

crop circle, where people had been working. Five people lay dead in that clearing, and as the lead farmer pushed through the wheat curtain to follow he saw the bodies and gasped.

Two people had been shot in the back of the head and were slumped together on the ground. One more had been shot several times. It was hard to see how many but there was blood on the man's face and a vacant expression in his open eyes. The other two looked human, but Ricky realized they weren't—they were some kind of mechanicals, human in shape and size and dress, but beneath their clothes their skin was sleek metal. One was missing its head.

The lead farmer scrambled over to the man with the vacant eyes. "Lionel? What happened?"

The man with the vacant eyes said nothing, just a bubble of blood popping between his pursed lips.

Ricky looked frantically around, searching for somewhere to hide or to get away. Up ahead, he spotted a great metal structure towering above the golden wheat. The thing looked like a tank or a war wag, great treads running along its side, but set at an angle, not as wheels but as a kind of conveyor belt. Ricky whistled as he took it in, wondering what the machine did. Some kind of processing unit, he guessed. The thing idled now, unused.

He turned back to the farmer, who still crouched over the voiceless Lionel. The others were through the clearing now, watching solemnly. "He's dead, man," Ricky said.

The bearded farmer looked up at Ricky, an expression of barely endurable pain on his face. "He's my cousin," he said. "Three months older than—" He stopped, choking back tears, and one of the women in the group trotted forward and put her arm on his, whispering words of consolation.

"All dead if stay," Jak reminded the group as he shifted his position under Krysty. She was out of it, her head rolling about on her shoulders, her eyelids flickering between consciousness and sleep.

"Jak's right," Mildred said. "We've got to keep moving. I know it's hard, but I guess your cousin wouldn't want you to be dead just because he is."

The bearded farmer nodded grimly. "I want to bury him."

"No time," Mildred said in a firm tone.

They ran on, scrambling past the idling hunk of machinery that dominated the wheat field, crossing a drainage ditch that ran parallel.

J.B. AND DOC ran deeper into the fields, regularly checking over their shoulders to make sure they were not being followed. They did not have an ultimate destination in mind just yet—all they knew was that to keep running was to stay alive.

Behind them, the barn continued to burn, its skeletal wreckage billowing dark smoke as the fire tore through whatever remained. Had they been able to hear, Doc and J.B. might have heard the sound of revving engines as a few of the bikers began to struggle back to consciousness and try their bikes, but for the most part the only sound was the tick-tick-tick of fire tongues licking at everything they could reach.

RYAN TOOK DEEP breaths as he raced through the field, batting aside stalks of wheat as he chased after his allies. Behind him, the drone of the bike engines continued relentlessly.

Five bikes were still active after Ryan's assault. Three of them raced to the farmhouse inferno, while the other two bumped off the track and began to tear through the fields, running at speed over the bumpy terrain, searching for stragglers.

Ryan glanced back over his shoulder, heard the engines getting closer. They weren't on him yet. He still had time if he acted swiftly.

Ryan ducked, almost throwing himself at the ground, and rolled until he was in a low crouch facing the direction he had come from. He had the SIG Sauer in his hands in a second. It was hard to see the bikers—they were close, no doubt, but the wheat was thick and the sound of their engines was disorienting, could come from any of three or four different places.

Ryan turned his head slowly, scanning the field. There was a dead body not a dozen paces from where he lay, a farmhand, a young woman in a ragged summer dress—now sporting a sickle at the top of her spine. Ryan continued to search, spotted movement and focused with his artificial eye.

The eye magnified and enhanced the scene. A moment before, all Ryan could make out was a dark blur moving among the golden stalks. With the eye's capabilities, he could now make out the figures, two of them, riding parallel to him, twenty feet from his hiding place among the crops.

One of the bikers wore a strap of grens over his chest and had a metal limb in place of his left arm, a mechanical monstrosity as thick as a child's torso. The mechanical arm stretched right up to his shoulder, where threads of metal lashed farther up like a spiderweb, threading under his skin right up through the corded muscles of his neck. The other rider wore a visor over his face that covered his eyes and hung down over his mouth in a grille. The eyepiece glowed with amber light as he scanned the field, feeding him information.

Ryan raised the SIG Sauer, timing the shots in his head to ensure he could take out both men. Two figures—no, three…four…ten… The image blurred before him and suddenly he found himself reeling with the sense of motion, a mirage across his vision as he tried to take the shot.

Compromised, Ryan eased his finger from the trigger and ducked lower to the ground, closing his eyes. His vision kept racing even after that, and for a moment Ryan had a strange sense of seasickness as motion continued to flicker past his senses even though he was still.

Twenty feet away, the bikes roared past, missing Ryan by the slimmest of margins, bumping past the female farmhand with the protruding sickle.

"LIVE ONES UP AHEAD," the biker with the visor shouted, raising his hand and pointing.

His companion with the metal arm smiled, a nasty slice of teeth in his scarred and beaten face. "I see them, Rusty. Let's finish them."

The bikes tore through the field, chasing after the group of survivors, oblivious to Ryan's fallen figure hidden in the tall wheat.

THE RESCUED FARMERS continued to follow Ricky through the field along with Mildred, Krysty and Jak. Some distance away, flames licked at the edge of the field. They would not have long to get out of there.

The heads of the riders bobbed up over the tall wheat like flotsam cresting an ocean wave. "They're getting closer," Mildred said as she dared a glance over her shoulder.

"Keep going," Ricky said, making a decision. He turned back.

There was no time to argue. The companions survived on trust—trust in each other's abilities and their own. As their newest member, Ricky could be unpredictable, but Mildred had seen him hold his own against incredible odds.

"You heard him," Mildred said to the others. "Keep moving! Get to the edge of the field."

As MILDRED DIRECTED the survivors, Ricky scampered back to the hunk of machinery he had seen dominating the field. He didn't know what it was—some kind of harvester maybe—but he hoped it could provide the shelter he needed to set an ambush.

The bikes hurried on, bumping over the rough terrain, struggling to gain purchase as they dipped and bobbed over the ground. The bikes were durable, but they had not been designed for this kind of riding. The tires slipped and the terrain seemed to be fighting them at every turn.

RYAN LAY ON his back, taking deep breaths. He felt sick. Reluctantly, he opened his eyes, winced as he saw the bright blue sky above.

"What the hell just happened?" Ryan whispered.

It could be some side effect of the heat. He had gotten pretty close to that fire when he had picked off the approaching bikers, doubtlessly inhaled smoke as he waited there. Smoke inhalation? He felt light-headed, that was true. It all kind of made sense.

But he had missed the shot. He sat up, looking down

the lines of wheat, trying to locate the bikers. His head
was still reeling; it wasn't good sitting up. For now, all
Ryan could do was hope Ricky had gotten the others
to safety.

RICKY WAS BACK at the hunk of machinery that loomed
amid the crops. Up close he could see it was a static harvester, the kind you needed to feed with crops that you
brought to it. It had four huge wheels set at its corners
though, and Ricky wondered if maybe he could get it
moving and use it to barge the bikers out of the field.
No, there wouldn't be time for that.

The two bikers were really close now. Only thirty
yards remained between them and Ricky. He slipped
behind the harvester and pulled his De Lisle carbine
from its strap across his back. The blaster used .45 ACP
ammo, and Ricky made sure that the magazine was in
place and secure. Then, with the towering harvester as
cover, Ricky began to fire, targeting the closest of the
bobbing heads that appeared over the line of golden
wheat.

Shots cut through the air, and the lead biker—visor
over his face—ducked lower to the crossbar and began
to weave. "We're under attack!" he warned his companion.

Both men gunned their engines, urging more speed
from them as they tried to find their latest attacker.

Ricky continued firing. There was no point in shooting at both—that just split his target and made it less
certain he would hit either, so he aimed for the first,
sending a burst of rapid fire at the figure. He gained
confidence as the man went down, disappearing behind the curtain of wheat, accompanied by the sound

of his engine suddenly hitting a higher pitch as he lost balance and the wheels lost traction.

The second rider was still coming, bearing down low to the frame of his bike so that he could hardly be seen above the tall stalks of wheat. Ricky was keenly aware that the inferno ravaging parts of the field was getting closer, and he cursed himself into action, waiting for the biker to reappear.

Suddenly, there was a flash from the area where Ricky was looking and a projectile raced through the air toward him. There was no time to process what it was—a rocket maybe or a shell? Ricky leaped, diving back behind the harvester even as the blast hit.

The harvester shook as the projectile impacted, and Ricky found himself knocked three steps forward from the aftershock. He recovered immediately, bringing the De Lisle around and searching desperately for the last assailant.

For a moment: nothing.

Then he saw a flash of black as the biker's head whizzed between a gap in the wheat, enough that Ricky could follow his path.

Ricky waited, his finger on the trigger, watching for another hint of the biker's movement. This close he could smell him coming, the distillery reek of the bike's alcohol engine.

He fired almost before he had consciously spotted the biker, then drew back as the biker fired something in his direction. He saw it this time, the familiar pineapple-shape of the projectile—a hand gren—not thrown but launched from something the biker held in his left hand.

The gren butted against the ground with a boom of explosive. Ricky was already scrambling, running backward.

The biker followed, reloading the strange attachment that took the place of his arm. He had four homemade grens kept on a strap across his chest. That wasn't the limit of his armament—two blasters were strapped to the back of the bike, a stubby shotgun with abbreviated barrel and a modified Smith & Wesson Sigma with no trigger guard.

The biker pulled to a halt, letting the engine idle a moment while he reloaded his mechanical arm cannon, peering through the wheat to catch a glimpse of his target. He saw him a moment later, Ricky's adolescent figure scrambling away on swift legs. The biker laughed. "Legs're no match for wheels," he said, sneering.

Then he revved the engine again, released the brake and powered toward Ricky. He was seven seconds away…six…five. The biker snatched the shotgun from its saddle strap and brought it around to take a shot on the fly, framing Ricky's back in his sights.

But before the biker could squeeze the trigger, the bike dipped and suddenly he was reeling, losing balance as he went caroming into the drainage ditch that ran parallel to the harvester. Ricky had been ready for that. The biker's shotgun went off as he lost control, sending a burst of buckshot uselessly into the dirt.

Ricky turned and brought the De Lisle around, taking his time to get the aim right. The blaster fired, sending .45-caliber death into the biker's chest, drilling a second shot into his face.

Ricky stood over the drainage ditch a moment, watching the man die as the bike's engine continued to whine in protest, wheels struggling against the muddy sides of the ditch.

Then he hurried away, leaving the cyborg rider to die alone.

Chapter Nineteen

Ryan caught up with Ricky's group a mile out from the farm's edge. The youth had encouraged everyone to keep moving, but they were slow and tired and the ground was too rugged to make good progress. Ryan found them as they ascended a dirt wall that ran on the far side of an irrigation ditch that had dried up some time before. The lead farmer—Trevor—explained that he and his neighbors, the Dodsons, had shared this border and had built this ditch to water their crops. Something had happened recently though to change that, but Trevor remained quiet as to what.

Ryan looked exhausted when he caught up to the group.

"What happened back there?" Mildred asked.

Ryan shook his head. "Took out as many as I could," he said evasively. "I saw that you people chilled the others."

"Ricky did that," Mildred told him. "The kid's a one-man war zone when he needs to be."

Ryan nodded grimly.

As they continued the trek away from the burning fields, Ryan checked on Krysty while Mildred asked about J.B. and Doc.

"Any sign of them?"

Ryan grimaced. "I couldn't go back to check. It was too dangerous by then," he admitted. "We'll start leaving them a trail and hope they can catch up with us. If not, we'll come back when the way is clear."

"Hope." Mildred repeated the word like a curse. "Seems that's sometimes all we have."

"It's all any of us have," Ryan told her with a fixed expression.

The black plume of smoke would be visible from miles away. It wouldn't do to stay here now, not with so many casualties on the other side.

With Ricky and Jak moving ahead to scout for danger, Ryan led the rest of the group out into the wilderness, following but remaining parallel to a road leading from the farm, away from the burning fields. The land here was ashy, like the aftermath of a volcano, and the companions could not help but notice that it appeared unnatural.

Krysty still looked exhausted, and she paled as they trekked through the ashy ground.

"Something bad happened here," she told the others.

"Bikers," Trevor the farmer said grimly.

Fire was the weapon of the bike gang—no, not a gang, Ryan corrected—an army. An army sent out to destroy everything that had been done to make life bearable in this remote corner of the Deathlands.

It was clear that Trevor already knew, but for whatever reason he had tried to cling on to his own little corner of Hell, even as the gang circled his property, systematically destroying everything around it.

Mildred helped Krysty to walk, but she had mostly regained her strength by now. She just looked tired and washed-out.

Two of the locals complained about leaving their home and possessions behind, argued about returning now if the bikers had gone—which was a very big

if—but the others quieted them. They had already lost
everything in the fire, including many of their own.
Farmhands lay dead in the fields, each chilled by a single bullet to the back of the head, and the robots who
assisted them had been destroyed. Arguing now would
only put the survivors in more danger. Ryan let them
settle their differences among themselves, and he asked
Mildred to give each survivor a quick medical checkup
while they remained on the move. Ryan didn't want to
argue with the locals, didn't want to argue with anyone. He had lost it back there, with the bike gang bearing down on him, and he had been lucky to survive.

A girl had died in the farmhouse, weeks shy of becoming a teenager. The group of farmers wanted to hold
a vigil for her while they were still in sight of the farm.
While it would slow them, Ryan had lost a son too, albeit under different circumstances. He was tough and
battle hardened, but he would not be heartless enough
to tell parents not to mourn the child. He urged them
to move swiftly and say their goodbyes on the road.

"Soon as we get the chance, we move away from this
track and find ourselves some shelter, a place we can
protect," Ryan told everyone. "You folks can make new
lives, but only if you still have lives to make."

The ginger-haired farmer with the goatee beard nodded solemnly at that. "Wise advice, friend," he said.
"I'm Trevor. You have a name you'd care to share?"

"Ryan," he answered, and he took the man's offered
hand, shaking it firmly. Trevor had the strong grip of
an outdoorsman, someone used to working the land
with his bare hands. "You know of a place around here
where we can go?"

"There's a ville twenty-five…mebbe thirty miles
from here," the farmer replied. "Place goes by the name

of Heartsville. We trade with them—or we used to, I guess that life's over now."

Ryan nodded. "Guess it is."

"They're fortified," Trevor explained. "Got walls and some old military hardware. Big trading post like that needs it, ya know?"

"I guess I do," Ryan agreed. He had been a trader once himself, part of the legendary crew of the man known as The Trader, in fact. Trading in the Deathlands was one way to obtain what you needed to survive, and it notched up a lot less dead bodies than the other way, which was taking. But traders lived by their wits. They were very often seen as the haves in this world of have-nots, which meant it wasn't difficult to find people willing to take a shot at them in hopes of getting their hands on the stock. Trader had protected himself by traveling from ville to ville in the armored War Wag One and surrounding himself with the best crew of chillers he could find. Other traders survived in other ways. Sometimes a trader set up a base that he fortified, using it as a trading post, maybe even setting himself up as its ruling baron. "Are these people going to let you in, Trevor?"

"They got no beef with us, Ryan," the farmer assured him. "We always treated them fair when we traded and I dare say they paid us the same courtesy. Made the trip there annually, occasionally more often."

Ryan nodded, peering off into the distance as something caught his eye. Down the road a little, he could see another farmhouse, this one burned-out like the one they had found. Ryan tapped into the magnification system of his new eye, focusing on the distant building. It looked as if it had been burned-out weeks, if not months, ago.

"Crops can be kind sometimes," Trevor was explaining. "With a lot of hands or a store, you can wind up with too much."

Ryan nodded. "You know this place?" he asked, indicating the burned-out farmhouse.

Trev nodded grimly. "Yup."

As they trudged past the fire-blackened farmhouse, Ryan noticed a number of the adults pause and cross themselves solemnly. He recognized the gesture as a religious sign, an affirmation of faith.

"Friends of yours?" Ryan asked as he saw Trevor do the same.

"Good friends," Trevor replied.

"What happened?"

"Same thing as you saw today, more or less," the farmer explained. "Three months ago a group of people came in the night, burned the place down while the Dodsons slept in their beds. Terrible thing—three generations of their family died, including eight children."

"You have any idea why?"

Trevor shook his head. "Is there ever any reason for hate? It just perpetuates and it sweeps wrong ones up in its fury."

Ryan looked around at the scene surrounding the burned-out farmhouse. Here, as at Trevor's, the surrounding fields has suffered too. A circle of crops around the building had burned down to stubble, a mosaic of ash carpeting the ground even now, all this time after from the destruction. An outhouse had survived, but its walls were streaked black with smoke, its door hanging awkwardly from metal hinges that had been melted into new shapes.

"Someone doesn't like farmers, I guess," Ryan said.

"Or eating," Trevor added grimly. "Once all the farms

close down, there won't be anything left here—no reason left for people to stay."

That was a good point, Ryan realized. He had seen a lot of stealing in his travels across the Deathlands, understood the use of force to get property and goods. And he had seen wanton destruction too, but it was usually territorial when you got right down to it. This however? From what Trevor seemed to be saying, there was no real reason behind it—not one he knew of anyhow.

Close to the farmhouse, Jak found a tree that was still standing and he placed the blade of his knife against it, carving a line there. It was a marker—hardly noticeable but enough for J.B. and Doc to follow if they got here.

The group trekked on. They were already two miles out from Trevor's burned-out farmhouse, but Ryan's team kept a wary eye fore and aft for any possible attack. Those bikers had been a strong group determined to raise hell. Figuring the reasons why could wait.

As they walked, Jak showed Ryan a path that took them out of immediate sight. Ryan commanded the group to stay close and together they followed the track, a snaking dirt line through a patchy forest made up of lemon trees and some mutie breed of apple that seemed to double-bud in Siamese couplings.

At the wreckage of the barn, a few tufts of flame were burning, littering the ground like tumbleweed while the fields billowed dark smoke into the sky. Little of the barn itself remained, just struts here and there, a beam that had somehow survived J.B.'s attack.

Around the farmhouse and the barn, the bikers arose, struggling from the ground where they had been tossed by explosions or racked by blasterfire. Some were dead, some had lost limbs, but fully two-thirds remained alive, staggering through the stinking curtain of black smoke.

"What the black dust happened?" Niles, the leader of the bikers said from his sneering blood-caked mouth. His mouth always showed that sneer, ever since the surgeons had rebuilt his face after the accident that had changed his life. He was a tall man with brown hair down past his collar, dressed in a scuffed jacket and pants made from some Kevlar-leather weave. The jacket had a logo painted across the back: an old restaurant managed by celebrities back before the nukecaust that was now not even a memory.

Beside Niles, his partner, twenty-three years old with hair as golden as the burning corn, wiped soot from her pretty face as she shook her head. "Some kind of funting explosion, Niles," she said, staring around in bewilderment. She too had been victim to that accident, where Niles's bike had hit a patch of rough ground on a cliff path and veered into hers, sending them both over the edge of the cliff.

They had been lucky to survive; lucky and something else maybe, something planned. Now the woman wore metal down her right side, a perfectly tooled curve of stainless steel to replace her shattered hip and three metal ribs resting below her right breast, covered in synthetic skin that looked identical to her own, but that never took a tan no matter how much sun she showed it. There was another line of metal twisted up through her arm, attached to her right shoulder to give her the same freedom of movement she had enjoyed before the accident, only now it gave her strength too. Her name was Amanda, and that, at least, had remained unchanged after the accident that had chilled her once.

There was a litter of metal and wood scattered around

the two of them. Their colleagues were strewed all about on the scorched ground, struggling in the tall stalks of corn like discarded rag dolls, as if a toddler had knocked over his toys on a colossal scale. Some people were picking themselves up, checking where they had been hit or had fallen, while others lay unmoving as black ash washed over them like a shower from Hades. Metal shone here and there from beneath their torn skin, prosthetic limbs, a metal plate in the skull, other parts, random but cruelly effective.

"Explosion is right, Amanda," Niles said, and he spit a gob of bloody saliva onto the smoke-black ground. "Someone ambushed us."

He looked around more warily, holding his hand over his eyes where the ash lashed at his face. The ash felt hot, the way spicy food tasted hot. He and Amanda had been some way back when the barn blew, their bikes running side by side as the explosion ripped through their colleagues. He had fallen into hers, his bike ramming into her front wheel and flipping both of them up and over the handlebars. The bikes were somewhere among the pileup of fallen wrecks, tossed across the dirt track and the fields that ran to either side. Thoughts of the crash reminded Niles of that day when he and Amanda had spun out on the cliff top. He would rather not remember that; it felt like another man's life now, like something he had only encountered in his dreams.

Niles wiped at the ruined flesh on the left-hand side of his face, where a line of brass rivets showed. He had been rebuilt once, after that other bike accident months ago that had taken away a whole chunk of his once-handsome face and the life that went with it. The rebuild had been exemplary, but it had left him with a puckered sneer that wouldn't leave his face, not even when he smiled. It didn't much matter—weren't nothing worth smiling about out here anyway, except maybe Amanda's tits with their dappled suntan on synthetic skin, patterned like a giraffe.

Others were struggling with a chorus of groans. Niles scanned them, seeing two figures standing close to the smoldering farmhouse and counting eighteen more emerging from the black-smeared stubble of the corn and wheat. Some were already testing their bikes. He switched his right eye to infrared vision, drawing on another of the enhancements that the people of Progress had gifted him, searching for more warm bodies amid the debris as more of his gang joined them from the far side of the property. There were three more of his crew still alive, struggling beneath the wreckage of the barn as well as a farm survivor, who had to have been making a run for it through the fields. He ordered his men to go find them, pointing them out where a human eye would have missed them. His troops chilled the farmer, blasting his brains out as he screamed at the pain he was in—it was what passed for mercy hereabouts.

J.B. AND DOC left the fields, drawing a wide semicircle around the burning crops until they reached the westernmost side of the property. It was there that they found the first marker that Ryan and the others had left. The marker was nothing more than a notch in a tree trunk, roughly the height of J.B.'s belt. The mark was an indent at eleven, twelve, or one o'clock to indicate the direction Ryan's group had taken. It was barely noticeable, yet easy enough to decipher if you knew to look for it. The first mark was at the eleven o'clock angle, indicating that they needed to track to the left and follow what path they found there. A road waited that way, a dirt track

with pools of cloudy water that stunk of pollutants—
that would be the way that Ryan's group had gone.

J.B. and Doc followed the road indicated, wondering
how far behind the others they were. They said little,
keeping their thoughts and concerns to themselves, and
also saving energy for the unknown trek ahead. Their
hearing had come back, but tiredness was setting in
with the comedown from adrenaline.

J.B. stopped at the side of the road that ran along the
edge of the farmland, pulled out his mini-binoculars
and held them up to his eyes, scanning the farm and
the barn beyond.

"Bastards are moving," he told Doc after a moment.
"Lots of activity. I can't make out the details, but it looks
like we took out fewer than we thought in that explosion. Either that or they had friends nearby."

Doc shook his head in weary disbelief. "Cockroaches
do have a knack of surviving," he stated, "no matter
how hard you beat them down."

"There had to be thirty in that 'roach army," J.B.
said. "Figure twenty-plus are still walking. Their machines mebbe didn't do so well."

Doc smiled grimly. "You call them an army, J.B.,"
he said.

"That many people coming to chill folks is a mi-
litia," J.B. reasoned, "no matter whether they wear a
flag or salute one."

"We should keep moving," Doc said.

His companion nodded, pulling the binoculars from
his eyes. The road ahead looked bleak.

Chapter Twenty

Twenty-four bikers survived the explosion, including Niles and Amanda. Niles grimaced at that. They had taken unexpected losses here. The farmers had to have set the ambush, but they had lost everything in the process. Even their own equipment was nothing but scrap now, but so were a lot of the bikes.

As Niles was making his observations, one of the crew mechanics drew his attention from where he knelt, examining a scratched-up bike. Nicknamed Hog, the man was rotund and wore a bandana over his bald head, covering the place where the surgeons of Progress had replaced the front of his skull with a metal plate after they'd messed with his brain.

"Lotto d-d-damage on the bikes," the mechanic said. "Can mebbe get nineteen or twenty up an' r-r-running in time, but—blast! Nuke-shittin' ash!" He swatted away the ash as it stung against the exposed skin on his forearms like an insect.

"Twenty rides?" Niles asked, bringing the man back to the present.

"Yeah," Hog said, nodding thoughtfully. "It'll take a while to get all of them up 'n r-r-runnin' but we got plenty of p-p-parts to scavenge from."

Niles nodded, surveying the litter of broken bikes. "Get what you can running and we'll head back," he said. "Those farm hicks won't get far, not on foot.

They'll keep. We'll take what we got, refuel and go hunting."

Hog let out a cheerful whoop at that, stuttered by the shitty job the surgeons did on his brain.

Amanda could ride with Niles until they could patch up something for her. They had come here to burn, and they wanted to get back on the road.

Amanda strode over to join Niles, the leather pants encompassing her long legs black and slick like an insect's shell. She reached for Niles, placing her hand behind his neck and pulling him into a savage, forceful kiss that he reciprocated in kind. "Are we going to ride, lover-mine?"

Niles smiled, the curl of his lip sneering where the brass rivets held his new jaw in place. "There's nothing left for them here now," he said, "so they'll head for Heartsville. That's the only pesthole left. That's where we'll find them. That's where we'll chill them. All of them."

They were indestructible, Niles and Amanda—metal shells wrapped in their original, outmoded flesh. And the drive burned inside them—the drive to chill.

THIRTY MILES, RYAN thought as he assessed his fellow travelers. On this terrain that was a two-day trek. Mildred had done what she could to patch up people, but at least three of the farm survivors would be classified as walking wounded, and there were kids to consider—kids who slowed them.

His own people weren't in much better shape. Jak was still coughing up junk after his excursions into the heart of the inferno, and Krysty had recovered but she looked pale, perhaps a reaction to the blighted landscape all around them. He knew how attuned to nature she could be.

They weaved along the trees that dotted a gentle slope, made their way onto the flatland beyond that had once been a feeder road. It was overgrown now, a yellow-green veld, populated here and there by road signs, the occasional roof of a truck or Greyhound bus poking through where they had been abandoned a hundred years before.

An orange grove waited at the edge of the road, the trees reaching for the sky, oblivious to the horror that had been unleashed just a few generations ago. Ryan's team moved through it, weapons ready in case of ambush.

"Stick together," Ryan ordered. "No stragglers."

Behind him, Jak was marking another tree with one of those eleven-twelve-one-o'clock ticks, showing J.B. and Doc in which direction they had gone.

Doc and J.B. made it to the Dodsons' farm just before the first of the bikers appeared on the road behind them. The old man had been searching around for the next marker while J.B. checked his maps, resting on a low wall that acted as the house's perimeter. The wall was smoke-stained black just like the rest of the old house.

"Klamath, Klamath..." J.B. muttered, following the snake of the old river as it wended past a few long-since destroyed towns.

"Found it." Doc cheered as he located the mark Jak had left on a nearby tree. There had been twenty trees to choose from, finding the right one felt like something of an achievement.

Looking up, J.B. tipped two fingers to the brim of his hat in acknowledgment. Then he heard the noise—engines approaching, nearby and getting louder. "Doc?" he called.

The old man was peering down the haphazard path that ran between the trees, judging how far they had to go and whether they might be closing in on Ryan's group. He turned back and recognized the grim look on J.B.'s face. "Trouble?"

"Coming fast," J.B. replied. "Come on, Doc, let's get to cover."

With that, J.B. strode swiftly into the tumbledown remains of the burned-out farmhouse, drawing his mini-Uzi as he ducked beneath the lintel. Doc followed, scrambling across the road, one eye on the bend in the road from which the sound of engines buzzed, back where the burning farm still churned smoke into the air in black shadows painted across the sky.

A moment later the two men were inside the farmhouse. It was a grim affair; fire had gutted the place, top to bottom, leaving just a vestige of what it had been before. Everything that remained was blackened and melted or twisted in on itself with the horrendous heat that had swept through the property three months earlier. Daylight shone through the house from high up in the rafters where a great gaping hole rent the roof, casting its beam down into the lobby like a spotlight on stage.

J.B. and Doc took up positions close to the front door, blasters ready, scanning the road. They waited there in silence as the first bike appeared, followed by two more. Their riders looked as if they were part of the bikes— barely human, great metal machines with pistons and gears and belts that whirled as they steered the handlebars and bumped over the rough track.

"Are they…automatons?" Doc wondered in a haunted whisper.

J.B. shook his head. "Don't know," he admitted. "That blast mebbe took some skin off them, showing us what's underneath."

J.B. couldn't be sure. Both men could see human parts mixed in with the cybernetic sections, here a beating heart exposed but kept safe behind a plastic screen, there a set of lungs that had been augmented with a bellows where one lung had collapsed.

"Neither human nor machine," J.B. said. "Either way, they're programmed to chill."

Doc gripped the handle of his LeMat tighter, waiting for the bikers to pass.

"I figure they're scouting for survivors," J.B. suggested, and Doc nodded. "We get into it with them, my guess is more will come. A lot more. 'till we're chilled."

Doc agreed with the Armorer's assessment. For now, all they could do was hide and wait.

IN SHORT TIME, Ryan's group was through the orange grove and out onto an open plain. The plain was bisected by the wide strip of blacktop that was cracked and overgrown with weeds and bushes. A hundred years before, this had been a major highway through California. Now it stood as the forgotten remnants of a civilization that had tried to finish itself in a blaze of nuclear fury. Road signs slunk down close to the ground, their metal legs warped and broken, names of long-forgotten destinations still clinging without hope to their bent and rusted placards, faded by the sun.

The companions stepped out onto the overgrown plain that had once been a highway.

"Trading post is that way," Trevor said, pointing off to the west. "Day's walk. Should have got us a horse."

Ryan didn't like this. He felt too exposed out here, with only the road signs for cover. "Keep moving," he said. "No stragglers."

Despite Ryan's advice, Jak held back, eyeing the sky, his nose wrinkled. His clothes and pale skin were dark with smoke, but otherwise Jak seemed to be fine now. His cough had gone and Mildred had checked him over twice as they moved away from the carnage at Trevor's. Jak's makeshift shirt-turned-gas mask had done enough to keep smoke out of his lungs, although his hair and clothes reeked of it.

"Not gonna make it," Jak said, holding his position.

"What's that?" Ryan asked.

"Storm," Jak said, pointing to the south.

Ryan looked where the albino pointed. The sky was the dark purple of a bruise, a sign of too many pollutants kicked up in the wake of the nuclear exchange all those years before. The weather could be deadly in the Deathlands, and Ryan had heard tell of men being stripped right down to the bone when acid rains hit, had in fact seen it happened.

"How long do you reckon we have," Ryan asked, "before we need to get under cover?"

Jak scratched at his head absently, dislodging soot from his usually pale hair. "Hour, mebbe less," he said.

"Not long," Ryan mused. He looked back at the sky, then ahead to where Trevor had said the ville was. "Anywhere closer than this Heartsville?" he asked.

"We come off track a little," the bearded man replied thoughtfully, "but ain't nowhere I can think of. Quickest by road."

"Be bad," Jak said, referring to the rain. "Smell bad already."

"Okay," Ryan said, raising his voice and his hands to get everyone's attention. The group was strewed across the undergrowth, moving in twos and threes, clumped but not tightly the way a military unit would have been. "I know you're all tired and having a shitty day already, but we need to get to cover now."

The kid with the dark bangs asked why. "Is there more bike men coming, mister?" he said.

"No, but my friend here says it's going to rain," Ryan told him, "and rain hard."

Already the sky above had become darker, the purple expanding as it reached for the place where the companions and their charges were poised.

Ryan could smell it now too, that dry tang in the air that promised acid rainfall. It caught in the back of his throat as he inhaled.

The rain was as black as a vampire's kiss and had a pungency to it, a cloying fruity tang like the smell of spilled gasoline. It was the smell of toxins and death and restless souls, a hundred-thousand bodies turned to ash by the nuclear bombs that had almost wiped the United States off the map a hundred years before. People turned into ash, and ash become darkness in the black rain, wafting over the lands they had once believed to be the home of the free. The rain rushed across the heavens in darkened clouds, purples, blues and greens in their depths where the pollutants thrown up by the nuclear exchange continued their endless race through the atmosphere, circling the planet again and again, like the story of Sisyphus and the boulder.

Mildred, Ricky and Krysty scouted for cover on the ruined highway. There were automobiles hidden among the overgrowth, smothered by weeds, their tires rotted away to leave them resting on their wheel rims.

"It's partly buried," Ricky said, trying a door.

"Get it the door open," Ryan said. "Everyone! Find a car, find a partner, get the doors open and get as many people inside as you can. The metal roofs should protect us."

Doc AND J.B. watched as the last of the bikers sped away. They had hung around outside the burned-out farmhouse for a few minutes, ten at most, but during those minutes the sense that the two allies would be discovered was palpable. Eventually, the bikers had raced farther down the road, shouting and whooping, leaving the space around the burned ruin clear.

"Let's get moving before they come back," J.B. said.

Doc stepped outside and stopped. He didn't like the look of the sky—it was too dark. Something wasn't right.

"Doc?"

"Smell the air," Doc said.

J.B. sniffed. "Brimstone."

"Look," Doc added. "There were birds in those trees not ten minutes ago. Now they've gone to ground."

"Think they know something we don't?" J.B. asked.

"When animals hide, it's wise to take their cue," Doc told him.

J.B. looked back into the soot-stained lobby of the burned-out house. He didn't like to lose ground, not with Ryan so far ahead, but Doc was right. They would wait. Whatever storm was coming, it could be deadly to get caught in it.

THE BIKERS FOUND a farmhand cowering beneath the burned wreck of a harvester. The man had dark skin the color of cocoa, and he wore the wide-eyed expression of someone unable to take anything in. His men held the farmhand's arms as Niles studied him. It was something to do while Hog fixed the bikes up, at least.

Up above, the sky was turning darker as clouds raced across it. The farmhand was babbling something about "being merciful."

Niles shook his head, ignoring the man.

"Bikes are ready," Amanda said. "We should go."

"Yeah," Niles agreed. "We'll leave soon."

The farmhand looked ready to bolt when Niles turned back to the men who held him. "Tie him down," Niles said. "Find a rope or something. We'll leave him here. The fires will chill him, just like everyone else."

"You dirty boys," the farmhand spit. "Let me go, I don't do nothing to you."

RYAN'S CREW HURRIED to find cars buried by the madness of vegetation, urgently hacking and digging their way to doors and sunroofs, pulling at them until they could make their way inside. In total, the group found four useable cars in the space of twenty minutes; not much, but somewhere to shelter when the rains struck. Some vehicles still had skeletons inside them, wedged into the driver's seat from when the nukes had struck, flash-fried as they drove to work or from it, or traveled to see family or friends or a million other inconsequential reasons. Their lives had come to an abrupt halt a hundred years before, hands stopped on the clock as civilization came to a halt.

Ryan kicked rust from the jammed side door of an old Chevy, pushed the overgrown brambles back so that he had room to open it. Around him, the other companions did likewise, clambering into automobiles defined by rotted upholstery and melted dashboards. By the time the rains hit, everyone was inside a car, watching through the foliage that webbed across the windshields.

The rain smelled of sulfur and it hissed like a snake where it landed. Anyone unlucky enough to be caught out there would have blistered skin where the rain struck them, Ryan knew. The world was ruined. Whatever the people in Progress thought in their towers, there wasn't much left to save.

THE BIKERS CHAINED the farmhand at the side of the road, lashing him to the stump of a fence with the fires still burning in the distance. He struggled there, shirt torn open to expose his bare chest as the fires cut across the field. He watched in horror, screaming for mercy as the fire drew closer. Niles and his gang walked away, pacing just far enough to watch without getting burned.

And then the rains came, the ugly sky opening up and unleashing its foul-smelling torrent in a downpour as black as night.

The farmhand whooped with delight as he saw the rain put out the fire. For a moment he thought he was safe. But he had misjudged his fate.

The hellwater smelled of sulfur and misery, and it burned against the farmhand's skin like steam from a kettle. The man began to cry out, begging once more for mercy as the burn took a hold of his chest, his arms, his face.

"My eyes!" he screamed. "It's in my eyes!"

Niles gestured to his gang, and they stalked over to what little shelter remained amid the burned fields, amassing under the few trees that had grown along the roadside.

The gang made bets on how long the man would last. He continued to plead for help, closing his eyes against the onslaught. Then the rain became heavier, turning from a downpour into a torrent. It was like being dipped in acid, countless different pollutants, the result of a thousand nuclear missiles, feeding that precipitation so that it had the potency of fire against the skin.

The farmhand's screams turned hoarse. Then, disconcertingly, he saw the black rain again and the trees where the bikers huddled and laughed. His eyelids were searing away, leaving him no protection from the downpour.

The last thing the farmhand saw before he blacked out was the effect the rains had on Niles and his leggy female companion. Where it touched them, finding a path through the clawed web of branches above, it seemed to strip their flesh away, revealing strips of metal beneath, revealing faces that only appeared to be human.

Chapter Twenty-One

The rain came, black like tar. It hammered against the roofs of the parked automobiles, stranded amid the jungle of wild plants that had overwhelmed the highway.

Ryan and Krysty shared a Chevy with three of the farmers, while Mildred, Ricky and Jak distributed themselves in the other cars, hiding from the lethal torrent with the survivors of the farm massacre.

The rains lasted through the day and half the night, their drumbeat against the metal roofs of the cars like a mutie orchestra tuning up for chaos. With nothing else to do, Ryan, the companions and the surviving farmers grabbed what sleep they could in the automobiles.

CATNAPPING IN a grounded SUV, Jak was awoken by a wail. He opened his eyes, sensing the change in atmosphere. In the front seat, a woman was crying, dragging a bundle of clothes toward her, trying the vehicle's door handle in the dark.

"Don't," Jak told her, reaching ahead to stop her from opening the side door. It was then that he saw the rain slick on his jacket's sleeve, felt its coolness there. The SUV had a sunroof and even in the darkness Jak could see the crack running through it—just a small, angled line, but enough to let in a slow trickle of water as the rains continued. The tinted plastic of the roof was bowing inward, struggling under the weight of that relentless rain.

Around the car, the other sleepers—a hardy-looking farmhand and a woman with prematurely graying hair—were waking up to the commotion. The farmhand jumped in his seat when he saw the water pooling on his shoulder.

"My Jessica," the woman in the front seat cried, clutching the bundle of clothes to her chest. She was wet with rain, Jak saw, face and chest glistening with water in the faint moonlight that seeped through the roof panel past the clouds, and so was the bundle of rags she held. He remembered now—the bundle contained a child, a baby not more than a week old.

"Dry here," Jak said. "Climb through."

The crying woman shifted in her seat, tried to turn around. "I can't. Oh, heavens—" She reached for the door handle again, about to open it.

Jak could see she was starting to panic so he reached through for the baby. "Pass me," he said calmly, keeping the urgency out of his voice.

Above them, the sunroof buckled, more water pouring in through the crack and around its seal. It came in thin streams, like barely open faucets, bringing the smell of sulfur into the vehicle.

"Oh shit," the man in the front seat said as the foul-smelling water splashed against his face. "Oh shit, oh shit!"

"Baby," Jak ordered, prioritizing the child. "Quick."

The woman reached around and, with a little effort, managed to pass the bundle of rags between the seats to Jak's waiting hands. The bundle was wet, and the dampness stung Jak as he grasped it.

Then the roof finally gave, dropping a cascade of

black water into the SUV. The farmhand and the woman shrieked as it struck the front seats, drenching them with the toxic brew.

"It burns," the man gasped, and he worked his door handle and—nonsensically—stepped out into the full fury of the storm.

"Wait!" Jak cried but it was already too late.

They heard the man screaming as the full force of the rain lashed against him, its black curtain enshrouding him. Jak watched through the windows as the farmhand started to run away from the SUV, placing his arms up over his head as he tried to find shelter. Then, his dark silhouette was lost to the blackness of the rain and the night, and all they could hear was his pained scream echoing back to them across the plain.

The two women were crying, muttering about getting outside, away from the rain. Jak shushed them.

"Safest here," he said.

"But the rain...?" the woman in the front seat pleaded.

Jak handed the baby to the older woman who had been sleeping next to him, then hunkered down in his seat until his shoulders met with the curve between seat and upright. Then, legs up, he kicked out at the sunroof, striking it firmly with the heel of his boot. The sunroof tilted in place, dropping a tirade of water into the front of the car over the dashboard. The woman in front screamed as a little of the black water splashed her, drawing her legs as far to the side as she could to keep out of the stream as it cascaded over the curve of the front shelf.

Jak kicked again, striking the sunroof a second time, wedging it back up into its seal. With the third kick the roof seemed to lock in place, and the torrent became a stream that, after a few seconds, became just a slow drip nudging through the crack.

Jak reached down then, hands scrambling on the floor until he had pulled up the mat that lay there. The mat was loose and made of some kind of rubberlike substance, and it had originally been used to protect the carpet of the SUV. Jak hauled it up and placed it over the sunroof. It was not a perfect fit, but it was enough to cover the crack and about two-thirds of the panel, effectively protecting the woman in the passenger seat. Jak adjusted it slightly, then took out four knives from his stash of throwing blades and used them to secure the mat in place. He hammered them hard through the mat and into the roof until they held it firm.

"Will that hold?" the older woman with the graying hair asked.

"Long enough," Jak said, hoping it would.

AT ONE POINT, Ryan awoke to discover he had been trying to strangle Krysty in his sleep. He could not remember what he had been dreaming about, it might even have been about her, and yet his hands were pressed against her throat with enough force to awaken her.

"You okay, lover?" she asked as he drew his hands away, shaken.

"Are you?"

DOC AND J.B. waited out the storm in the confines of the Dodson farm. The roof leaked and the windows were missing, but there was enough cover to keep them dry, plus a few unfortunate rats who fell victim to one of J.B.'s traps and made for a meal when they were boiled in water over a fire. The water had come from the meager supplies that Doc and J.B. carried—there was no way they would have consumed the poison-laden gunk that was pouring from the skies.

They got a little sleep, taking turns to keep watch while the rain hammered against the walls like a lunatic in a padded cell and the wind made everything bluster and creak. They saw no further sign of the bike gang, who presumably had the sense to get under cover while this storm from Hell rallied its anger, and no one came looking for them.

The rain finally started to ease off before dawn, switching from downpour to irritating drizzle. Eventually it petered out entirely, the clouds moving across the sky like bruises on the skin.

Keeping watch, J.B. woke Doc and told him they were moving now, before something else delayed them. Doc agreed, snatching up his sword stick and checking his LeMat—a daily ritual necessary for survival—before making his way to the door.

"I do not think I was really asleep anyway," Doc admitted. "Not properly."

"Catnaps," J.B. said, picking a piece of rat meat from between his teeth with the nail of his index finger. "Wake up more tired than when you went to sleep."

Both of them felt cold, that cold down in their bones that felt as though it would never go away. It was the effect of their tiredness and of sleeping in a cold building during the storm. There was nothing they could do about that now. They just had to keep moving, and hopefully find Ryan and safety.

The two men stepped outside. In the storm's wake, a heady smell, cloying and acrid, remained—evidence of the awful pollutants that were rife in the atmosphere all these years on from that terrible nuclear exchange. The dirt road was littered with vast puddles, some as big as a train carriage, and the trees lining the road had suffered a battering from the assault.

Doc scanned the trees, searching for the mark he had seen the day before. "There," he said. "Due west."

"Mebbe we can catch up with Ryan before something else catches up with us," J.B. said.

"Fortune favors the brave," Doc replied.

RYAN AND HIS companions emerged from the grounded automobiles, clambering from doors wedged closed to protect them from the vicious downpour, some of them climbing from cracked sunroofs whose tint had done nothing to protect their original inhabitants against the rockets' red glare a hundred years earlier. Now those same sunroofs had protected against black rain that mixed ash with water, like a joke in a crematorium. All except the one in Jak's SUV.

They stepped onto the vegetation, flattened now by the violence of the storm, saw the dark puddles that pooled in the cracks of the asphalt road beneath. The wild vegetation stank of smoke, mist circling the steam-rolled leaves, wafting darkly away on the breeze.

"Next time we'll pack an umbrella," Mildred muttered, hefting her satchel of medical supplies over her shoulder.

"Everybody in one piece?" Trevor asked, scanning the foliage for his friends and family as he pulled himself out from the bent door of a modest family hatchback whose sides had turned brown with rust.

Slowly, the members of the farming group made themselves known, calling in like army recruits. The farmhand who had run from Jak's vehicle in the night was sprawled beneath a skewed road sign. Ryan and Trevor hurried over to the man, but it was clear even

from a distance that he was dead. His skin had turned
coal black with the rain, and traces of red threaded
through it where the flesh had been stripped of its skin.

Jak handed the baby back to her mother, but the child
had not survived the night. Like the farmhand, the girl's
week-old skin had been flayed by the rainwater, leaving it a raw red as if burned.

"We must bury her," the mother said through rack-
ing sobs, and the farmers agreed.

Trevor checked with Ryan if they had time.

Ryan looked at the baby, curled in on herself, her face
red as if she had just a moment ago been crying. As he
stared, the camera affixed in his artificial eye snapped,
storing the image of the dead child in its memory.

"Bury her," he told Trevor. "Do the right thing by
her and by the mother."

"Terry," Trevor said, calling to the woman. He joined
her, outlining the service they would enact for the de-
ceased child and for the dead farmhand whose name
was Judd.

Ryan nodded to the group and, as they set about their
ceremony, Krysty joined him.

"Tough losing a loved one," she said, "even one so
young."

"Tough all over," Ryan agreed.

They stood together, watching the farmers' ceremony for their dead, touching one another's hands as
the ceremony continued. It was a necessity, Ryan knew,
a way to let go and say goodbye—not just to Jessica
and Judd, but also to the others they had had to leave
at the farm, and to the life they had built there. Simple
things that humans needed, Ryan thought.

As the burial service continued in the shadow of the
rusted road signs, Ryan and his companions took a few

moments to check over their weapons, ensuring they were loaded and ready should anything more trouble-some come their way. Something would; sooner or later, something always did.

BY FOLLOWING THE tree markings and keeping to a slow jog, J.B. and Doc finally caught up with Ryan and the others by midafternoon. Ryan had urged his team to remain on alert but had ordered frequent stops, partly because they needed it, especially the farm women, and partly to give J.B. and Doc a chance to catch up if they were able to.

The reunion was typically understated. Jak noticed the two men approaching from a swathe of forest be-hind them, and so the companions had waited. Ryan acknowledged his missing companions with a brief greeting, before asking J.B. about what had happened back at the farm.

"We saw an explosion," Ryan said.

J.B. nodded, slowing his stride and dropping back a little farther to give them some privacy as the farmers and their allies continued the slow trek to Heartsville.

"The barn?" J.B. said. "Sure. Those coldhearts at the farm had backup. A lot of it too. A big gang of bikers came up the main track, armed and looking for trouble."

"Yeah, I met with a few myself," Ryan told him.

"I figured me and Doc had to give them pause, the best way I knew how," J.B. said, a grin crossing his face.

"What did you blow up?" Ryan asked.

"Lot of equipment stored there," J.B. recalled. "High tech stuff, too."

"Is that so?" Ryan asked, intrigued.

"It looked almost new and was really technical,

Ryan," J.B. said, a note of warning in his voice. "Really technical."

"Not good?" Ryan queried.

J.B. shrugged. "Mebbe yes, mebbe no. One thing's for sure—it doesn't belong out here with these sodbusters. If you ask me, it looked almost military."

Military-grade equipment being used on a farm? New military equipment? Just what had they stumbled into here?

They continued their long walk, passing burned-out farms and the remains of a walled ville as they made their way to Heartsville.

Chapter Twenty-Two

They reached the ville a little before dusk on the second day. The sun was crouching low on the horizon, spreading the last of its rays with its golden knife.

Heartsville took up a quarter square mile in total, and it was surrounded on all sides by cleared scrubland to prevent a sneak attack. By the time Ryan and his crew reached it, they could already sense the blasters pointed at them, following their every step as they moved from overgrown blacktop to the dirt expanse that led up to the ville itself.

The ville was located on a mound, up above the surrounding scrub, with walls constructed of wood and scrap. Included in those walls were cars and trucks, some of them standing upright to create rigid barriers that set against the walls to create nooks in which the ville snipers could hide. There had been an industrial park on the site once, the kind of place where IT companies had been located, and one side of the ville jabbed out where one of those buildings still stood. Just two stories high, its ancient glass facade was now reinforced with scrap-built pillars of stone, concrete and wood. One pillar appeared to be made of repurposed tarmac, lifted straight off the road in a great line, now standing upright and supported by a wooden post with metal spines wrapping around the mélange of scrap. It looked a lot like they were hugging, like mutie art.

The ville was heavily armed, with two big Gatling guns poised to either side of the high, portcullis-style gate. Their long snouts pointed downward, framing a patch of scrub thirty feet square in front of the gate itself. Atop those blasters, two figures sat in bucket seats that rotated with the blaster barrels, while two more figures stood to the sides, armed with automatic weapons but ready to help operate the larger blasters if required.

Ryan made a gesture to his crew, and with that simple wave of his hand they knew to hang back and wait. Krysty, Mildred and Doc spoke with the farmhands, urging them to hold back too while Ryan and Trevor, the farm's default leader and someone known to the ville, walked up to the gate.

Ryan approached warily, holding his SIG Sauer loosely at his side, the Steyr Scout longblaster strapped across his back. Unarmed, Trevor kept pace. "Is it safe walking up like this, Trev?" Ryan asked as he scanned the blaster emplacements with the magnification lens of his artificial eye.

Trevor nodded. "They know me and my family," he assured Ryan.

"They ever shoot someone they know?" Ryan asked. Besides the Gatling guns there were a number of blaster ports located along the mismatched walls of the ville, small, flip-back doors through which weapons could be jabbed and fired while blessing the shooter with the maximum of shielding. They would be a bitch to target accurately without a scope, but Ryan figured that didn't matter much so long as the ville sec men got the first shot in.

Trevor snorted with amusement. Then seeing the fixed expression on Ryan's face, he realized that the man had not meant his question as a joke. "I never saw them shoot at anyone, Ryan," he said seriously, "but I don't imagine that means they never have. This place has survived this long while others have fallen."

Ryan halted fifteen feet out from the gate, slap-bang in the middle of the target range, and Trevor stopped by his side. The sec men had been watching them the whole time, blasters trained on the approaching party from at least a half mile away. They had scopes up there, simple lensed affairs through which to scan the distance.

"You want to introduce us?" Ryan urged Trevor, his voice kept low.

Trevor nodded and called up to the sec crew manning the gate. He explained who he was and what had happened, showing them his empty hands and assuring them that he had no hidden weapons on him.

"What about your friend?" the sec man to the left of the main gate called down. He was olive-skinned, with a black gunslinger mustache that drooped to his chin.

"We offered them protection," Ryan explained, stepping forward and holding out his SIG Sauer blaster for the sec man to see.

"And what about this?" the sec man asked, and he turned in place and pointed to his own back to indicate that Ryan should turn around.

Ryan turned slowly, both hands held high in the air, the SIG Sauer still clutched in his right.

"What is that, a Colt carbine?" the sec man asked.

"Steyr," Ryan said. "Foreign-made."

"You find that 'round here?" the sec man on the other side of the gate called down. He was a ruddy-faced man with broad shoulders and rust-red hair.

"Yeah, close by," Ryan lied. He would rather not get into a discussion of the progress across the Deathlands that he and his companions had made before reaching this point. But at the same time he knew that maintaining a friendly appearance right now was the main thing keeping him from getting chilled. People were mistrustful in the Deathlands, and walled communities like this one kept a tight rein on who did and did not enter. Chilling a visitor for his weapons was an everyday story in places like this, too, and it was something Ryan hoped to avoid. Blasters played such a crucial role in survival that discussing them was akin to discussing breakfast— just another way to pass the time and build up the social links that had all but evaporated with the nukecaust.

After further discussion, wherein Ryan's companions were made to declare what weapons they were carrying, the gate was finally drawn up and the group were granted entry into Heartsville.

Inside, the ville was a smorgasbord of prefabricated huts, dilapidated office blocks and scratch-built homes made out of whatever scrap had been available at the time. Three school buses had been welded together, their wheels removed, to create a tunnellike building that housed several workshops, including a blacksmith working at a forge with his red-faced, teenaged girl assistant. The blacksmith looked up as Ryan and his crew strode slowly past accompanied by three sec men, saluting them with a still-glowing iron held in red-hot tongs.

"Looks like a friendly place," Doc proclaimed, gazing around with a sense of wonder.

"Looks can deceive," J.B. reminded him quietly. He was watching the way the portcullis gate had been brought back down to its defensive position, blocking their exit and sealing them inside the ville—a ville peopled by potential enemies.

Jak and the others stayed alert to the alleyways between buildings as they trekked through the ville's open

center. The center was a paved area, with a well and
water pump in its middle and rows of cabbages growing to the sides. There were other vegetable plots too,
wedged between the buildings and along their dirt-
encrusted roofs where they could best catch the sun.
Chickens wandered across the main square, and a few
shoeless kids chased after a ball as the ville's adults
went about their business.

Surprisingly, the ville had electricity. As the settle-
ment had been built on the site of an old industrial park,
it had its own power substations. While these were no
longer connected to any national grid—indeed, such a
thing had long since been abandoned—they retained
the facility to produce electricity in limited amounts via
generators. As the darkness of twilight descended, the
companions saw dim lights begin to flicker on behind
the windows of the buildings, a haphazard pattern of
illumination. There were no working streetlamps, however, and no porch lights—just the illumination coming
from within the lit buildings themselves.

Ryan admired the setup. It seemed that the people
of Heartsville had enough to live on, and the heavily
guarded walls gave them a degree of freedom to come
and go within the ville itself as they pleased, safe from
danger.

THEY WERE ESCORTED to the ville hall, which was located
in the reception area of one of the old office buildings.
The reception area was large enough to house several
wags, which made a grand impression when Ryan and
his crew entered. Within, the space was kept mostly
empty, although tomato plants grew in compost set in
strips along the edges, where the glass in the windows
acted as a greenhouse. This created twin lines of foliage

on either side of the room, channeling any visitor toward the chair and desk that had been set at the far end.

Behind the desk sat the ville's baron, a young man, thin with narrow shoulders and sunken cheeks. He wore round-framed spectacles and had swept his dark hair back in an impressive quiff that loomed over his face like a rooster's comb. He wore an open-necked shirt, and the feet he'd propped on the desk were encased in beautifully polished cowboy boots the color of mahogany.

The man was mighty young, Ryan thought, to be baron of a ville. That was generally a position reserved for those with a little more experience behind them, and usually fell to the most ruthless or the most cunning.

Two women knelt on cushions at either side of the desk. They were dressed in short, formfitting dresses that left their knees bare, showing off their tanned legs. One was blonde while the other had black hair, both trimmed in the same style—a long bob that brushed against their shoulders—and both wore matching sunglasses that made their eyes look like those of a bug.

The baron smiled at the new arrivals. "Trevor, my friend!" he exclaimed. "You look tired. What brings you here to my ville?" His gaze swept over Ryan and his companions.

"We seek refuge, your highness," Trevor said, genuflecting. Ryan could see that the man had dealt with this baron before, and he knew just how he was expected to behave.

The baron smiled more broadly as he observed the older farmer bowing. "And what do you bring me in exchange for this refuge?"

"We have nothing," Trevor admitted grimly. "The

bike men took everything, burned it to ash. My house, my crops…my cousin."

This was the first time Ryan had heard the farmer speak of the people who had died in the fire, and he realized how carefully the man had been restraining his emotions.

"But we'll work the debt," Trevor continued. "You give us a patch of land and we'll work it, all of us."

The baron looked thoughtful for a few seconds, mulling the farmer's words. "Fire," he finally said, rolling the word around as if to taste it. "We've witnessed them use weapons, shoot arrows and bullets, even used vehicles to ram and crush people and their property. And now they've turned to fire."

"They have," Trevor agreed, "and they've become more vicious."

"There's another farm burned-out not far from Trevor's homestead," Ryan stated grimly.

"The Dodsons," Trevor added.

The baron nodded solemnly. "They're getting closer then, circling us. Bolder too."

"But what's driving them?" Ryan asked.

The baron looked Ryan slowly up and down, taking him in as if for the first time. "Do I know you, sir?" he asked.

"Ryan Cawdor, Baron," Ryan said, stepping gingerly forward and offering his hand. As he did, the women at the baron's sides tensed as though ready to pounce. Sec men, Ryan thought—or sec women anyway.

The baron seemed momentarily surprised, then he stood and reached for Ryan's hand, shaking it firmly. "And what do you bring to all of this, Ryan Cawdor?"

"Not much," Ryan admitted. "We were traveling on

the road at the time, passed Trevor's farm and saw the smoke. That's really all there is to tell."

"Not true," Trevor insisted. "Ryan and his people risked their own lives to rescue my family from that blaze. Just like that Good Sam Marathon guy I heard about in the Bible."

"Samaritan," Doc corrected under his breath, but no one noticed.

"Well, that's a fine recommendation," the young baron admitted, "but what we deal in here is trade. If you folks don't have anything to trade, we cannot help you."

Before Ryan could reply, J.B. stepped forward and opened his satchel. "We've got ammo," he said, flashing the baron a glimpse of the shiny contents of his bag. "Enough to trade, if that might interest your high and greatness."

"It might, it might," the baron said in a singsong voice, his smile widening.

"I'm an armorer too," J.B. continued, "a blaster man. You need someone to check over those big blasters on top of the gate or anywhere else, I'll throw that in, do a good job."

"J.B.'s the best," Ricky added by way of support.

The baron looked from the teenager to J.B. to Ryan, adjusting his spectacles as he took them in. "And what would you want in return for all this?" he asked, addressing the question to Ryan. Evidently, the man recognized a group leader when he saw one.

"A safe place to sleep down till morning," Ryan said. "Nothing more than that."

The baron dipped his head a moment to glance past Ryan, and he saw that the sun had almost set. "That sounds like a wise idea, Ryan Cawdor," he said. "Consider yourself under the protection of Baron Hurst."

Ryan expressed his gratitude to Baron Hurst and within a few moments he and his companions were being escorted from the chamber by a pair of sec men. Trevor and his family remained behind to negotiate the nature of their prospective new life as indentured farmers.

"The baron seems like a good man ," Ricky said as they exited the building and walked across the ville square.

The sun had sunk low, now just a red-orange semicircle peering above the high, west wall of the ville. Ryan watched it for a moment, observing the way his cybernetic eye adjusted to its brilliance. He was seeing the world in new shades, new dimensions, and each time he noticed something new he wondered how much his world would change.

For now at least, Ryan and his companions had a safe place to rest in that dangerously changing world.

Chapter Twenty-Three

Ryan couldn't see the surgeons at first. Instead, he saw their instruments, shiny metal barbs like the sting of a nettle, glinting under the fierce light of the operating room.

Ryan felt the assistants holding him down before he saw them. They were strapping his head to a gurney, using thick rubber belts to pin him there. One belt was strapped across his forehead, another across his nose and a third cinched tight across his throat, so tight it made breathing a struggle.

He strained at his bonds, looking at the tray of surgical instruments. There was something else there too, something round and bloody and staring back at him— an eyeball. The iris was green and a snake tail of optic nerve trailed from its rear, dangling from the wheeled trolley upon which the sterile metal tray rested. Ryan looked at the eye, recognizing it, instinctively knowing its source.

Then the surgeons filed past, dressed in black shrouds, inverted ghosts. They approached the gurney solemnly, heads down, marching in step, following one after the other, six in all, ready to work on him from all sides. They were muties, creatures more like gorillas than men, black faces with probing eyes and pronounced jaws that emphasised their elongated canine teeth. Their breath smelled of cleaning fluid, that harsh bite of alcohol that made the nose wrinkle, the eyes sting.

The lead surgeon reached for the eyeball, bringing it toward Ryan's face, iris first. Ryan saw his own reflection in the iris, luminescent and green, like everything else reflected there.

"I don't want it," he shouted, struggling against his bonds.

The surgeons held Ryan's head in place while he thrashed and fought against them. And then he felt rough hands play across his face, reaching for his left eye and plucking it out

The surgeon held the plucked eye close to Ryan's face for a moment, palm flat, and the eye seemed almost to dance there, turning left and right as it studied its surroundings. Ryan watched as it throbbed in the surgeon's hand, pulsing with the rapid beat of his heart, his fear.

Then he felt more pain as the other eye, the new one, was forced into his socket, pushed there the way J.B. would shove plas ex into a lock to blast it open.

There was pressure and then the eye was in and it was working, sending new signals to Ryan's brain. The eye was green, and seeing through it everything went green too, like standing beneath a thick canopy of vegetation. "Earth Mother," Ryan muttered to himself, translating what he saw in a way he couldn't have expected.

A woman had joined them by then, although Ryan had not seen her enter: Krysty Wroth, beautiful, her cascade of red hair flowing down her back and swishing over her face like a waterfall. She was dressed in what he knew was a surgical gown, pastel green with ties at the back, and she held her head low. There was blood on the gown. Krysty shuffled toward the gurney listlessly, her head slumped. Ryan wanted to reach for her, wanted to say something, wanted to apologize.

The surgeons pulled her hair back, kicking her forward at the same time so that her head was drawn backward, revealing her face to Ryan for the first time. There was a bloody hole where her left eye had been, scabs circling the socket in a thick, wine-red line.

"No!" Ryan screamed. "I don't want it! I don't want her eye!"

Somewhere, distant but close, a bell was ringing. It sounded like one of the surgeons had dropped a metal implement but instead of landing it kept striking against the floor, over and over.

THEN RYAN WAS AWAKE. Beside him, Krysty was calling his name gently from where she sat at the edge of the bed, buckling her holster back on over her blue jeans. The bell continued to ring from somewhere outside the room.

"Ryan, wake up," Krysty said. "There's trouble."

A bell was ringing in the distance, over and over: an alarm.

"What?" Ryan asked, not fully awake. He took in the room at a glance, recalled its tight confines, the small window with a ragged drape drawn across it on a rail. The room had been a storage room, the bed that he and Krysty slept on had no mattress and was made up from spare blankets. Still, it was comfortable enough and safe—or so he had hoped. Through the window, edges showing around the side of the ragged curtain, Ryan could see it was still dark, moonlight highlighting the violet-blue sky. "What is it?"

"Someone said bikers," Krysty said. "A lot of them. Even more than before"

Ryan leaped out of bed, reaching for his SIG Sauer blaster where he had placed it cautiously beneath his pillow. He had slept in his clothes. "Fireblast! They must have followed us."

"Now it's all hands to the pump, lover," Krysty replied, flashing one of her stomach-flipping smiles at him before she stood.

Before Ryan could reply, Ricky appeared in the doorway, slapping his palm against it. "They need us up front, guys," he said. "Now!"

OUTSIDE HEARTSVILLE, FORTY-ONE bikers riding twenty-nine vehicles drove in a slow circle like a wag train, bumping over rough ground as they closed in on the ville's high walls. A dust trail kicked up in the wake of the passing vehicles like a wall, grit and dirt flying high in the air as it was disturbed by the passage of the tires.

At their lead, Niles rode his metal steed with Amanda clutching tightly to his back. The vehicle was a low-slung two-wheeler, with an extended front bar that thrust the front wheel ahead by almost the length again of the bike. Its engine cover was black and gold, hand-painted by Niles years before he had become the leader of the gang, back when he was still just a recruit who had turned to the bikers for safety against the woes and the predators that lurked in the radioactive terrain. The gang was bigger now. He had seen every road that was left in mainland California, driven right up to the edge of those ancient highways that had been cleaved in two by the quakes that had submerged half the state into the ocean.

Now he rode at the head of the gang, leading them to this one last site in the area that still housed humans, this one place where people survived against the terrible odds. His face showed more metal than it had before, where the replacement skin had torn away after the bomb blast.

"THEY'RE GETTING CLOSER," said the sec man standing beside the Gatling gun at the crest of the portcullis. He was staring through an extending telescope, watching the dust cloud that rose in the bikers' wake like a wall. It flickered in the moonlight, flecks of grit momentarily catching the light. Around and below, the alarm bell was tolling as it was repeatedly struck by one of the women whom Ryan's team had seen accompanying the baron earlier.

Crouched beside the sec man on the gate, J.B. had his binoculars pressed against his face and was scanning the horizon for the bike gang. "How far away do you make them?" he asked.

"Three-quarters of a mile mebbe," the sec man replied.

"Look," Jak said, pointing to the north and the south, away from the east-facing gate. "All 'round us."

Jak had been with J.B. checking the blaster emplacements—part of their agreement with the baron—when the alarm had been raised. The albino didn't use binoculars to scan the distance—he simply looked hard.

"Jak's right," J.B. stated grimly. "They're surrounding us, likely prepping to attack from all sides."

The sec man lowered his scope and looked up at the large Gatling gun that rested on its rotating base to his left. An identical gun stood on its own base on the other side of the gate, its two operators checking the horizon beside it.

"We've got firepower here," the sec man insisted.

"Seen off worse asshats than these. Everyone here fights, 'cause we all got a stake."

"Yeah, but I'm guessing that your other attackers mostly came from the front," J.B. speculated, "where the guns are strongest. What other ordnance you got here, pal?"

"A lot of blaster emplacements at ground level," the sec man said thoughtfully, "plus two war wags, primed and ready to roll."

J.B. nodded. "War wags against bikes," he mused. "Seems like good odds, but even a bee sting can take out a man sometimes."

The sec man waved his hand dismissively. "Your friend worries a lot, huh?" he teased, directing his observation to Jak.

Jak's haunting red eyes glared at the sec man. "Worried man lives longest," he responded.

The sec man shrugged. It was a good point.

TWO HOURS EARLIER, Niles and Amanda had made love, wild and free in the ashy shadow of a burned-out shopping mall. She had kissed the ruined flesh of his face, kissed the metal plating that lurked beneath like some ancient buried treasure. And when their lovemaking had become more passionate, more intense, she had bitten at the frayed edges of the ruined skin, exposing more of the metal. Now, almost the whole of the metal jaw was exposed, and so too was the plate-and-rivet cheek that had been put in place of the flesh that had scraped away on the cliff face all those months before. The effect made Niles's sneer more prominent, more cruel.

"Tonight we chill," Niles boomed in a voice that carried above even the roar of the engines. "I want everyone dead by dawn! Everyone!"

Around him, the other members of the gang cheered their agreement, bloodlust burning brightly in their single-minded brains. Chilling was good. Chilling was the only good.

Chill the humans.

Chill all humans.

Chapter Twenty-Four

The alarm bell continued to ring, clanging like a dinner bell in a mess hall.

Like most people who lived on the road, Ryan slept like a cat. It took him just a few seconds to bring himself to wakefulness and from there to be ready, mind and body, for action. Ricky led the way through the warren of corridors that crisscrossed the building they had slept in, a reconstructed building propped around an inner core that had once been a power generator. The generator still worked, or had been made to work again, providing the building with dim illumination in the narrow corridors accompanied by a low thrumming that seemed to drill through a person's heart, making Ryan's bones shake.

The corridors were busy with other people, residents of the building who had heard the alarm call and were readying themselves for the worst. Villes like this had grown up to offer protection first for families who co-opted their resources, later for people with skills and the survival instincts needed to function in this broken new world that had been born from the remnants of a destroyed civilization. Villes grew wary of outlanders, because villes were seen as the places of plenty in a world where most people had nothing. Everyone who could hold a blaster would be armed, and if there weren't enough blasters to go around then they would resort to whatever else they had for weapons, right down to the same tools they had used to till the soil in the daylight.

The companions followed the locals through the door to the outside. The door had been propped open by a skull—human or mutie, Ryan couldn't tell for sure.

Outside was pandemonium. They were under siege.

"I HAD BEEN asleep not five minutes," Doc groused as he hurried across the main square to join the throng of locals to defend the ville.

Beside Doc, Mildred sighed as she checked her target pistol. "Count yourself lucky. That's five minutes more than I got," she told him. As so often happened, news that Mildred was a healer had traveled fast, and she had spent almost every minute since arriving in Heartsville dealing with the ville folks' ailments.

Around them, several dozen people were making their way swiftly to the defense positions that were scattered along the high wall. Some posts were high up while others were simply retractable slits located at ground level, allowing a defender to poke out the nose of his or her blaster to cover a narrow area outside.

Reaching the side wall, Mildred and Doc met a sec man with a patchy blond beard, wearing a tattered baseball cap, checkered shirt and jeans. Trevor was already there, learning how to use a remade automatic longblaster that was nicked and scratched from use.

"I'm Rog," the sec man said. "You newcomers got weapons?"

"Aye, that we do," Doc said, brandishing his formidable LeMat for the sec man to see.

Rog frowned at the blaster then nodded appreciatively. "That's an impressive piece of hardware, Pops," he said. "You build that?"

"My goodness, no," Doc replied, smiling, "but I dote on it as I would my own child."

The sec man laughed, then pointed out two emplacements located high along the wall that could be reached by a wooden ladder. "You two go up there, get comfortable and don't wait too long to start blasting," he told them. "We've had trouble from these bikers before. They're devious and mean, but they scare off pretty easy. We're hoping that the blasters on the main gates will take out their leaders and they'll back down, but with the circling pattern they've adopted we're gonna have to stay sharp."

"Sharp is my middle name," Doc assured the sec man, who shook his head in confused response.

"Hell of a coincidence that," the sec man muttered as he made his way to instruct the next group of defenders.

OUTSIDE, THE FORTY-STRONG biker army had reached the quarter-mile marker, closing on the ville in a slow circle, engines roaring, the stench of alcofuel hanging in the air like a heady wine.

At the lead, Niles held one hand aloft and slowed until his bike came to a halt directly in line with the Heartsville gates. Behind him, the line of bikes pulled to a stop, spread out across the wilderness, surrounding the ville in a radial web. The sound of engines ticking over hummed through the atmosphere like an angry beehive.

Niles eyed the gates, the magnification software in the artificial eye that the surgeons had given him bringing the Gatling guns and their operators into sharp focus. Up there, he could see a number of heads peeking out over the high wall, narrow blaster windows sliding open as the ville folk prepared to defend their home from ransacking and worse.

Perhaps they expected to negotiate, Niles thought. But that was not what he was here for. He wanted only the destruction of the people who had settled this land.

Niles raised his open hand, sensed the eyes of his gang upon him, heard Amanda behind him hold her breath in anticipation. Then he closed his hand into a fist, sending the signal to attack.

It was time.

THE FIRST ATTACK came from a fleet of bikes, six in all, roaring toward the high walls from all directions like an approaching thunderhead. They came at the points of the clock, one at twelve, the next at two, then four and so on, timed to arrive together, chrome engines glinting in ghostly fashion as they caught the moonlight in the darkness.

The sec men of the ville readied their blasters, targeting the approaching figures hurtling through the night, unsure whether they should shoot or wait to see if the bikers would negotiate. Baron Hurst stood atop the high wall on the south side of the ville, urging caution. It would be better to warn these attackers off peaceably than to get into a firefight. Even with the ville's superior numbers and firepower, they remained caught in a tricky position, locked behind the walls with no facility to survive a protracted siege. Barons may come to power through strength and intimidation, but they retained it by their ability to negotiate. Hurst knew that and he hoped he could triumph this day without bloodshed.

Standing beside Baron Hurst, the beautiful blonde held up a pair of binocs to his eyes and a second pair to her own. One lens on her pair was cracked, a cobweb pattern across the glass.

"They're getting close," she said. "We should do something."

"No, we wait," the baron insisted. He had dealt with outlanders like these before, and he knew that as soon as one party fired a shot negotiations were over. His own people would wait for his signal, and until the rotary cannon residing on this wall fired, no one else would make a move.

The bikes roared closer, one of them coming directly toward where the baron waited with his people. They were fifty yards away now, then thirty, then just a dozen. As the nearest biker closed in, he drew back his arm and Baron Hurst and his people saw he was holding something there. It was a jerrican, fourteen inches high and designed to carry spare fuel.

With a swing of his muscled arm, the rider threw the can. It swept up into the air, rotating as its contents sloshed about inside, hurtling toward the side of the two-story wall. For a few moments, all attention was on that hurtling can, eyes following its path as it crested the wall. The biker was watching too, a 9 mm Smith & Wesson blaster in his hand. As the can breached the summit of the wall, the rider squeezed the trigger and sent a bullet through the jerrican, ripping its metal surface, a spark igniting the fuel within.

In a fraction of a second, the can exploded, sending torn needles of red-hot metal in a burst over the people watching from the wall, even as the fireball hurtled into the ville itself.

All around the ville, the other bikers were doing the same thing, launching their homemade bombs at the ville. Some of the projectiles were jerricans, others scratch-built. In the space of five seconds, the night sky above the ville seemed to erupt with fire, a half dozen burning comets streaking through the air before exploding inside the walls in a violent conflagration.

The baron ducked back, covering his head even as the jerrican exploded. He felt fiery spines of metal lash against his arms and back. All around him, his people were suffering from red-hot lacerations, while the burning remains of the can landed in a flaming streak inside the ville walls.

"Blast him!" Hurst commanded. "Shoot him down!"

Beside him, the sec man working the rotary cannon snapped at the twin triggers, sending a stream of bullets from the high wall out at the retreating biker. The heavy cannon had been acquired from a military helicopter that had been grounded a hundred years before, and its rotating chamber spit its stream of bullets at a rate of four thousand rounds per minute. Its lethal issue carved a path in the ground, kicking up dust as it tracked the retreating biker speeding away until suddenly his bike was caught, erupting in a fireball.

But already, the second attack wave was approaching. More bikers followed in the wake of the first, coming at different angles, with passengers setting light to their missiles on the move, launching blazing tangles of kindling toward the high walls. Flaming missiles smashed against the walls, sending out great splashes of fire as they struck. Others cleared the top of the walls, hurtling over before crashing back down to earth in great skidding bursts of flame, sending fire in all directions. One missile caught the top of the wall where Mildred and Doc had been stationed, and they reared back as Rog, the sec man who had shown them to their position, was caught in the explosion, lighting up like a human campfire.

"Drop and roll!" Mildred shouted, hurrying toward the sec man as he danced on the spot, screaming and trying to remove his burning clothes. "Put out the flames! Somebody get this man a blanket!"

Confusion reigned in the ville as great scorching meteors hurtled through the air, a third wave of attack as the ville folk tried to defend themselves. The sounds of blasterfire echoed through the night, like branches snapping all around, but it was accompanied by the deep drumbeat of heavy artillery, as the Gatling guns and rotary cannons were brought to bear on the attackers.

WAITING OUTSIDE, HIS engine idling, Niles watched as pillars of smoke twisted into the night, coloring the dark sky a shade darker. Fire dotted the ville walls and issued from within, the great cleanser, the great leveler.

Even here, a quarter mile from the closest fire, Niles fancied he could feel the heat brush against his synthetic skin, warming the plates of metal that replaced his skull, his ruined limb. For a moment he smiled grimly, watching the flames and the smoke rise higher, the last great funeral pyre to humankind's failed ambition.

Around Niles, the other members of his gang were bringing their bikes back around, ending their circling as they converged on the spot where he and Amanda waited. There had been losses already—a rider and passenger had gone up in flames when their missile had exploded too soon, caught by a well-placed bullet from a ville sniper, two more died in return fire. But still they were strong—nineteen riders and a handful of armed passengers, raring to wipe Heartsville off the map forever.

Why?

Niles didn't ask that question. There had been a reason, years before, when he had hit the road, searching for fuel and the freedom that came with it. But that was before the accident, before his rebirth at the hands of the surgeons of Progress. Now all he could really remember was how much hate he had, hate for all of humankind.

All he desired—all he yearned for—was to chill the human scum.

Chapter Twenty-Five

The sound of motorcycle engines droned through the air like a swarm of angry hornets.

Fire licked the ville walls. Inside flames were scurrying across the ground and a number of the buildings.

The ville folk were working their blasters, firing from high positions over the walls or using the fortified nooks to take potshots at the bikers as they came around again for another attack.

A temporary field hospital had been organized in the ville square, its volunteers dealing with early burn victims who had been caught up in the first wave of flaming missiles.

Ryan, Krysty and Ricky were with a number of people at the north wall, taking shots at the bikers as they hurried toward the walls with their burning missiles. But those attacks had ceased now, and word came through that the bikers were amassing before the main gates.

Ryan ran across the ville square, the Steyr Scout longblaster in his hands, Krysty and Ricky just a couple of steps behind him. He dashed through the field hospital, ducking into and then out of one of the bivouac-style tents that had been set up to give the patients some privacy as those who knew some healing techniques did what little they could to help them.

Ryan ran past the main square, sprinting at full speed

toward the main gates. He could hear the sounds of
the bike engines, and something else too—great thuds
as missiles were tossed against the towering gate. The
Gatling guns raged in reply, sending lethal streams of
bullets out into the wastes that surrounded the ville even
as flames raced toward them from the burning walls.

Another missile struck the gate, and the companions watched as it shuddered and cracked, the dazzling
light from the fire beyond bleeding through the narrow splits. Then another flaming object came hurtling
over the gates, rushing through the air with an audible
whoosh of wind before crashing to the ground twenty
yards from Ryan. He watched as the roof of the trip-
let school bus began to burn, the acrid tang of sizzling
paint almost immediate in the air.

They were forty feet from the gates when they saw
something else hurtling over the wall to their left side.
The operators of the big blasters were trying to track
it, rotating the weapons as swiftly as they could even
as it launched over the wall and into the compound itself. The thing landed with a howl of joyous laughter—
it was a bike, suspension rocking as the rider steered it
out of a skid and righted his balance.

The rider was laughing, blasting shots from a revolver in his hand, picking off the sec men at the walls
like shooting at a duck gallery. Three sec men tumbled
from their high positions on the walls, while a fourth
cried out in pain as his shoulder exploded in a red blos-
som of blood.

Ryan ran, firing a quick shot from his Steyr—an
unwieldy weapon in this instance, designed as it was
for distance work—shooting the longblaster from the
hip. The biker's face turned to a red splatter, a spray
of teeth flying through the air as he howled in sudden

agony. He had lost control of the bike by then, and it raced onward before slamming against the exterior wall in a violent crash.

Ryan, Krysty and Ricky kept moving, watching grimly as a second bike leaped over the wall. How the nuking hell are they doing that? Ryan wondered.

AT THE GATES, J.B. and Jak had seen the whole thing. The bikers had brought a ramped length of wood with them that they had carried tied on the back of one of the quad bikes. The wood sheet was long and narrow.

Even as the Gatling guns sent lead slugs toward them, the bikers had moved swiftly, setting up the wooden sheet on the run, balancing it between two quad bikes and holding it up at a forty degree angle in line with the wall. Then, as the quad bikes slowed, one of their two-wheeled companions had sped up and raced toward the wooden ramp, hitting it at some velocity and using it to launch himself up and over the wall.

The Gatling guns roared, cutting into the first biker as he leaped. He had misjudged his trajectory, and went crashing into the top of the wall by the gates before sagging back under a hailstorm of bullets.

But the next rider managed to jump over the wall, skimming the top by a matter of inches before plummeting into the courtyard of the ville, where Ryan had ultimately ended his attack.

The next ones came faster, one had barely left the ramp when the second hit it, twin bikes hurtling over the wall one after the other. J.B. ducked back as the next sailed by overhead, squatting and rolling out of its path.

The bikes' headlights whizzed overhead like shooting stars as the bikers vaulted the walls.

Beside J.B., Jak called out a warning, spying the

second bike coming straight toward the Armorer. J.B. sank down on his back and held the M-4000 shotgun toward the heavens, squeezing the trigger twice. The first shot missed the bike by a good ten inches. But the second caught the vehicle as it hurtled above J.B.'s torso, and he turned away as fire erupted across the bike's belly—even as it cleared the wall and went dropping back earthward.

The bike he hit veered wildly off course as the rider was pushed up in his seat by the explosion. Bike and rider landed together on their flanks, the bike crushing and mangling the rider's right leg as it pressed on top of him.

The first rider was still alive however, which left Jak and a number of the fast-acting sec men to try to take her out before she created any more havoc within the ville itself.

Buildings and crops were burning, great spots of flame dotting across the ville. Jak pulled the trigger rapidly. Bullets spit from his MSG90, joining a barrage of shots from the sec men's longblasters. Jak had snagged the battered Heckler & Koch MSG90 longblaster from the sec men's stores. The weapon featured a scope and had a 20-round magazine.

The female rider sped off, her long black tresses whipping out behind her like the wings of a crow.

Jak slung his longblaster and leaped, determined not to lose the woman. He dropped from the high ledge that ran along the wall, his alabaster skin showing like a ghostly blur in the moonlight. In a moment, he was on the ground, landing in a crouch that he turned effortlessly into a run, tearing after the bike as it wove down the alley between two nearby buildings. Jak took the most direct route, running straight at the single story

building to the right and kicking out at the very last
moment so that he literally ran up the wall. Speed and
determination carried him five feet off the ground before the tug of gravity caught up, and by then Jak was
high enough to reach the roof with both hands and pull
himself over.

An instant later, Jak was sprinting full speed across
the low roof, his head cocked as he tracked the motorcycle by the furious sound of its engine.

AN EXPLOSION SHOOK the north wall. Close to the impact,
Ryan, Krysty and Ricky were thrown to the ground.
Thirty feet away, a weak spot had been created in the
wall, and a great chunk began to topple forward, hunks
of it crumbling away as a second explosion ripped
through it.

People were stationed there, professional sec men
and residents just trying to defend their homes, caught
up in the explosion and its aftermath. Two people died
in the explosion, while three more were crushed by the
wall when it toppled.

"Wall breach!" somebody cried, and the sounds of
blasterfire redoubled.

The roar of twin-stroke engines grew louder in the
aftermath of the explosion. Ryan's head was reeling but
he forced himself to move, turning to watch through
the dust haze churned up by the ruined wall. Three figures appeared, riding high on their motorcycles, standing on the footrests as they bumped over the debris and
into the ville.

"Ricky, Krysty—come on," Ryan commanded, pulling himself back to his feet. As he did so, the first of
the bikers aimed his outstretched arm at the nearest sec

man and blasted, unleashing a vicious burst of buckshot
from the end of his limb with a cacophonous boom.

JAK SPRINTED across the low rooftop, following the roaring sound of the motorcycle engine. Below him, he
could hear shots ringing out as the female biker blasted
locals with a handblaster. The shots sounded blunt and
abrupt in the tight confines of the alleys as she sped
from one into the next to generate as much fear and
chaos as she could, and Jak grimaced as he heard another innocent scream in agony over the growl of the
throttle.

A gap between rooftops was just ahead of him—five
feet across and appearing as a patch of blackness on the
moonlit roof. Jak leaped without slowing, resting one
hand on the longblaster that hung across his back to stop
it striking him and throwing his balance.

He landed, then hurried across that roof, cutting the
corner and leaping to the next roof and then down into
the alley Painted by a narrow strip of silver moonlight eking between buildings, the alley was just four
feet wide.

Jak stood resolute, whipping around the weighty
longblaster as the bike screeched around the corner,
the rider's foot stomping on the ground, tires spinning
to grip the loose dirt as the vehicle turned. The bike
roared forward, its rider clutching a blaster in her right
hand, pressed hard against the handlebars as she steered
the sharp turn at speed.

The bike was eight feet from Jak and, that close, he
could see the rider. She was young with a wide jaw and
a mean smile, black hair splayed out around her as it
caught the breeze She looked surprised as Jak brought
up the muzzle of his weapon and began to fire. The

bullets raced toward the bike in a cough of propellant, drilling through the front tire, handlebars and across the biker's chest in an instant.

Still firing, Jak leaped backward, driving himself flush to the wall as the bike and rider went screaming past. The bike skimmed past him, engine roaring, missing his knees and feet by a fraction of an inch. The rider was shaking atop her motorcycle, a line of dark holes running up her torso, the familiar shocked expression on her face that Jak recognized from so many gunshot victims.

A moment later, the vehicle slapped hard against a building, overturning and throwing the rider high into the air. Jak watched the grim spectacle, training the longblaster on his target as she was thrown against the highest reaches of the building, where wall met roof. She tumbled down a moment later, her bike still revving below her, crashing into it to create a mangled mess of human and machine.

Jak turned away, knowing his job was done. He dropped the magazine from his weapon and reloaded. Seconds later he heard laughter coming from behind him—a woman's laughter, playful and mocking.

INSIDE A GARAGE located behind the baron's buildings, two mighty war wags rumbled to life. The war wags had been converted from predark vehicles. One had been a sec van, a bulky square vehicle with reinforced walls and bulletproof glass that had once been used to transport money between banks. The other was a converted camper van, twenty-three feet in length with twin sets of wheels at the back. The camper van had been remodeled, its chassis strengthened and the exterior reclad in sheet metal leaving only the narrowest of slits through

which driver and passengers could see. Both vehicles
had been fitted with blaster turrets on their roofs and
automatic machine gun barrels fixed in place on their
hoods that could be operated from the passenger seat,
as well as a few extras specific to each vehicle. The
sec truck included an antitank rocket launcher poking
through a gap in its back door. The war wags had been
converted to run on alcofuel, which could be distilled on
site, and as their engines started up they reeked with the
sweet tang of alcohol, so strong it made the eyes water.

The war wags were operated by three- or four-man
crews who could work the armament as in coordination
with the drivers. The crews were relentlessly drilled.
Right now, the drivers were strapping themselves in
while their crews took up their positions inside. Then
the war wags powered ahead in a blaze of headlights,
tires screeching as they exited the garage and rolled
toward the ville gate.

The sec men were ready at the flaming gates, and
even as more bikes vaulted over the wall, the ville gate
was drawn open and both war wags thundered out in
single file, hurrying from the ville like bullets from a
blaster.

The ground itself seemed to shake as the war wags
flew through the open gate. Both vehicles were heavy,
granting them a top speed of just fifty miles per hour.
The drivers floored the accelerators and diverged as
they exited the ville walls, with the armored truck going
to the right while the camper peeled off to the left.
There were plenty of targets out there—a whole cluster of bikers had been circling the ville and at least fifteen of them were amassed at the main gates when the
war wags emerged.

The sec truck drove straight for a group of bikers

who blasted shots from their light weaponry as they
retreated from the approaching behemoth. One biker
reacted too slowly, and both he and his bike slammed
into the war wag's grille before being tossed high over
the hood.

To the left, the six-wheeled camper van took a wider
curve, rounding on the bikers, herding them closer to
the ville walls to give the faster-moving vehicles less
room to maneuver. Then the top cannon began to blaze,
twin barrels blasting out .50 caliber bullets in silver
streaks that churned up the ground and drilled holes in
those bikes that didn't weave out of the way fast enough.

The bikers fought back, blasting at the truck with
handguns and custom-built cannons that had been fixed
to their bikes. A few used physical attachments that had
been grafted to their bodies in place of missing limbs.

The fight was on.

JAK TURNED BACK, swinging the longblaster around on
its strap with both hands. The female rider was there,
captured in the mangled ruin of her motorcycle, blood
staining her clothes and streaming down her face. She
was laughing at him, her eyes fixed on Jak's as she
stood up amid the wreckage of her vehicle, chrome
and flesh torn together like some hideous nightmare.

And then she began to run at Jak, leaping to extract
herself from the ruined motorcycle, issuing that awful,
throaty chuckle like a taunt.

Chapter Twenty-Six

A biker was using a machete to hack at everything and everyone he passed, wielding it low to the ground and using his bike's speed to his advantage.

Ryan watched as the biker hacked through the lower leg of a sec man, speeding onward but still framed in the Steyr's crosshairs. The sec man's right calf exploded in a splash of blood.

Ryan inhaled, held the breath for a moment, then slowly let the breath out, squeezing the trigger on the exhale. The Steyr bucked against his shoulder, sending a single 7.62 mm bullet toward the bike's rider. Ryan watched, his artificial eye magnifying the impact, as his bullet cut through the man's forehead and he lost control of his bike.

RICKY AND KRYSTY were just a few feet away from Ryan, and they had their own targets in their sights. Two more bikers roared down the ville's main street, firing blasters and a weird hand-cannon attachment at anyone who got in their way.

Krysty winced as one of the bikes slammed into a brave sec man, knocking him off his feet as he tried to take a shot at the rider. Behind the rider, his passenger—a slender woman with a swishing ponytail floating out behind her—wielded a Mossberg shotgun one-handed, sending lethal bursts of shot at everything that moved.

"We have to do something," Ricky said, watching in horror as the other biker used the hand-cannon molded into his arm to blast a child and mother cowering in a doorway. Both child and mother collapsed to the ground, a blast of buckshot peppering the door where they had stood before.

"You're right," Krysty agreed, steadying her two-handed grip on her Smith & Wesson .38. A moment later, she fired at the biker who had rammed the sec man—but her target was traveling too fast, and Krysty's shot missed. "Dammit."

The rider and his ponytailed passenger sped off toward the tents that had been set up in the ville square.

Before Ricky could ask, Krysty emerged from cover and began to give chase, her legs and arms pumping as she ran across the street after the retreating bike. She ran past the burning blacksmith's shop, feeling the heat wash against her side in a fierce wave.

"Krysty, look out!" Ricky screamed, as he spotted the other biker turn his handlebars and begin bearing down on her. It was no good—Krysty could not hear him over the roar of the engines.

Ricky moved, an automatic response to seeing his beautiful ally in danger. He was out from the cover of the cart in a flash, his Webley firing once, twice, a third time, sending three shots at the rider with the metal arm.

Ricky's first shot missed, while the second struck the bike's chassis and ricocheted away in a flash of sparks. The third shot, however, struck the rider in the fleshy part of his thigh, generating a spurt of blood. It was a minor wound, not much more than a flesh wound, but it was enough to make the biker lose control momentarily.

He pulled at the handlebars in flinch reaction, swerving to the right away from the direction that Ricky's bullet had come from. Ricky watched as bike and rider bumped over a tangle of blankets that had been left out close to the temporary medical center, and in a moment one of the blankets had caught in the bike's back wheel, forcing it to spin out of control. The bike slipped over, skidding across the street with its rider still clinging to it, before striking the wall of a burning building in a shower of sparks.

Ricky ran after the bike, the Webley thrust before him, his eyes fixed on the fallen rider. He had seen these people get up from worse than that back at the farmhouse, so he was taking no chances here.

IN AN ALLEY between buildings, Jak processed what he saw in a fraction of a second. The biker woman was running at him, her raven tresses flowing out behind her like a black shroud, her expression fixed in a hideous, inhuman grin. He could see the flesh hanging from her arm where she had struck the wall, a long gash crossing from her shoulder right up to the side of her face. And beneath it, there was metal lined by torn skin and blood, as if she was some kind of robot. Jak wondered briefly about that, but there was no time to think.

The woman ran at Jak with incredible speed, a broken pipe from the crashed motorcycle dropping away from her side as it slipped from her body. Her right arm snapped out in a vicious punch. Jak ducked, squeezing the longblaster's trigger three times in rapid succession. The discharges sounded loud in the confines of the alley, as if someone was drumming against his skull.

The woman's punch missed Jak by a fraction, and her fist drove instead against the building behind him.

Against…and into! Jak's bullets raked across her body at
the same time, hacking tiny chunks of her torso away in a
stutter of flesh, blood and metal. The woman didn't seem
to notice, or if she did she didn't care. Instead, she was
concentrating on following up her attack, bringing her
knee up to strike Jak in the groin with a powerful blow.

Jak shifted the longblaster in his hands, bringing it
down even as the woman's knee knifed toward him,
deflecting her attack as he struck the top of her leg.

The biker followed through with a left jab at Jak's
face, and he rolled with the punch, ducking and staggering as it glanced against him. The woman was already attacking again, her left leg whipping up in a high
kick that struck the barrel of the Heckler & Koch as Jak
tried to bring it around to shoot her. The blaster's barrel shifted upward, sending the round skyward as Jak
pulled the trigger.

Then the woman was on him again, her right arm
powering forward, her balled fist striking Jak in the
chest like a thrown hammer.

The albino stumbled back until his heels met the wall
behind him. The woman flew at him like an unleashed
rocket, her arms and legs flailing at him, almost faster
than his eyes could follow. His bullets had had no effect,
and nor had the bike's collision with the wall. Jak saw
metal beneath her flesh, hidden there where the skin
had been torn away. Metal meant machine, so whatever
she looked like, however she acted, Jak figured she was
just another damn machine.

The woman brought her arms out in preparation to
slap Jak on both sides of his head. As she did so, Jak
squeezed the trigger of the longblaster again, working
the trigger over and over to send a half dozen rounds
into the woman's foot. The 7.62 mm bullets shredded

the leather of her boot and tore her flesh and bone to a bloody pulp. The woman cried out, howling like a wolf in pain, and in that moment her attack on Jak was forgotten.

So she's got flesh, Jak thought. Real flesh. Flesh that could be hurt.

Raising his weapon, Jak turned it on the woman's torso sending shot after shot into her gut as she stumbled before him, searching for the soft human parts that remained in her otherwise artificial body.

The biker woman shook before him, stumbling like a drunk as the bullets strafed her body. Jak saw the spot he wanted then, and he eased his finger from the trigger, letting the longblaster hang on its strap. Before him, the woman was still stumbling, blood and sheared metal showing through her clothes where the bullets had torn them.

Jak moved his wrist in a practiced gesture, freeing the leaf-bladed throwing knife he kept hidden in a sheath in his sleeve. The blade dropped neatly into his hand even as he drew his arm across his body. An instant later, Jak's arm whipped out in a graceful arc, sending the knife hurtling through the air until it met his attacker front and center, between the second and third ribs on her left side. The blade pierced the woman's heart, her still-human heart, and Jak watched as she sagged to her knees, the unvoiced cry of agony stuck in her throat.

"Machines in human parts," Jak muttered with a shake of his head. He didn't know what that meant yet, but he was sure it was bad for Heartsville.

OUTSIDE THE VILLE, bullets cut through the air with the cacophonous drumbeat of death as the bikers fought

with the war wags. Twin rockets blazed from the rear
of the converted security truck as it hurtled past the exterior wall, throwing bikers from their machines and
forcing others to take evasive action as the antitank
missiles struck.

The bikers regrouped swiftly, turning their maneu-
verability to their advantage as they bore down on the
war wags. Three bikers came at the war wag from either
side, tossing grens at the high-sided vehicle as its weapons crew hurried to reload the rocket launcher. Grens
struck both sides, rocking the war wag as it roared over
the uneven dirt outside the ville.

Inside the cab, driver and passengers were shaken
by the impacts. The driver clung tightly to his steering
wheel, fought to keep the vehicle on course as his body
strained against the binding of his safety belt. Beside
him, the codriver who operated the forward blasters fell
forward, his head striking the dashboard, pulling back
with a bloodied nose.

In the truck's rear, the two-man crew was thrown
from their posts. The man on the blaster turret tumbled
from his seat and slammed into the back wall, while the
rocket operator jabbed his leg out against a side wall
to stop himself from toppling over while still holding
a primed rocket.

One biker, who rode a bike with a sidecar that carried all manner of tools, weaved in close to the smaller
war wag and tossed a lit Molotov cocktail at it. The
bomb struck, sending a fiery burst of flames streaking
up the driver's door and across the armored windshield.

The flaming war wag swerved, tires churning up dry
dirt, bull bars knocking a cactus flat as the driver tried
to hold his course. Then the driver hitched the wheel
hard to his left and the heavy war wag came barreling

toward bomber and his bike, nudging against the side-car in a squeal of metal against metal.

The biker steered into the impact, locking his bike against the war wag and throwing a second Molotov cocktail at the vehicle's side.

For a moment the old sec truck was lost in a blinding stream of flames. Then the driver's door opened—fire racing up its side—and a hand reached out, jabbing a blaster in the biker's face. The old man's skull exploded in a red blush of blood, flesh and bone.

CLOSE BY, THE converted camper van had circled a third of the way around the ville, all blasters blazing as the crew tried to herd the bikers away from the gates. Three bikers went down in a hail of bullets, two of them dropping almost simultaneously as they tried to steer away from a pillbox outcropping in the ville's side that was also spitting bullets in their direction.

The camper came level with another bike, a straggler whose companions had outpaced him. The driver swerved, bringing the war wag closer to the walls as they continued to chase around the moonlit, dusty terrain. Beside the wag, the biker found himself with an ever-decreasing corridor to drive along, the high and irregular wall of the ville to his left, the high-sided war wag to his right. He struggled to free his shotgun from its holster behind his saddle, whipping it up and pulling the trigger even as the war wag nudged closer.

The shotgun boomed, a brief burst of propellant lighting up both vehicles as they came closer to one another in a roar of straining engines. Then, with a sudden turn of the wheels, the war wag nudged against the remaining biker and pushed him the final few feet until he struck the ville wall. The bike's handlebar caught the wall first and its rider suddenly found himself unable to steer. Then the bike was sandwiched against the wall, and a shriek of metal and human misery rent the air as both bike and rider were crushed against the unyielding wall.

Chapter Twenty-Seven

Doc spun at the sound of the engine. He was working in a bivouac-style tent, a single sheet of canvas propped up at an angle using two posts, utilizing the edge of a building as its other wall. At some point during the attack, he and Mildred had been enlisted to help in the makeshift medical tents that dominated the center of the ville. He was tending to a sec man whose face, chest and shoulders had been horribly burned by one of the jerrican grens when the snarl of a bike's engine came suddenly close.

Turning, Doc saw the motorcycle race through one of the other tents in the compound, a shotgun in the passenger's hand blasting away, wheels running over two patients who had been stretched out to recover from other wounds.

Doc winced at the violence, feeling helpless as the bike slammed into another patient before bumping out of the tent. Doc had been a man of learning once, but time and circumstance had transformed him into a man of action. He turned his attention from his patient and reached for his LeMat blaster, which he had left on the floor at his side, whipping it up and targeting the approaching bike. Doc fired at the approaching bike, the shot unleashing a noise that sounded like a thunderclap.

The bike swerved, and the LeMat's lethal issue missed the bike's driver entirely, punching a hole instead through the shotgun-wielding passenger riding pillion. The woman was knocked off the bike, and she tumbled over and over as she struck the ground at speed.

The effect of suddenly losing his passenger saw the bike's driver struggling to retain his balance; the bike bucked and weaved beneath him as he tried to keep it upright.

Doc watched with irritation as the bike disappeared under the cover of another bivouac tent, riding rough-shod over the legs of a burn victim. He tracked its path with his blaster, his teeth gritted.

STANDING ON THE street by the blacksmith's, Krysty watched the bike disappear into another of the tents that had been set around the compound, and she bit back a curse. His rider had fallen but she couldn't catch the man, not from this distance, nor could she hope to shoot him with the way he was weaving.

"Gaia!" Krysty spoke the word through gritted teeth, drawing once more on the power of the Earth Mother to grant her a surge of strength that she might use to stop these maniacs. "Great mother of all, creator of the Universe, hear me in my hour of need." She felt the power course through her veins, igniting her muscles. The change was like the difference between being asleep and awake, as if without the power given to her by Gaia she was sleepwalking through the waking world.

As the power charged through Krysty's body, she ducked into the school bus that served as a blacksmith's shop. The roof was on fire and the smith's unmanned forge was rapidly raging into a full-blown inferno.

Krysty's eyes pierced the smoke, searching for something she could use. There. The poker used to stoke the fire was just what she needed. Krysty grabbed it, feeling the heat of the handle where the fire had played too close to it.

Then she was running—indeed she had never stopped—and she emerged into the street just as the bike reappeared on the far side of the canvas cover, Doc's bullets following it. Krysty drew back her arm, aimed, then launched the poker like a javelin, not at where the bike was but at where it would be in four seconds.

THE BIKE WAS through the tent and out the other side now, zipping across the ville square, its rider laughing grimly despite losing his passenger. Chilling frenzy had taken over him. The laughter echoed around the square, but was abruptly cut short as Krysty's missile landed between the spokes of the bike's back wheel. In an instant, the rear of the bike came to an abrupt halt while the front wheel continued forward, resulting in the bike flipping entirely. Bike and rider flew off the ground for a heartbeat before crashing to earth. The rider landed first, the bike landing on top of him where he still clung to the handlebars. He howled in terrific pain as the white-hot poker scored against his chest.

DOC DIDN'T HAVE time to figure out what had happened; he was too busy running toward the fallen passenger, the LeMat thrust out before him, ready to blow out her brains. The LeMat blasted the moment he saw the woman, struggling to get up from where she had fallen. Her head exploded like a ripe melon beneath a hammer blow. A moment later he found the rider struggling to raise a weapon and executed him in the same fashion, cutting short his screams of white-hot pain.

THE BIKER WAS six feet tall and heavily tattooed, and right now he was sailing through the air as the motorcycle beneath him exploded in a fireball where Ryan's perfectly placed bullet had pierced the gas tank. The bikes didn't run on gasoline, of course—they used a refined alcohol-based solution that powered the converted engines and made the exhaust eye-watering in its stink. Ryan had tracked the biker as he sped through a flaming gap in the exterior wall, waiting until he was sure that no one would be caught up in the blast before shooting out the gas tank. The bike went up in a red-orange burst of exploding fuel, sending its rider twenty feet in the air until he crashed to earth in the ville square. Ryan watched the man disappear as his flailing body tore through the canvas covering of one of those swiftly erected tents, and he hurried to follow.

Inside, Mildred was patching up a pregnant woman when the biker crashed through roof of the tent. She leaped aside, dragging her patient with her as the biker dropped to the ground and shattered the lamp she had been working by, casting the tent in sudden darkness.

With a growl of irritation, the biker rolled over and drew a revolver from his vest. He reeled off a shot, delivering a bullet into the forehead of an elderly cobbler who had already been caught up in an explosion in the initial attack.

Miidred reached for the pancake holster she wore at her hip, pulling the ZKR pistol from its hiding place there. As she did so, a figure appeared silhouetted in the doorway of the tent, broad-shouldered and familiar.

"Ryan, look out!" Mildred cried in warning, recognizing her companion as he hurried through the doorway.

Ryan ducked as the biker shot at him, and the bullet went wide, zipping over his head and disappearing into the night.

THE SEC-TRUCK-TURNED-WAR-WAG powered toward twin bikers who had handled the ramp mechanism. The war wag looked to be in pretty bad shape now. The driver's door was buckled inward and both sides and the rear showed evidence of grenades and fire damage, with a great hole showing across the back edge close to where the rocket launcher was located. The rocket launcher itself was out of commission now. A well-placed gren had been shoved in its barrel during the frantic battle, leaving it looking like a fountain frozen in ice.

The top blasters blazed however, twin barrels spitting heavy caliber bullets at the retreating bikers as they left the ramp mechanism and made a dash for safety. The driver smiled grimly as he watched them race toward Heartsville's wall across from the main gate. He had them now.

Then the bikers skidded to a halt, locking their handlebars and pulling out in unison so as to create a space between them. The war wag hurtled on, bouncing over the rough terrain, its top blasters and side barrels still firing. Without warning a curtain of fire came to life before the wag as the two bikers used an accelerant on the ground to create a line of flames. Then, on command, one of the bikers blew up, exploding before the war wag in an impressive display of bones and flesh and metal. The burning debris slapped against the war wag's windshield, feeding the fire even further.

Suddenly unable to see, the sec man driving the war wag slammed his foot against the brakes—but it was too late. The war wag sped out of control, the front end a pillar of flames as it barreled straight into the high wall of the ville before coming to an abrupt halt. The wall gave as the wag struck, a reinforced section crumbling around it, great chunks of debris crushing the engine and grille even as the flames continue to roar.

The driver opened the door and leaped free from the

burning vehicle, his crew working their own doors as they hurried to safety. But safety would not be so easy to find. Driver and crew were briskly rounded upon by several bikers and they suddenly found themselves in the center of a pitched blaster-fight with enemies on every side.

The war wag crew fell in seconds to the relentless charge of the bikers.

ELSEWHERE, THE SECOND war wag had been herding bikers toward the gun emplacements in the ville walls where they could be cut down without risk. But the bikers had become wise to that, and as blasterfire filled the night, the converted camper van found itself surrounded by angry bikers brandishing heavy weaponry.

Somehow, one of the bikers had acquired a bazooka and the war wag found itself dead in its sights. The driver jerked the wheel left and right as he saw a gren hurtling toward the windshield, jounced over the rough earth as the explosive skimmed by.

A moment later, the gren struck a dead tree twenty feet behind the war wag, cutting the trunk in two and sending viciously sharp splinters the size of chair legs in all directions.

The war wag barreled on, its driver not quite in control as the attacks came thick and fast from all sides. Suddenly, something exploded under the front, left wheel, the bright burst of the explosion dazzling through the narrow gap in the windshield. Then the war wag struck a ditch and the vehicle lurched over, tipping forward and sideways as it struggled for purchase.

The driver gunned the engine, trying to keep upright as the front wheels caught in a trench in the earth. The engine complained, gears clashing as the driver tried to keep moving forward. A moment later, a dark shape hurtled through the air toward the struggling vehicle, and in an instant that shape turned into an explosion.

Caught at a fatal angle in the ditch, the camper van went up like a funeral pyre, its remaining ordnance exploding like popping candy as more firepower was turned against it. The driver and passengers were roasted alive inside.

IT WAS DARK inside the tent, and Ryan switched automatically to night vision, recasting the interior in greens and grays. He would rely on the artificial eye while he was inside the tent, knowing its report would be better than anything his opponent could make out in the darkness.

As he switched vision, Ryan ran at the biker, wielding his Steyr rifle two-handed like a staff and swinging the butt toward the man's tattooed face. It connected with a crack, the sound of the biker's jaw breaking, and Ryan's opponent toppled backward. He moved in again, driving the butt of the longblaster into the man's face. The biker yelled in pain, spitting blood and broken teeth as he tried to avoid the next blow.

Ryan scanned the man through the artificial eye. He was unarmed, no threat, just another enemy who needed to be put down. Ryan drove the rifle into his face one last time before turning to Mildred.

"Thanks—" Mildred began. But before she could finish, Ryan was driving the butt of his Steyr Scout at her face.

Chapter Twenty-Eight

The bikers were getting bolder now. Both war wags were down, and they felt they had no opposition left. Inside the ville, fires burned and the dead and wounded outnumbered the living.

At the ville gate, J.B. watched as a determined wave of attackers circled the compound like a flock of screamwings, peeling off in ones and twos to attack specific areas where they had presumably identified weaknesses.

The Gatling guns had ceased firing many minutes before, out of ammunition and with no time to reload. Instead, the sec men who manned them had been drawn into the ground fight, bringing handblasters and long-blasters into the fray as biker upon biker breached through gaps in the wall to create more carnage.

J.B. watched from his high position as the remaining bikers made another circuit outside. He had their speed now, could see the patterns they were using, which ones would break away and when.

Reaching into his satchel, the Armorer brought forth something he had been saving for just such an occasion—old-fashioned fragmentation grens designed to cause the maximum spread of damage from the minimum explosive charge.

As two of the bikes peeled away, J.B. dropped the gren. He didn't even need to throw it, he just let it plum-

met over the near side of the wall where the gap had
already been created—the one that the bikers planned
to use to enter the ville.

J.B. was running before the fragger struck, sprinting
along the shelflike walkway that ran along the top of
the wall, dropping two more grens as he ran.

The first gren went off with a boom, ripping through
the first of the two bikers and catching his companion
with enough force that he was driven back out of the
very gap he had been using to enter the ville.

Outside, the next two grens went off in quick succession, blasting close to the exterior wall and sending
a shower of metal flecks against the wall and the bikers
who were hurtling past. Those caught up by the explosion were knocked from their saddles, flung across the
wasteland that waited just beyond the ville gates. Before they could recover, sec men moved in, using long-
blasters and long-range assault weapons to pick them
off and chill them.

J.B. kept running, eyes on the space beyond ville
limits, searching for his next target in this small but
deadly war.

THE BATTLE WAS playing out all over the ville. The nihil-
istic bike gang launched wave after wave of vicious attacks, reveling in the destruction and the loss of human
life. The ville's residents defended as best as they could
against an enemy that seemed to resent even its own
right to live, to survive.

The bikers seemed impervious to pain. Set light to
them and they just kept coming, blast them with any
one of the dozens of weapons available in the ville, and
they seemed to shrug off the bullets with a laugh and
redouble their efforts to chill everyone in their path.

Chill their colleagues, and it just made them try to chill you even more.

Baron Hurst, now sporting a thick bandage across his head where he had been struck by a flying chunk of broken wall, suspected that their enemies were high on jolt, fueling their anarchic, destructive behavior. It was an insightful guess, but he could not have been further from the truth.

The truth was far stranger than anyone yet suspected.

RYAN'S LONGBLASTER SWISHED toward Mildred. She moved fractionally faster, stepping just clear of its path. Its butt sailed by with a rush of moving air. But Ryan was already stepping in for the chill, bringing his left hand up and aiming for Mildred's throat.

She saw the flash of metal in that hand—the blade of Ryan's panga as it caught the moonlight through the rip in the tent's roof.

"Ryan, no!" Mildred cried and used her right hand—the one still holding the ZKR—to intercept the attack and block it. "It's me!"

Ryan didn't seem to hear. He just kept driving the blade toward Mildred's throat, a cruel and determined expression on his scarred face.

"Die, you abomination," Ryan gritted through his teeth.

It was all Mildred could do to block his attack.

RYAN SAW THE enemy standing in the darkness. The eye showed him its face, melted like a wax candle, teeth bared—sharp like a shark's.

"Die, you abomination," Ryan gritted through his teeth as he pushed his panga toward the foul monstrosity's throat.

His foe fought valiantly, pushing the blade away with all his?—her?—its?—might.

MILDRED STRUGGLED TO push the blade of Ryan's panga away.

"Ryan, no! It's me," she yelled, working to get the words out as she fought to hold the blade away. "It's Mildred."

For another long moment, the blade was pushing toward her. Ryan was stronger than she was and a more proficient fighter. Mildred shrieked with the effort of keeping the knife away.

"Stop it, Ryan," Mildred pleaded, hot tears streaming down her cheeks with the exertion. "Please stop." She had seen men driven wild with bloodlust, men turned insane by the chilling they had witnessed around them, men turned mad with shell shock. Ryan had seen it all, she knew: his father's murder, the loss of an eye at his brother's hand and the loss of his son, Dean, not once but twice. If anyone had just cause to go crazy, it was Ryan. "Please stop," Mildred begged again, glancing from side to side for help as the blade inched closer.

THROUGH THE NIGHT-VISION of his artificial eye, Ryan saw his enemy glaring back at him. He heard its words but they sounded like gibberish, animal sounds mimicking the human voice box.

But as he looked, the face changed, warping from that melted wax appearance into something more human. A biker, a woman, black hair, dark skin. A human. A human who needed to be chilled.

Ryan drew back the blade and readied to lunge.

AS THE BLADE drew back, Mildred let her strength ebb, and suddenly she was providing no resistance to Ryan's

gripping hand. In that moment, his grip became effectively too strong, and he pulled Mildred toward him
even as he lunged at her with the knife.

Mildred's forehead collided with Ryan's in a loud,
hollow-sounding strike like clashing coconut shells.
The knife swished behind her before Ryan dropped it,
overcompensating and cutting not Mildred's throat but
merely the fabric of her sleeve.

Ryan stumbled backward in the aftermath, his free
hand going to his face, feeling for the pain that the head
butt had caused. His head was spinning. He had to get
out, breathe fresh air before he was sick.

Three steps and Ryan was through the opening of
the bivouac, outside on the street by the well.

SCANNING THE AREA for targets, J.B. saw Ryan and called
to him.

"Ryan? You okay?"

Ryan turned, his eyes narrowed, murder in mind. It
was as if he was looking at something repellent or dangerous, something that Ryan had never seen before. He
eyed J.B. the way he might eye a rabid dog, as if waiting for it to attack.

"What's up with you?" J.B. said, scanning around
for more attackers. "Cat got your tongue?"

"I'm just fine," Ryan said, and in the next moment
his left fist swung out toward J.B., cuffing him across
the chin.

Ryan felt a wave of elation as he saw J.B. fall. He
looked different now—the familiar lines in the Armorer's face seemed alien, like cracks in warped wood, and
his eyes behind the lenses of his glasses seemed pen-
etrating and feral, as though they were sizing Ryan up
for a coffin. Different but the same.

"What the hell?" J.B. spit angrily as he regained his balance, swiping his chin with the back of his hand and wincing.

Ryan did not answer. He merely took a step closer to his oldest and most-trusted friend and sent his fist toward the man's jaw in a vicious right hook even as the battle raged on all around them.

J.B. was ready this time, and he stepped backward and blocked the punch with his forearm, moving instinctively.

Ryan was on him in a second, stepping closer and using his long legs to drive more power into his follow-up punches, a left cross, a right jab and then another, the latter two aimed at the Armorer's gut.

Dancing on light feet, J.B. was still trying to process what was happening as he stepped out of each of Ryan's attacks, batting each one aside in a painful clash of fist on muscle. "Ryan, what's going on? What are you doing?"

Silently, his lips pulled back from gritted teeth, Ryan drove another punch at the Armorer, using his greater height to come in high and strike down at the man's face. J.B. brought up his left arm before his face to block, grunting as the powerful blow struck his forearm.

J.B. staggered back against the onslaught, glancing briefly over his shoulder to get his bearings. The well was located just a half dozen steps behind him, its low wall in line with his knees.

As J.B. struggled to recover, Ryan stepped back, watching his old friend with a grim expression of hate.

WHILE THE TWO friends were engaged in their dangerous squabble, the larger battle was raging all around them.

Mildred picked off two bikers with her ZKR, firing from the shadows of the tent. Doc turned his sword stick on another biker, rapping the rider across the knuckles with the sheath before skewering him with the sword, driving the blade through his chest just two inches from his breastbone in a shower of blood and electric sparks.

Other skirmishes were playing out all around. Sec men turned everything they could on the invaders, dropping boiling water on passing bikers from hidden positions on low rooftops, blasting bikers from the street and throwing debris all over the streets in an effort to slow them or throw them from their rides.

One thing became clear though—the bikers were not just relentless, they cared little for their own lives. This was more than just nihilism; they seemed to believe themselves invulnerable, and to some extent that proved to be true.

Gradually, the locals learned and they adjusted tactics accordingly. With Ricky and Jak leading the charge, a group of sec men used ropes and nets to capture invading riders rather than try to chill them, ensuring that they could not escape and cause more destruction. Alive, they could be detained—death, by contrast, proved frustratingly elusive.

BY THE WELL, the battle between J.B. and Ryan continued.

"Whatever the joke is, Ryan, you better explain it to me bastard quick," J.B. said, rubbing at the pain running up his forearm where he had just been struck.

Instead of answering, Ryan took another step back then began to run at his friend, closing the distance between them—just six feet—and sweeping his right leg up and out, kicking at J.B.'s chest.

The Armorer ducked, dropping almost to the ground and rolling out of the path of that vicious blow.

Ryan followed through with another kick, this one lower to the ground and coming upward, driving his left foot against the side of J.B.'s leg so that the older man stumbled backward.

"Going to chill you," Ryan growled. "Worthless meat bag."

J.B. heard the words, even as he struggled to recover from his stumble. Already Ryan was moving toward him again, right fist drawn back to punch J.B. in the throat. The smaller man moved quicker, throwing himself aside and hefting his satchel full of ammo and armament into the path of Ryan's fist. J.B. grimaced as he held the bag firm, blocking the other man's blow.

The Armorer had to move quickly. Ryan was a natural fighter and a well-trained one as well. He was already moving into his next attack, his left leg sweeping out to hook J.B. behind the knee and unbalance him. J.B. cursed as the leg hooked him, toppling onto his back and striking the dirt with a rush of expelled air from his lungs.

"Ryan, you've got to stop this," J.B. said, struggling to get his breath back. "You got to—"

Ryan stepped back and smiled, a cruel grin that J.B. had never seen on the man's face before, and the words died in J.B.'s throat. Before he could say another word, Ryan took a heavy step toward him and kicked, the toe of his right boot driving sharply into J.B.'s side. The older man felt the pain, and he rolled across the ground from the force of the blow. Ryan was not stopping—no matter what he said. It was crazy.

Ryan came at him again, trotting forward the few steps before kicking his old friend once more in the flank. J.B. hissed in pain as the breath was forced once again from his lungs.

The Armorer scrabbled across the dirt as Ryan lunged at him with a second kick, and the bigger man's foot scuffed his side.

Moving swiftly, J.B. brought himself up from a crouch to a standing position, but he was bent over, struggling to catch his breath. His sides and chin ached where Ryan had clocked him, but what hurt more than that was seeing his friend turn on him like this. He had known Ryan for the longest time, trusted the man like a brother, and he would follow him through the gates of Hades itself. But now, J.B. realized, he was forced to fight him—because if he didn't, Ryan would chill him without a moment's hesitation.

Ryan drew his SIG Sauer from its holster and calmly checked the ammo.

Still doubled over, J.B. bunched his fists as Ryan came at him again. The moment Ryan was within striking distance, J.B. moved, lunging at the bigger man with his outthrust fist, striking him hard across the jaw and turning the blaster away with his other hand. Ryan was not slowed, he merely seemed to shake his head and keep coming, his own whirlwind fist driving at the Armorer, striking small but brutal blows against J.B.'s face, chest and gut as the Armorer held the blaster away.

"You're going to make me hurt you," J.B. spit through gritted teeth. "Is that it?"

Ryan glared at him, his eyes fixed on the Armorer's, one of them a mechanical device that glistened in a way no human eye ever had. "Spoiled human meat, past your prime," he said with a sneer, wrenching his blaster hand back to take a shot.

J.B. lunged forward in that moment, ducking low

and powering into Ryan like a bowling ball striking a pin. The SIG Sauer barked in Ryan's hand once, the 9 mm bullet tearing through the canvas wall of one of the nearby medical tents. Ryan stumbled backward at the same time, with J.B. scrambling across the ground to force him back even farther.

And then the back of Ryan's knees struck the low wall around the well, forcing him to an abrupt and unbalanced stop. But his momentum carried him, and his knees bent under the impact, sending his body dipping backward as though he was trying to sit down.

J.B. drew back awkwardly as Ryan continued to fall, and in a moment his oldest friend collapsed behind the wall of the well, issuing a yelp of pain and surprise.

Ryan's hands scrambled for the edge of the wall, dropping the SIG Sauer as he did so. J.B. watched the blaster drop to the ground beside the well, and he ran toward it. Once there, J.B. kicked it a few inches clear of the well and kept his foot on it as he peered over the edge. Ryan was still there, clinging on with his arms and legs outstretched, like a turtle struggling on its back. He was wedged tight.

"J.B.?" Ryan gasped, and there was surprise in his breathless voice.

J.B. pulled his mini-Uzi from its strap beneath his coat and pointed it at Ryan, keeping his distance. "What's going on here, Ryan?" he asked. "You want to tell me?"

Ryan's wide eyes absorbed the barrel of the blaster pointing at his face then switched to fix on J.B.'s. The Armorer saw the haunted look there.

"Ryan?" J.B. urged.

"You've got to help me," Ryan said, as his fingers began to slip from the edge of the well. If he let go he

would fall, J.B. knew, and that was a nasty drop with
no easy way to get back out.

"Why don't you tell me what the nukeshit you
thought you were doing first?" J.B. pressed, not lowering his weapon nor moving to help his friend.

Ryan looked at J.B. and his face was a tortured mask
of pain. "I can't stop it, J.B.," he said. "You have to
help me."

"Stop what?" J.B. demanded, confused by Ryan's
words.

"The voice inside me, telling me to chill," Ryan said.

"What voice?" J.B. asked, his aim never wavering.

Ryan looked at his old friend, fear clear in his scarred
face. "My voice," he replied. "It's my voice telling me
to chill everyone. My own voice."

Chapter Twenty-Nine

The aftermath of the biker attack was grim. The night before, Heartsville had been home to 314 people before the incident, including Ryan, Trevor and their respective entourages. By dawn it was home to 122 living and 192 corpses not including the bikers, many of whom were in urgent need of burial. Of those 122 survivors, less than thirty had got away without any serious wounds, and that included Ryan and his team.

J.B. bore a superficial graze down his right cheek and a cut on his chin, as well as a handful of abrasions on both arms where he had wrestled one of the invaders to the ground from a moving quad bike.

The others had suffered similar wounds, but they had, at least, all survived. Right now Krysty was lying down, trying to regain her strength after channeling the Gaia power, and Mildred tended to her.

Doc meanwhile continued to tend to the numerous wounded who had been housed not just in the bivouacs but also in several of the surviving buildings that made up the ville.

Of those buildings, three had been entirely gutted by fire while five more had sustained significant damage, two of them rammed by the burning remains of bikers when they had been wounded too badly to do anything else to create more havoc. And havoc, it seemed, had been the intention of the operation—the whole at-

tack had been calculated not to take over the ville but
to destroy it.

The gang's leader, Niles, had been captured by a
brave team of sec men who had drawn a chain across a
street as Niles sped toward it, pulling it taut and whipping him and his lover from the back of the bike. With
the speed that they were traveling at the time, the pair
had suffered terrible injuries including a number of broken bones, and the woman—Amanda—could no longer
stand up straight due to the serious damage inflicted on
her spine in the fall.

The sec men had captured Niles and Amanda, using
the same chain to tie the man to one of the broken
streetlights that dotted the old complex and that had
not worked in a hundred years. His woman, meanwhile,
had been taken away to a storeroom in one of the building's basements, where she had been locked away and
left to cry out her pain, paralyzed. Medical attention was
reserved for the ville's residents, which meant Amanda
would get nothing, not even sympathy. The best she
could hope for was a quick death at the hands of her captors, second best to be released back into the outlands.

Baron Hurst was dead, chilled by a biker waving an
ornamental sword, the kind ancient Japanese warlords
had their executioners use to behead people. Hurst had
not been beheaded, just stabbed clear through the chest
with enough force that both lungs had been pierced. He
had died trying to take another breath; trying and failing.

Now the ville was aching to recover from all that
had happened. There were so many wounded, so much
death. Walking down the main street was like walking
through Hell on an especially bad day, burned-out buildings, vehicles, corpses and the air heavy with the tang
of burning human flesh. It was terrible.

J.B. sat on the wall surrounding the well, working the screw back in one arm of his glasses where it had come loose during the attack. He looked up as Ricky stepped across the sunlight, casting a shadow on his work. "That you, Ricky?" J.B. asked, squinting.

"Yeah," Ricky said, a resigned sigh in his voice. "How's Ryan?"

J.B. sensed his upset. "Guess we all survived, at least," he said, working the screw with a tiny-bladed screwdriver until it caught the thread. "Krysty okay?"

"She's lying down," Ricky explained. "Like we all should be. Hell of a night."

"You've been with us long enough to know the score out here, Ricky," J.B. said, checking over his handiwork. "Everyone wants what they haven't got yet, and they'll chill for it sooner than discuss it."

Ricky nodded slowly, eyeing the ville. The place was smoldering with smoke, protective walls holed and ruined, buildings turned into funeral pyres. Fires still sputtered in a few of the gutted buildings, sparks trying to catch alight once more and continue their busy work.

"But why, J.B.?" Ricky asked. "Can you tell me that?"

"Destruction for the sake of destruction," J.B. opined, shaking his head. "Chilling for the sake of chilling. Trust me, Ricky, I've seen enough of everything in my travels that there aren't any bastard surprises left. Not from coldhearts like these anyhow."

"How did you know to blow up the bikers, J.B.?" Ricky asked. "When we first saw them at the farm, I mean."

"Sometimes you choose a side, boy, but most times the side chooses you," J.B. replied.

Ricky nodded thoughtfully, mulling over J.B.'s words. He looked up to J.B., trusted the man to steer him right

in the hellscape of the Deathlands. It was a wild world
out there, one where even the rain would try to chill
you if you were dumb enough to let it. Companionship
was all they had, and trusts had been betrayed over that
long night.

As THINGS IN the ville wound down, J.B. and Doc pulled
Ryan from where he had become dangerously wedged
within the well. Ryan's moment of lucidness passed as
rapidly as it had appeared, and he became consumed
with rage as Ricky secured a rope for Ryan to climb up.

Ryan ascended, hand over hand, but when he emerged
his face was red with fury and he barely made sense as
J.B. tried to talk to him. Ryan had lost none of his mis-
placed anger. He seemed more driven by it now; more
insane.

"Chill you, fucker," Ryan spit as he emerged, reaching out for J.B.'s neck with clawed hands.

J.B. dropped, felling Ryan with a leg sweep. Ryan
slammed against the dirt, noisily expelling his breath
through clashing teeth. Even as he fell, Ricky stepped
forward with a second rope, lassoing it around Ryan's
legs using a slipknot and cinching it tight. Ryan lay on
his back, bellowing with nonsensical rage. Whatever had
given him those brief moments of lucidity had passed
now—he was nothing more than dark anger held within
a human form.

Whatever had possessed Ryan had taken away his
ability to reason, J.B. realized. All Ryan seemed to
want to do now was fight, hissing curses at his one-time
friends. Eventually, J.B., Doc and Ricky managed to tie
Ryan securely enough that he could not easily escape,
taking his weapons for safekeeping. Then Doc asked one
of the surviving locals—a man sitting on the curb while

Mildred tended to a cut on his head—whether there was anywhere to hold a prisoner captive.

"Law office," the man explained, pointing in the direction of a single-story building located close to the baron's hall.

Mildred left her charge to check on Ryan. He strained at his bonds as he tried to take a swing at her, and when this was unsuccessful he spit in her face.

J.B. took Mildred by the arm and pulled her away a few steps. "He's not Ryan right now, Millie," J.B. said as the woman wiped spittle from her face. "I don't know how, but he's seeing things the rest of us isn't. Mebbe he's seeing himself in a way he shouldn't either."

Mildred nodded solemnly. "He needs to be helped."

J.B. brushed her cheek gently, a flash of the deep concern he felt for Mildred crossing his face. "We'll do what we can," he said. "For now, we need to calm him down and get him out of this street. It won't do for the locals to see one of us like this. Trust is in short enough supply out here as it is. It's not good to be seen to be harboring a crazy."

Glancing back at Ryan, Mildred nodded grimly. Ryan was still straining at his bonds while Ricky and Doc kept their distance, holding the ends of the ropes from either side the way one would hold a leash on a savage animal. "I have some tranquilizers in my bag," Mildred told J.B. quietly. "They'll calm him down."

"Go get them," J.B. said.

Then, the three men made their way to the so-called law office, dragging Ryan with them. The law office was a small building made up of two rooms including a disused toilet. At some point in the past, J.B. guessed it had served as a sec station for the industrial park that had become Heartsville. Now, it served as a staging post and meeting house for the ville's sec men, with local maps pasted along one wall accompanied by rosters and a carefully kept ledger of the weapons and ammo held by the ville. At a glance, J.B. could see that the sec men had kept a record of every bullet they had fired— presumably one reason why the ville had been so successful until this latest devastating night attack. Ryan struggled and fought every step of the way, trying to bite J.B. when he came close.

There were six chairs in the center of the main room, beside a bank of low desks like a counter. Ignoring Ryan's complaints, J.B., Doc and Ricky worked their companion into one of those chairs and tied him there. They used the leather reins from a horse to wrap around Ryan's torso, and several lengths of rope and chain to tie his wrists and ankles as he fought.

Ryan was made to sit in one chair with his hands secured behind him, while his legs were hoisted up and tied to another chair. That way, if he tried to escape he would likely tip one or other chair and land in a more difficult position to free himself from. Ryan cursed the whole way, a stream-of-consciousness rant at J.B., Doc and Ricky. He called them "a blight," over and over, repeatedly stating how they should be eliminated.

Doc and J.B. stayed on guard while Ricky located Mildred.

"What do you think all of this is about?" Doc asked J.B. as Ryan babbled furiously at them both.

The Armorer shook his head wearily. "Beats me," he admitted. "I've never seen Ryan in this state. I don't know what triggered it."

"He keeps talking about chilling humans," Doc said. "Did you notice that?"

J.B. nodded.

"Doesn't that strike you as peculiar?" Doc suggested.

J.B. pushed at the bridge of his nose where the glasses had started to pinch; it had been a long night with no sleep. "Ryan's chilled a lot of people in his day," he said. "Nothing too unusual about what he's saying."

"I disagree," Doc argued. "This is not the rantings of a man with a specific target in mind. This is the cry of one who is angry with the world and everyone in it."

"Lot of world to be angry at, Doc," J.B. said.

AT THAT MOMENT, Ryan was consumed by hate. He could not see the room's walls or door, the countertop or the chairs that dominated the little space. All he could see was the two figures standing just out of reach, discussing his fate in grunts and coughs. To his mind, Ryan saw J.B. and Doc not as friends but as evil red scars on the world, burning cancerous holes in reality, destroying everything they touched. Humans.

When Ryan had left Front Royal as a youth, he had entered a world filled with muties, twisted caricatures left in the wake of a destroyed world. The muties were humans deep down, humans gone wrong—or maybe fixed from the evil that they had been, the evil that had brought about the nukecaust and so destroyed everything that had been, everything that humankind had worked to create. The muties were humans at heart, their spite and limitations made flesh, bubbling to humankind's surface in telling revelation of man's true nature. Men and muties—worthless, hateful things. They should all be chilled.

And then there were humans themselves. All of them fueled by sick desires, the need to dominate and to destroy. Humans were at fault, humans were to blame. It was all so obvious.

In those moments of red rage, everything had become clear to Ryan.

"HE'S OUT," MILDRED SAID, standing over the long counter in the sec room.

While Doc and J.B. held him, Mildred had administered a tranquilizer shot to Ryan's arm, jabbing the needle into his vein as he strained against his bonds. The medication was old, and there was a chance that its potency had ebbed.

Ryan had thrashed against the chair for almost a minute before his body had finally become slack, in the way a balloon will deflate with a slow puncture. Now he sat forward in the chair, his head dipped low, his chin on his chest, the ropes and chains holding him upright.

"How long will that last?" J.B. asked.

Mildred replied as she replaced the hypodermic syringe in her satchel. "Ryan's built with the constitution of a horse," she said. "He'll start to come around in two hours, maybe less." After securing the syringe in an inside side pocket away from her other medical supplies, Mildred buckled the satchel closed. Hypodermics were hard to come by in the Deathlands, and while it wasn't ideal she would sterilize the needle using boiling water so that it might be used again.

"So, what do we do now?" J.B. asked. removing his hat and scraping a tired hand through his thinning hair.

Doc shook his head. "'Tis a grim business this," he said. "Whatever has possessed our friend may just as swiftly come for us. Any of us. And then, where would we be?"

Chapter Thirty

As nominal leader of the companions in Ryan's absence, J.B. gathered the group for a meeting in one of the buildings lining the west wall, within sight of the law office. The building had once been divided into office units, but these had been repurposed under Baron Hurst's rule to be shared between living quarters and small workshops where tools and equipment could be constructed and serviced. Two whole rooms were turned over to storing ammunition that had been salvaged from various military bases, gun shops, target ranges and hunting clubs. Ammo was a crucial part of modern life, and thriving villes would frequently have dedicated teams who conducted salvage missions, investing numerous hours in what was seen as a way to guarantee their safety.

This particular room had been used for entertainment, and incorporated a theater stage area—not raised, but left clear for performances, with a few boards of painted backgrounds that served as sets. J.B. stood on the stage while the companions took up seats in the audience. Krysty looked exhausted as she joined the others, slumping in a seat at the rear of the small room, near the doors, as though she didn't have the strength to get any farther. After calling on Gaia three times in a short period, the woman was spent. Mildred took a few moments to check on her, while J.B. explained the Ryan situation.

"Now we're not sure what happened to make Ryan wig out like that," J.B. finished, "but just now Mildred is keeping him under sedation to make sure we don't see a reoccurrence. I'd just as soon not get into another fight with Ryan."

Jak ran his hand through his alabaster hair in confusion. "It catching?" he asked.

J.B. shook his head. "Can't say for certain, Jak. It could be that all of us have got infected with the same thing. Mildred?"

"It's hard to say," Mildred opined. "On one hand, Ryan seems very clearly to be not in his right mind. On the other, there was no clear trigger that any of us saw."

"Ricky? Krysty?" J.B. asked. "You were with him when this all started. You see anything to make you think that mebbe—?"

"He wasn't bitten or anything," Ricky said while Krysty shook her head. "I had to wake Ryan up when the alert went out, but that was all. He seemed just like Ryan to me then."

Doc harrumphed at that before taking the floor. "Young Ricardo here makes a valid point. Is this man actually Ryan or has he, mayhap, been possessed in some fashion."

"Ghosts and spirits?" J.B. asked doubtfully. "I don't believe in things I can't shoot, Doc. Let's try to keep this within the bounds of reality."

"Not a ghost," Doc said. "I was thinking that it may perhaps be something more…man-made. A hypnotic suggestion, mayhap, the kind that the military are known to have dabbled with in the twentieth century."

J.B. scratched at his chin. "That's possible," he said.

"But when would Ryan have been hypnotized, and why? We've all been together for as far back as the last mattrans jump."

"Could it have been during Ryan's surgery when we were in Progress?" Ricky suggested.

"Or during recovery?" Krysty added.

"He was in that fixing tank for over a week," J.B. recalled. "Plenty of time to plant a hypnotic suggestion."

"That doesn't make sense," Mildred said. "Firstly, we were allowed to check on Ryan anytime we wanted to. Secondly, even if that was the case, what was the trigger? No word came, no instruction. From what I saw, Ryan just flipped out in the middle of the firefight."

J.B. nodded. "Which puts us squarely back at the starting line while the race carries on ahead of us. Let's take a little time to think about this, and see where we go from here. Millie, can you keep Ryan quiet?"

Mildred glanced at the supplies she carried in her satchel. "For a few days, yes."

So, the companions went about their usual business, all the while pondering Ryan's condition.

J.B. took it upon himself to fieldstrip, oil and reload his blasters and those of his companions, including Ryan's Steyr Scout and SIG Sauer in a kind of rustic therapy.

Jak wandered the streets of Heartsville alone, emotionlessly taking in the damage that had been wrought by the bikers' attack. He had seen worse than this, cruelty magnified to almost-impossible proportions. Death held no fear for him, and he showed no hint of disgust as he stepped over the fallen bodies of allies and foes.

Ricky sat with Doc on the curb outside the sec house where Ryan was held, while Mildred went inside to ensure Ryan was comfortable. Ryan shook as he sat bound in the chair, not conscious but something more than simply unconscious. Mildred had seen this kind of behavior before, the restless struggles of a disturbed mind.

Outside, Doc was content to watch the world go by, and so Ricky kept quiet. The ville was in ruins, whole buildings burned to the ground, leaving the stench of smoke in the air. People had not even begun to tidy up yet. First they needed to patch up the ruined walls, tend to the wounded and bury the dead. Once all of those things were done, perhaps they could start again on the life they had created here in the Californian hellscape.

Krysty meanwhile found a quiet room where she could lie down and try to gather her strength.

Chapter Thirty-One

"I'm going to talk to him," Krysty insisted as the others discussed Ryan's fate. She had found them—Doc, Mildred and Ricky—with J.B. in the workshop he had occupied to check over their weaponry. The Armorer's face was smeared with oil.

"Krysty, dear, I do not think you ought—" Doc began, but J.B. indicated he say no more. Their discussion had been going around in circles for over an hour. Perhaps Krysty could provide some insight into Ryan's condition that had eluded them.

Nodding once, Doc continued. "That is to say, I do not think that you should be with Ryan alone just now. If I may accompany you mayhap—?"

Krysty flashed a look at Doc, enough to show she would agree to his recommendation.

OUTSIDE, THE MORNING sun was nudging slowly into the sky. All around, ville folk were trying to clear away the mess of the night battle. Many of the helpers looked to be in worse condition than the buildings they were patching up, with crutches, splints and bloody bandages the norm.

Doc kept a tight grip on his sword stick as he strode with Krysty toward the sec house where Ryan was held. The people of Heartsville had proved welcoming initially, but Doc had seen these kinds of traumas before and knew they could effect trust between parties. All too often he had witnessed locals turn on strangers, casting them as scapegoats when tragedy befell their community.

The shedlike law office was unguarded, but the door had been locked. Doc flipped back the bolt and gestured for Krysty to step inside.

Ryan remained tied in the chair, his ankles held up and tied to the second chair. His head was lolling, a glistening sheen of sweat clear on the skin of his forehead, and he muttered angrily to himself. Krysty gasped when she saw him, then bit down on her surprise.

"Ryan?" she asked.

In the chair, Ryan continued to mutter, head lolling on his neck like an abandoned ship cast adrift.

"Ryan, do you hear me?"

The lolling head stopped its incessant movement as if trying to focus. In that instant, Krysty dashed closer to Ryan, the heels of her cowboy boots clattering on the tiled and dirt-streaked floor. A moment later, she was standing just a foot away from her lover, reaching out as though to touch him. Standing at the door, Doc sucked at his teeth and warned her not to.

"Mildred has dosed Ryan with sufficient medication to quieten him and keep him comfortable," Doc explained, "but I warn you he's very much not himself."

Krysty turned back to Ryan, leaning very close to his face. "Ryan," she whispered. "Lover. Do you hear me? Do you know I am here?"

Ryan grumbled something, and his head drew back slowly until Krysty could see his face. His hair had become stuck to his sweaty forehead, and a few rogue strands brushed the top of his nose. Behind those strands, Krysty could see that Ryan's eyes were open—

the real one looked unfocused, gazing off into infinity, while the left-hand eye—the artificial one—showed a tint of red as if it had been dipped in blood. There was a crust of sleep around the artificial eye too, a thick line of yellow-gold scabbing at the inside edge and flaking in Ryan's black eyelashes.

"Lover, please," Krysty continued. "We need you. Come back to us. Wherever you are, come back."

Ryan murmured something but neither Krysty nor Doc could make sense of it.

IN HIS HEAD, Ryan could hear Krysty's voice. He could not pick out where exactly it was coming from, but he knew she had to be close.

There was the other voice too. The one that sounded like his own but bullied at him to do the awful things, to chill people: innocents; his friends. Ryan could not be sure it wasn't himself, his own thoughts, that demanded he do these awful things.

He focused on Krysty's voice, letting it wash through him like water through a man's hair. The words were ones of compassion, of love.

Weak words. Human words. Worthless human emotions, the other voice insisted, spitting out the statement as fact.

No, Ryan thought, fighting back at his own voice, his own words. Not weak. Love is many things but never weak. He knew that for a fact. His son had been taken from him—not once but twice—and the drive within him, the love for the boy, had been so powerful that it was all he could do to force himself to take another step without him. If breathing had taken conscious thought, Ryan was sure he would have stopped breathing after that first time, when Dean had been taken away by Sharona. He had bottled the feelings inside, but they had been there nonetheless.

Krysty loved him, and he loved her. That was the one thing that made life bearable as they trekked from the endless highway of life, encountering atrocities that no one should ever have to see.

You lie to yourself, Ryan. Human love is a burden, a failure, the other voice said. *Where was love when the world was blown out, when the nukecaust set fire to everything humanity had cherished?*

"Krysty…" Ryan replied, clinging to the name like a drowning man to driftwood.

"HE SAID MY NAME," Krysty said. She was standing with Doc at the doorway to the sec house. They had been about to leave, Ryan's plight a seeming hopeless cause.

Doc turned back to observe the bound man in the chair, tilting his head to hear. "I confess I did not hear clearly," he admitted.

"He whispered it," Krysty said, pacing back across the room to where Ryan was held. She crouched before him, bending her knees and resting on her haunches, bringing her head almost level with Ryan's. "Ryan? I'm here, lover. I'm here for you. Tell me what happened. Speak to me."

RYAN HEARD KRYSTY'S words but he struggled to make meaning from them. They were like the first autumn leaves falling from the trees, dropping one by one, withering and lifeless as they turned on the wind. You could no more make sense of those words than make a tree from those leaves.

"Krysty," Ryan said again. His tongue felt thick in his mouth, as if it were too wide to allow him to speak.

A mutie and a human, the other voice said. *The worst of all possible types. Eradication is too good for an abomination like Krysty Wroth. Purge everything she ever touched, every human who meant anything to her. Chill them all and cleanse the Earth.*

Ryan tried to ignore the voice, but it was his own voice, the words his own words. Something played across his brain then, a clear visual in his mind's eye as if he was reading from a sheet of paper. It read:

HATE LIST
03. Harvey Cawdor.
02. Krysty Wroth.

"What's 01?" Ryan asked.

You know what's number one on the hate list, Ryan. Think back. Who do you hate the most of all?

Sharona? Ryan asked, but he knew that was not right. The Magus?

No, neither of them. Try harder.

Ryan saw the people he had chilled, hundreds of them in a life of brutality and survival. Hundreds, perhaps thousands.

"People," Ryan said. "Humans. I hate humans."

Yes, the voice replied slickly. *You've chilled enough to know you have the taste for it. You've known all along.*

Krysty's voice interrupted the dialogue. "Please say something, Ryan. If you can hear me, please…just say something."

"Krysty," Ryan said.

KRYSTY ALMOST JUMPED as Ryan lifted his head and opened his eyes, staring right at her.

"Ryan," Krysty said, slapping her palm against the floor to keep from toppling.

But Ryan's eyes were still blank, unfocused, as if he were looking through her.

"Ryan, please," Krysty said, not knowing what else she could say or do.

"Krysty, that's enough," J.B. said from the doorway. He had been waiting just outside, had entered when he heard her cry out. "The man's on tranqs, he can't hear you."

"He spoke to me," Krysty replied without taking her eyes off Ryan, "said my name."

J.B. shook his head. "Even if he could hear you he couldn't answer. Not with the way Mildred's doped him up."

BUT RYAN COULD hear Krysty, although it was a struggle to make sense of her words. However, he could not see her. When he opened his eyes all he saw was a schematic of the room he was in, made up of gridlines and fed to him by the artificial eye.

Let me see Krysty, Ryan shouted at the voice in his head. I know she's there. Let me see her.

You can't chill her like this, the voice replied smoothly. *You need to get out of this trap, and then you can chill her.*

I don't want to chill her, Ryan growled.

You need a plan. Otherwise, you'll never feel her blood running through your fingers, never see her take her last breath.

I don't want to… Ryan said, but this time it seemed to take more effort. He was arguing with himself, and—dammit all!—he was losing.

Let me see Krysty, Ryan pleaded.

See her dead? the voice replied, and an image flashed across Ryan's brain of Krysty hanging naked and upside down from a tree, her once flawless skin turned ghostly pale, the blood draining from her body into a pool below, the way a hunter drained an animal of its blood.

No, Ryan said. I don't want that.

Don't want what? The perfect future, free from the mutie-human invasion? All life eradicated to ensure a cleansing of this nation that humankind tried to ruin? You'll only be finishing what man himself started. You must see that.

Ryan forced his eyes open wider, like how one might try to open one's eyes in a dream, willing with all his strength. The gridlines waited in their static positions, showing Ryan where he was in relation to everything in the room.

The next time you see her, she'll be dead. And you'll smile for the joy that death will bring, his voice assured him.

No, Ryan muttered to himself, remembering something as he tried to peer through the simulation of the artificial eye. He had taken a snapshot of Krysty beside the river when they were in Progress. He had taken that picture and he had stored it right here, in the artificial eye—the one feeding him the room schematic. He closed his eyes and called upon the memory function of the eye.

The first image that came forth was from the battle in Heartsville, when he had glanced swiftly at the attacking bikers and lodged the scene in his eye so that he could examine it at his leisure without getting shot. Ryan filed past it.

The next image was of the burned baby after the rains, an image he had not meant to take but had somehow been focused on for too long and ended up with it seared in the artificial memory of the eye.

Yes, the voice inside whispered. *Chill them at birth, before they can fight back and pose a threat.*

Ryan ignored the voice, clicking through to the next image. It showed the burning farmhouse and the attack by the bike gang as they tried to corner Ricky.

After that, came the image of Krysty, standing by the Klamath River, close to the hydroelectric dam, the wind catching her hair. She looked beautiful.

Chill her, chill her, chill her, the voice chanted.

No, Ryan told the voice.

Chill her, the voice repeated, but Ryan ignored it, focusing instead on the digitized image he had kept inside the mechanism of his new eye.

Chill her.

RYAN HAD SAID nothing for almost five minutes as Krysty continued to crouch at his side. Eventually, Doc stepped in and helped her up, prompting her to reluctantly leave Ryan.

"No one is happy about this situation, my dear," Doc insisted. "And no one here thinks any less of you for trying to aid Ryan."

"We all know what he means to you, Krysty," J.B. added solemnly from where he waited in the open doorway. "We've all been friends a long time."

"Then what are we going to do?" Krysty asked. "Just leave him?"

J.B. shook his head uncertainly. "Ryan's been like a brother to me for a long as I care to go back," he admitted. "There's no man I'd sooner have at my side in a blasterfight. Ryan made the worst shit bearable."

"But—?" Krysty prompted.

"If there's nothing we can do," J.B. said, "and that's still an 'if' just now, then we'll have to consider letting him go."

"You'd chill him?" Krysty asked, incensed.

"I flat-out don't want to do that. Mebbe he can be kept in a prison somewhere. You didn't see him when he attacked me," J.B. replied. "There was chilling in his eyes."

"His eye," Krysty corrected automatically. "Ryan has one eye. The other is a…a thing."

J.B. nodded. "As you said."

Krysty looked from J.B. to Doc to Ryan, as if an answer would present itself. "We can't just abandon him. I won't let you."

"We won't," Mildred said, appearing in the open door behind J.B.. "One time Ryan stuck his neck out for me when he had no reason to," Mildred said, recalling the time she had been infected by a cannie virus. "I'll bet you can each tell a similar story too."

The others nodded, thinking of how much they owed Ryan Cawdor.

"So we find a way," Mildred said. "The same as Ryan always did for us. We find a way and we stick to it and we work it out. We're not losing Ryan, even if I have to keep the tough bastard tranqed up for the rest of his life until we find a way to fix this."

J.B. nodded in grim agreement. "If we can fix it."

WEARY FROM BATTLE, Jak paced the length of Heartsville alone. The biker he had fought had had metal parts, like a machine. Jak had seen machines before, chilling machines designed to exterminate humans. But these were different—the biker had bled real blood, and her movements had displayed that unpredictability of a human.

Jak peered at the wreckage of the ville. There were people stretched out on the ground, some alive, some dead, all of them streaked with blood and grit and soot. One of the war wags protruded through the east wall, blackened from where it had been set alight, its front end dented and scraped where it had impacted with the wall as the driver finally lost control.

Beside the war wag lay a motorcycle and rider. The rider was a woman, her head shaved to leave just a top-knot that wended to midway down her back in a scorpion tail. Jak looked at her, saw that her leg had become caught under the bike when it had toppled. The bike's front wheel was bent on its rims, and the shocks and gas tank showed dark rings where a barrage of bullets had struck.

The rider was dead, Jak could see. But he could see something else too—a thin line of metal glinting beneath her left pinkie finger and running up the length of her hand.

Jak bent and took the woman's hand, examining it closely. The line of metal was the width of a pencil, and at its edges the skin was frayed. The fraying was unnatural, and it reminded Jak of the way plastic peeled and curled as it burned.

Running his fingernail along the rent, Jak picked at it until he could pull it back, exposing more of the metal beneath. The skin tore with an unnerving shushing sound, and after a few moments Jak saw blood forming at the edges as he reached muscle and flesh. The line of metal was just a bar, he saw, running from elbow to wrist and working what appeared to be an artificial hand.

Part human, part machine. Just like Ryan had become.

Chapter Thirty-Two

Jak found the others standing outside the sec building where Ryan was held, discussing what to do.

"Robot bikers," Jak said without preamble. "All got machine inside. Ryan now too."

Mildred, Doc and J.B. all turned to face Jak as he continued with his breathless explanation, while Krysty stood by the door to the sec building, her eyes fixed on Ryan. Ricky had found a window ledge to lean on, but he paced around the building to join the others as he heard the conversation developing.

"Ryan robot eye," Jak continued. "Mebbe eye something else too. Tells him to chill."

J.B. nodded grimly while Doc spoke.

"Jak could be right," Doc said. "Ryan's artificial eye is connected through his optic nerve to his brain. Any corruption in the data could be passed directly up into his brain where it would feed his thoughts."

"And if the bikers have mechanical parts too…" J.B. began, looking pensive. "Well, those would also be linked to the brain in some way, otherwise they wouldn't be able to move them, right, Millie?"

Mildred nodded slowly. "To move an artificial limb of the types we've seen would require a connection to the nervous system. That ultimately would connect those parts to the brain giving the commands, for sure."

"But could the process be reversed?" Doc pondered. "Could a limb send instructions to the mind?"

"It already does," Mildred stated. "Whenever we touch something, our fingertips tell us how that thing feels, whether it's hot, cold, sharp, wet, whatever. Our skin gives us a constant update on the immediate conditions around us, our muscles tell us how much pressure they are being put under."

"You get stabbed in the foot, you know you got to scream," Ricky added with a smile.

"Precisely," Mildred agreed. "But to send a more complex instruction through the nervous system…?"

"Wait, what are we saying here?" Krysty asked. "You think that the bikers and Ryan are following the same… program?"

"Krysty's right," Doc stated, turning his head to encompass each of the companions. "We are in the realms of speculation here, with no evidence to support such claims."

"I don't agree," J.B. said, gesturing to the chaotic ruins of Heartsville. "Look around you, Doc. I think we've got just about all the evidence we need."

"Circumstantial," Doc insisted. "We can all see the destruction, but what guided the motorcycle group's intentions and what caused Ryan to have this…breakdown may well be two separate and entirely unrelated factors."

The group went silent then, each person pondering where to go next. Jak snarled with irritation. He just felt sure that the two things were connected somehow.

"They captured the leader," Ricky stated, breaking the silence. "A man by the name of Niles, I think. The sec men dumped him and his lady in one of the storage sheds."

"You know which one?" J.B. asked.

Ricky looked uncertain. "I saw them take the two of them—chained up—around to the west," he said. "Sheds out there store food, I think. They might have used one of those."

"Let's go find out," J.B. said.

BARON HURST WAS lying in state outside his baronial hall, attended by one of the women—presumably one of his "wives"—whom the companions had first seen guarding him.

J.B. removed his hat as he, Doc and Jak walked past solemnly while a small crowd of seven people offered the woman their condolences.

The baron's other woman was nowhere to be seen, and J.B. guessed she had either been wounded or chilled in the biker attack.

The three companions made their way to where Ricky had indicated, locating the bike gang leader—Niles—by the hoopla going on around him. Niles had been staked to a lamppost in what had once been a parking lot, with burned-out wags to either side creating a corridor effect, and a high wall behind him so that he had no way to escape.

A sec man was standing at the far end of the parking lot like a carnival barker, using a cone to amplify his voice, encouraging the ville folk to take a pop at the man who couldn't take Heartsville down.

"See him squirm in pain!" the barker teased. "See him cry out for mercy or release! This inhuman son of a bitch, who thought he could destroy our wonderful ville, our wonderful lives, now lies ruined himself. Ruined and pleading for the mercy he never even offered us."

Walking past the barker, the companions couldn't

help but recall the mess of ruined villes and farms they
had passed on the way here. While the bikers had ultimately been stopped, they had sown seeds of terror right
across Northern California, taking countless human
lives. It had been almost a ritual purging, a genocide
against the living.

The barker spoke up as J.B., Doc and Jak passed.
"Hurt him! Show this foul creature your disgust! Brain
him for me, good citizen!"

It was understandable. The people of Heartsville
were hurting. They had lost their baron, their security
and many of their own. The base human instinct was
for revenge, to see someone suffer for the suffering
they had wrought.

Though chained up, bruised and bloody, Niles was
screaming bloody murder at his tormentors. His girl-
friend had been stuffed in one of the sheds that had been
used to hold spare parts for the wags, but whether she
was still alive now—in light of the terrible injuries she
had suffered—no one cared to check.

Niles himself was suffering at the hands of the survivors of the bike attack when J.B., Doc and Jak saw
him. Having been pulled from his moving bike, Niles
now showed signs of a beating. His face—what was left
of it—was raw and bloody, with lines of metal showing clearly through the torn flesh where bone and sinew
should be.

"You all die," Niles shrieked as a brood of children—
two of them streaked with black, presumably from a
lucky escape from the fires—stood shouting insults and
pitching stones at his head the way a kid might practice
pitching a baseball. "Sooner than you think, everyone
here will be dead. Even you blighted kids."

A sec man with a scarred left cheek had been posted

to monitor the bike gang leader where he was chained up, and he had a bucket filled with stones and bits of broken wood that he offered to the companions as they appeared.

"You want to toss something at this fuck-wit?" the sec man encouraged.

In reply to the sec man's offer, J.B. shook his head *no*. "Mighty generous offer, but we just came to talk to him," he explained.

The sec man eyed J.B. and his two companions warily. "You sure that's all you're gonna do? Have I seen you around before, hat?"

"Arrived yesterday afternoon," J.B. told him.

"You have every right to be cautious," Doc said, placating the man, "but I can assure you none of us are here to free this violent reprobate, nor to object to whatever punishment you ultimately decide to inflict upon him."

The sec man looked from J.B. to Doc, then his eyes fixed on Jak and he smiled. "And what's your story, whitey?"

"Fought for ville," Jak said. "Would do again."

"Jak's summed up our position pretty darn well," J.B. said. "Now, you are you going to let us talk to this idiot, or you just going to insist we throw stones at him?"

As J.B. spoke, a young couple passed the strange scene, a man and woman, he sporting a sling over his left arm. They carried a heavy bucket between them, and as they passed Niles they upended it over him in a shower of feces and rotten scraps. "That's for my sister," the woman said, spitting a gob of saliva at the chained-up biker.

"She was one of the lucky ones, dead-thing," Niles hissed back but the couple had already hurried on. "All

of you are dead. Whatever is alive is just a thing waiting to die. Plague on earth, waiting to be expunged."

The stench of the biker's impromptu shower made
J.B.'s nose wrinkle as he neared the man, while beside
him Doc was trying to hold back a choked cough. The
kids hurried away, shouting rhyming taunts in their
wake as they skipped down the road past buildings damaged in the midnight attack.

Once they had gone, J.B. stepped closer to the
chained man until he stood over him. "Need to ask
you some questions," he said.

"Dead," Niles replied. "All of you. I can see you
right now, see what the bones look like when they got
no more flesh to hold on to them."

"How can you see this?" Doc asked, his face a grimace as he tried not to smell the stink of human excre-
ment on the man.

Niles pierced the white-haired man with a fearsome
look of deadly earnest. "Everything human will die to
wipe the slate clean," he said. "You, him, all of you—
you're just sacks of meat waiting to get fried."

"But you're human too," Doc reasoned, trying to un-
derstand the man's logic.

"Doesn't matter," Niles growled. "You're dead,
deader with every step, every breath."

As he spoke, the sec man with the bucket produced a
stone about the size of a child's ball and threw it at the
chained biker. "Shut up, scum! The only death you're
gonna see today is your own, and mebbe your girl-
friend's."

Niles spit out a gob of bloody saliva and cursed the
sec man. "Dead thing tells me I'm going to die," he
taunted with a braying laugh. "Dead thing that smells of
death and walks like death and gets death seeping into

his brain-dead brain, dying with every dead breath he takes." He continued in this vein a while longer as the companions stood there, but most of it failed to make much sense.

Jak hung back, watching the chained man's movements with keen eyes. Those movements looked natural enough, but there was something forced about them, a pattern of repetition to the way the captive biker shook and struggled. He was human, smelled human, had that undefined aura that Jak knew came only from living creatures. But he also had a system to his movements that, for all its apparent randomness, was as precise as the movement of hands on a chron.

"This is getting us nowhere," Doc complained as the chained biker continued to rant.

More locals had arrived, some of them with their own projectiles and makeshift weapons to take out their frustrations on the helpless bike leader. J.B. stepped aside, drawing Doc and Jak away from the mob as the next group came to pay horrific tribute to their tormentor. A bearded man led them. He was holding a strip of wood with two nails protruding from its edge. As J.B. and his companions walked away, they heard the man begin to beat Niles. In response, the bike gang leader just laughed, barking more insults in his babbling, dreamlike way, stating how everything he saw was dead anyway and how none of this mattered.

At the end of the corridor of felled wags, J.B. turned back, his hand on his holstered blaster. "I should chill him, put him out of his misery."

Doc placed a steadying hand on J.B.'s arm. "Do not waste a bullet, John Barrymore. Repellent as it is, the ville folk deserve their revenge. They have lost so much

this day, and this process—however awful—is their
hope for catharsis."

J.B. shook his head with regret. "Chill him like a
man—the one thing he'd hate," he said. But he returned
his blaster to its holster and, after a moment, turned
away from the horrific scene of revenge.

AS THE TRIO trudged across the ville and back to where
Ryan was being held, Jak outlined what he had ob-
served. "Bike Man move like machine," he said.
"Clever-made, but machine all same."

"Are you sure?" Doc asked.

Jak's brow furrowed with vexation. "Smell human,"
he explained, "but move like puppet."

J.B. scratched his nose thoughtfully. "A control system?" he said. "One that takes over the person's body,
mebbe?"

"That would certainly tie in with what we have speculated regarding Ryan," Doc agreed.

"Yeah," J.B. muttered.

"But what can we do about it now?" Doc asked.

"Remove the program," J.B. concluded.

"How?" Doc asked, and Jak looked similarly intrigued.

"Pluck out his eye," J.B. stated.

Chapter Thirty-Three

Getting Ryan back to Progress would not be easy. The man had to remain doped up, otherwise he could turn violent and sabotage the plan. J.B. looked out on the wreckage from the battle of Heartsville and started to wonder what they could do.

"I see the little cogs working inside that mind of yours," Doc teased as J.B. stood smoking a hand rolled cheroot a sec man had given him. Mildred frowned on the habit, but J.B. occasionally indulged. And at the moment, he wanted to indulge.

"We could use the bikes to get back to Progress," J.B. suggested.

Doc followed where the Armorer was looking, saw the wrecked remains of a dozen vehicles including the burned front end of the war wag where it was being hauled back into the compound. "It does not look like there are a lot of bikes left," he said.

"Not complete, mebbe," J.B. agreed, "but the parts are all there. We just have to figure a way to combine them to make something that'll survive the terrain till we get where we're going."

Doc held his hands up as if in surrender. "The workings of the combustion engine are rather beyond my field of expertise," he admitted.

"I know a bit, and I figure we can recruit some of the ville folk to mebbe help us."

"They have a lot on their plates already," Doc told him.

J.B. blew a trail of gray smoke through his nostrils. "No harm in asking," he said. With that, he made his way to the ville's garage.

TWO DAYS LATER the companions had bikes. They were not pretty-looking machines, nor were they especially comfortable, cobbled together as they were from the wrecks left over by the attack. But they functioned and were hardy enough to take the terrain, albeit with an average top speed of below 40 mph.

J.B. had convinced the mechanics to help him out by petitioning the baron's wife and successor, who had taken temporary charge of the ville during the extended mop-up. When he outlined their theory about the source of the attacks and how one of their own may hold the key—J.B. was very careful to avoid stating that Ryan was infected—the new baron agreed to help for the good of the ville.

"If it means keeping these coldhearts away from the ville in future," she said, "then we'll do everything we can to assist."

"Everything" proved to be repurposing the wrecks of over a dozen motorcycles into five functioning vehicles, one of which included a camperlike box over its four rear wheels where Ryan could be transported while under heavy sedation.

Five bikes sped out of the repaired gates of Heartsville, with J.B. and Jak leading the way. Mildred rode the camper-type trike with Ryan held securely in its riding compartment, Doc and Ricky shared driving chores on a slope-sided bike balanced on thick wheels taken from one of the destroyed war wags, and Krysty rode alone beside Mildred, keeping pace with her and remaining close to Ryan.

Behind them, the ville retreated into the distance, patchwork walls still showing evidence of the night attack from two days earlier, the gate blasters repaired and serviced by J.B. in part-payment for the bikes.

The engines roared as they left the expanse of cleared ground and struck out toward Progress.

Chapter Thirty-Four

"There she is," J.B. said as the bikes pulled up at the top of the valley overlooking Progress. "The perfect ville." He said that last with a hint of caution.

The smell of alcohol was strong in the air. The bikes ran on alcohol, which meant they were easy enough to fuel but they stank like a distillery when ridden. J.B. didn't mind that so much; it just kind of made him long for a drink. They had ridden for the best part of a day, setting out from Heartsville an hour after dawn and only now pulling up in sight of Progress as the sun sank below the horizon.

It had been hard riding, some of it on cracked roads, but they often utilized dirt tracks and paths through the overgrowth where plants had reclaimed the ruined wasteland. J.B. had pushed his companions on. He hadn't wanted to stretch this out any longer, not with Ryan the way that he was. Plus he knew that the longer they spent on the road, the more exposed they were to other threats. Unpopulated didn't mean the same as untraveled, and sometimes the most unlikely villes existed just out of eyesight.

They had traveled a different route to the circuitous one they had used to reach Heartsville, following the roads but keeping to an easterly direction. They had passed two burned-out villes set back from the road, both smaller than Heartsville, but with evidence of pro-

tective high walls and sec measures that had proved
to be inadequate against the attacking bikers. They
knew it was bikers who had done the deed because
there was bike wreckage left within the undergrowth—
bent wheels, broken exhausts and other parts gleaming chrome.

They had also passed more than a half dozen farms,
these too destroyed—buildings gutted by fire, the fields
swept clear by the same.

At one point they had driven past a stream littered
with the detritus of wrecked boats used to house people, now monuments to fire and death. Someone had
gone to a lot of effort to lay waste to this little corner
of the Deathlands, someone who wanted to make sure
no one ever lived here again.

They had passed a different kind of ruin at one point
too, a predark town, its streets overgrown with weeds
and grass, its shops and offices and homes reclaimed by
the elements until they looked like nothing more than a
washed-out painting, colors faded, its definition gone.
Maybe people had tried to resettle here after the great
shake-up of the nukecaust, but it was hard to see any
evidence of life here now. There was no time to search
for items that would have been useful to the group.

At the end of all that destruction, Progress looked
like a perfect jewel, its pale towers gleaming in the
last rays of the sun, the clear waters of the Klamath
River rushing by with their unending rhythms, bringing with them a sense of tranquillity. Ryan had confided
to his companions that the leadership of Progress had
wanted to create the perfect world, to bring about per-
fection from the mess that had been left in the wake of
the nukecaust. Looking down on that perfect-looking

ville now, J.B. could well believe that they would do just that—that they might just succeed.

"John Barrymore, I do not know if this is such a good idea," Doc said as his engine idled. "I have been thinking about our bike-riding foes and how they had been enhanced the same way that Ryan was."

"Not exactly the same," Ricky pointed out. "Some of those dudes have robot arms and legs and stuff."

"But technology all the same," Doc interrupted. "Progress seems to be the source of that technology. Who is to say that we should trust them?"

J.B. nodded, deep in thought. "My mind's been plowing a similar furrow, Doc, and I got to wondering about the farm we came on—Trevor's place. There was a load of tech in that barn we blew up, and from what Jak says there were robots in the house and out in the fields."

"Big harvester out there," Ricky confirmed.

"Now, where do you think all of that technology came from," J.B. asked Doc, "if not from Progress?"

Doc eyed the pale buildings of the ville below them as he considered that. "Could there be two villes dedicated to the development of technology? One good, one bad." He sounded uncertain even as he spoke, conscious of how ridiculous it sounded.

Mildred spoke up before anyone could deny Doc's proposition. "This area was once called Silicon Valley, right?"

"Hereabouts," J.B. said, recalling his maps.

"Well, then. For a while, this whole area was a hub of technological innovation," Mildred told them. "This won't be the first time we've seen the legacy of the twentieth century influencing what's happening now."

"But two villes," J.B. said doubtfully. "Both producing tech on a grand scale…? Sooner or later they'd come into competition."

"And then—whammo!" Mildred said.

"Could be that the bikers are that whammo," Krysty pointed out. "They might have been sent out by one ville to trash the tech of the other."

J.B. rubbed at his face, processing all of that. "We're speculating," he said. "The only thing we do know is that these people can help Ryan, assuming we can trust them."

"Which seems an assumption of huge proportions," Doc stated.

J.B. fixed him with a grim look. "Doc, you've had a hate-on for whitecoats ever since you were plucked through time and dumped here. Not that I blame you for that, I should add. But what they did for Ryan was a miracle and—well—we're fresh out of options to fix it."

Doc nodded, accepting the Armorer's point. "We shall proceed then," he agreed, "but I must remind everyone to remain alert."

"Always do," J.B. said, patting at the mini-Uzi he wore hidden beneath his jacket.

THE CONVOY OF bikes wove its way down to lower ground, following the snaking paths that led through the mountains and into the valley below. They came out onto flat ground close to the east gateway to the ville, with the river and the hydroelectric dam. The sound of the rushing river was loud in the valley as it echoed against the high walls.

"Well, they've got power," J.B. said, pulling the bike around toward the open gate. "The hydrodam provides near-limitless electricity if they can harness it."

"They have lights, building equipment, electricity," Mildred recalled. "The ruling council told Ryan they wanted to make the perfect future. I guess that takes a lot of power."

"In all senses of the word," Doc said, a note of warning clear in his voice.

"The gates are open," Ricky pointed out as they approached.

Astride her patchwork motorcycle, Krysty pushed errant strands of hair from her face that the wind had caught, before addressing the others. "They said we could come back at any time," she reminded them. "Get Ryan's eye looked at, checked and repaired."

"Serviced," Mildred recalled.

J.B. sighed heavily. "We'll ask," he said, "but keep Doc's words in mind—we ask with one finger on the trigger."

Together the bikes drew up before the arching gateway of the ville. As they got close, figures appeared, dressed in pale-colored, floor-length robes and strolling almost casually toward the gateway to meet the visitors. If they were sec men, then they were just about the most easygoing sec men that J.B. had ever encountered.

In the lead, J.B. ease off the accelerator as the figures stepped across his path, and the companions followed suit. The robed men had shaved heads with unmemorable faces, a few generic lines and wrinkles, otherwise lacking distinction and portraying no emotion. At their belts they wore short, batonlike staffs slipped into sheathes that hung down to their knees.

"Hey," J.B. began as he switched off his engine. "Don't know if you remember us—we were here a few days ago, spent a couple of weeks here in fact. My friend had surgery—a new eye, artificial. But, well…I guess we been getting some teething troubles. Your surgeons here said it would be okay to return, you know, if we got…troubles."

The bald men looked at J.B. blankly, took in the others with a sweep of their gaze, then nodded. "Enter," the man on the left said. "Follow the green marker until you reach your destination. You will be met there, and you may leave your vehicles there also."

J.B. tipped his fingers to his hat. "Mighty kind of you." Then he switched on the engine and rode slowly under the arch and into the ville, looking around for the marker he had been asked to follow.

"Green, green…" J.B. muttered, looking left and right. And then he spotted it, a glowing green line that seemed to materialize on the road at his feet, a foot wide and pulsing lightly as it trailed off down the street and into the body of the ville. "Green!"

Progress was just as they had left it. Clean streets and towering buildings, with people going silently about their business, walking or employing simple vehicles that gave off no visible pollution and traveled noiselessly along the streets. All the people were dressed in floor-length robes, just like the men at the gates, and many of the men were bald. They seemed disinterested in the incursion by J.B. and the noisy, patched-together bikes—disinterested or oblivious.

As he rode, J.B. looked around him, trying to discern from where the marker had appeared. He was certain it had not been there the last time he was in the ville, and he was also pretty sure that it had not been there when they entered. It had just appeared, projected somehow onto the road in light of his conversation with the men on the gate.

THE GLOWING GREEN line led J.B. and the group into the heart of the ville, past the low structure that housed the mat-trans and the military base that had surrounded it and around until they were at the back of the building where Ryan had stayed while he recovered from surgery in the nutrient bath.

The green glow ended in a square pen, a little like a horse corral, with white walls from the building towering on three sides to leave the area itself in shadow. There was a double door in the building, slightly raised with a gentle ramp leading up to it. As the companions pulled up, the green glow faded, leaving no evidence of the way they had come.

The companions came to a halt, drawing their bikes up against the walls, leaving enough space for everyone. As they turned off their engines, the doors swept silently open and Roma appeared—the woman who had helped Ryan get his bearings when he had first awoken from surgery, a woman well-known to all of the companions from their stay here. It was reassuring to see a familiar face given the urgency of their circumstances now.

"Welcome, friends," Roma said, her arms wide-open. "Or should that be 'welcome back'? Whichever it is, it's always good to see visitors in our midst."

J.B. eased himself out of the saddle. He would be glad to get off the bike. The day's ride had been uncomfortable and exhausting. Around him, his companions were also dismounting, stretching arms and backs as they tried to loosen the kinks that the long ride had formed.

As they did so, more figures filed through the doors—a dozen robed men, each one armed with wide-barreled blasters cast from a mirrored metal. J.B. looked up and swore.

"Now, if you'd be so kind as to come with us," Roma began, "and not try anything stupid."

Chapter Thirty-Five

The companions were disarmed while the semiconscious Ryan walked on unsteady legs from the rear of Mildred's bike. While the others were being disarmed and their weapons were stored in a closet in the large, white building, Mildred made a successful argument to keep hold on her bag of medical supplies.

"Our friend is in a lot of pain right now," she told Roma, "and I'm his designated caregiver. If he begins to deteriorate, I want to be able to administer the right help right away."

While the guards watched, Roma checked Mildred's satchel before she agreed. "We can care for his needs, but carry on."

Then, disarmed, the companions were led into the towering structure that dominated the skyline of Progress where they were shuttled by elevator to the room where Ryan had met the mysterious ruling council. Despite being sedated, Ryan was brought along, held up by Doc and J.B., his head lolling on his shoulders, mumbling incoherently.

Tiny lights twinkled behind the glass panels that lined every wall, including the raised area where the council itself appeared. The companions waited while the council filed in high above them, seven shadowy figures in hoods and robes that disguised their physiques.

"Welcome," their leader, Emil, said in his rich, resonant tones.

"You call this a welcome?" Ricky spit, outraged.

Mildred held her hand up to calm him. "Ricky, no…"

"This is your second visit to Progress," Emil observed. "Please explain why."

Handing Ryan off to Doc, J.B. stepped forward and spoke on the team's behalf. "Your doctors did a repair job on my friend Ryan there, fixed him with a new robot eye that was full of tricks."

"I recall," Emil said from the shadows above. "I designed that device."

"Thing is, it isn't working right," J.B. said, scratching at the back of his neck self-consciously. "Ryan got himself into a confused state about what he was looking at during a little altercation out west of here. Started attacking his friends as well as his foes. Came at me with a blaster and his fists."

A woman spoke from the high wall, another member of Progress's ruling elite. "You believe the device to be responsible?" she asked.

"I do," J.B. said. "Mebbe some kind of glitch. Or could be it's overheated. We ran into a fire when we left here. Mebbe smoke got into the workings and gummed something up."

In response, the council remained silently in darkness. J.B. waited a half minute but, when they didn't respond, he decided to elaborate.

"We've seen some things out there," J.B. said, "that may interest you. Farm machinery that's well in advance of anything I've ever seen before. Robot gangs running rampage over the land. I figured someone's been taking your tech and corrupting it."

"No," Emil said, but the word was emotionless, just a statement.

J.B. waited while the other companions shuffled uncomfortably. "If you're trying to tell me it isn't happening, friend, well, it is," J.B. said. "Me and my friends have all got the bruises to prove it."

"No," Emil repeated with that same lack of emotion, "no one is corrupting our technology. It is working perfectly, including the item placed in your companion's eye socket."

Krysty shook her head, her fists bunched in frustration. "Ryan complained to me that the eye had fed him confused information when we were out in the field."

"And he mistook me for an enemy," Mildred added.

"Because you are," Emil replied. "All of you."

The already icy room seemed to get colder.

"What did you say?" Doc asked from where he stood propping Ryan up. "How can we possibly—?"

"Humankind tried to destroy the world on January 20, 2001," Emil interrupted. "Nuclear weapons were launched by many parties in an attempt at mutual destruction."

"I hardly think—" Doc began, but another of the ruling council took up the discussion.

"At that time, the United States of America was the most powerful nation on Earth," the man called Turing stated. "Safeguards were put in place should the United States of America become compromised, including plans to defend home soil from enemy invaders. What you have seen is the result of that plan."

The companions were dumbfounded.

"Are you trying to tell us," J.B. said, "that you've been following a hundred-year-old plan to safeguard a nation nobody even remembers?"

"We are not following the plan," Emil corrected.

"We are the plan," Una stated.

"We are the safeguard," Turing elaborated.

"We are the future," the seven figures in the council said as one.

J.B. and the others suddenly felt even more unprepared than they had when they had been disarmed on arrival in the ville.

"So the bikers are—what?—your own personal army?" J.B. asked.

"They follow their base instructions," Una said. "To destroy enemies wherever they find them."

"And whoever they are," Mildred muttered, shaking her head. "Even kids."

"What about the farm machinery?" J.B. said. "If you wanted those farmers dead, then why help them to grow crops?"

There was silence for almost a minute, until finally another member of the ruling council spoke up. "The first plan proved too slow, and so we refined it into the form you have observed."

"First plan?" J.B. asked.

"To create small pockets of abundance that would instill jealousy and resentment in the rest of the population," the shadowy figure explained. "From this, conflict should have arisen."

"But the farmers surprised you when they began to trade their surplus produce," J.B. said in realization.

"Employing neither cruelty nor using it to dominate or control others," Mildred added.

"So the plan was revised," Turing said. "We recreated humans who would bring nihilism and so wipe out the plague of the invaders."

"The invaders being humans," Ricky stated.

"All humans," J.B. added.

"And now we have revised that plan again," Emil stated. "You will be upgraded shortly, as your colleague Ryan is in the process of being."

"Upgraded?" Doc asked.

"Your thoughts will be replaced," Una told them emotionlessly. "You will feel no pain during the process and, once complete, your lives will have new purpose. You will be tasked to wipe out the last humans to ensure no further invaders can step on U.S. soil, as per the plan."

"You're going to turn us into robots?" Ricky gasped.

"And all because we told you Ryan's eye was faulty," J.B. said, turning his back to the council on the raised platform. "Boy, you guys sure don't take criticism well, do you?" As he spoke he caught Mildred's eye and winked. She saw the move, knew just what it meant. It was almost time to bust out of there.

Casually, not making any sudden movements, Mildred's hand reached into the satchel she held on a strap over her shoulder and fixed around the handle of a scalpel she had slipped into the lining for just such an occasion.

In front of the group, J.B. was still holding audience with the council. "Well," he said, "I'm sorry we have wasted your time, but none of us are planning on being 'upgraded' anytime soon."

"You have no choice," Emil told him with grave certainty. "Guards."

From the shadows surrounding the elevator, a half dozen guards marched forth to escort the prisoners from the room. Led by Roma, the guards were dressed in pale, floor-length robes with sleek blasters holstered at their hips. Mildred reversed her grip on the scalpel as she removed it from the bag, slipping it up against her wrist where she could hide it from view.

J.B. was ushered back from the room of circuit board walls and together the companions were herded back into the elevator. The curved door sealed closed around the group, and the elevator began its descent.

As soon as the door had closed, Mildred moved, lashing out with the hidden scalpel and drawing it across the wrist of the closest of the guards. J.B. worked in conjunction with her, reaching for the man's blaster even as he reared back from the assault.

Beside them both, Jak dropped two knives into his hands from their hiding places, twirling in place before drawing the two blades across the throats of two more sec men.

The other companions were reacting too, even as the sec men began to respond. With a twist of his sword stick's handle, Doc had his sword free and he drove it through the chest of the sec man guarding Ricky. Beside him, Krysty reached back and flipped her own guard over her shoulder, slamming him to the floor in a swirl of flowing robes.

By then, J.B. had his hands on the blaster's trigger and he began firing, chilling them all before they even realized what was happening.

WHEN THE ELEVATOR reached street level and the door opened, it revealed a scene of carnage where the companions had dispatched their captors. Each of the companions had taken one of the silver bands that their enemies wore like wedding rings, the bands that could be used to open the doors of Progress.

"Okay, change of plans, people," J.B. said, hefting the newly acquired, mirror-finished blaster in one hand.

"Let's retrieve our weapons and get Ryan into surgery. Mildred, you're up."

Mildred did a double take. "I'm *what?*" she asked J.B.

"Somebody's got to get that eye out of Ryan's skull," J.B. said as the companions hurried across the lobby and out of the building. "You just got volunteered."

Chapter Thirty-Six

"I can't remove a man's eye, J.B.," Mildred insisted as the companions moved stealthily down the open streets of Progress, keeping to the shadows between buildings. "Not even an artificial one."

"Why not?" J.B. challenged as he and Krysty carried Ryan's deadweight between them. "You're a doctor."

"I'm a doctor, but what you're asking for is a specialist operation," Mildred told him. "I'm not qualified to—"

"No one is qualified anymore, Mildred, my dear," Doc interrupted wistfully.

Mildred shot the old man a withering look. "Still, I can't do it," she insisted.

While Ricky and Jak checked up ahead, J.B. turned back and fixed Mildred with a hard stare. "I can field-strip a blaster, Jak here can throw a knife that'll pierce a man's heart and Krysty can take on the power of a titan.. But none of those abilities can get Ryan through this. Yours can."

"J.B., you know I'm not a surgeon and that my skills in that area are limited," Mildred said.

At that moment, Ricky and Jak used frenzied hand signals to indicate it was safe to step out from the shadows and get across the street, so long as they moved quickly. The companions moved in single file, hurrying to the protection of the next building where they

hoped to not be seen. Behind them, back at the building that housed the council room, several sec men were
beginning to congregate after the attack in the elevator.

"You said it yourself," J.B. told Mildred as the other
companions slipped through an open side door of the
building. "That we didn't let go of one of our own. That
Ryan had done everything he could to keep each one of
us safe. And now it's our turn to help him."

Mildred shook her head uncertainly as she disappeared through the door. "I don't know, J.B.. If I could
ever do this, it would take years of practice and men-
toring."

"Two things we don't have," J.B. told her, struggling
to get Ryan over the two steps that led into the door.

Krysty turned pleading eyes on Mildred as she
helped lift Ryan over the steps and up into the building. "What would you need, Mildred, to perform the
operation?"

Mildred shook her head, started to say something,
stopped, started again. "Surgery requires a sterile environment. And I can't be interrupted."

"They got sterile rooms here," J.B. recalled. "We get
our blasters back and we can protect you while you get
this sucker out of Ryan's head."

"Our blasters?" Mildred looked at the Armorer. "Are
you planning on starting a war with these people?"

"We're already in a war," J.B. replied. "This thing—
this virus—it's been put inside Ryan and those bikers,
mebbe others too. It's reprogramming human minds to
chill people wherever it finds them."

"Like soldiers in a war," Doc muttered, shaking his
head.

"You figure how to get the evil eye out safely," J.B.
told Mildred. "The rest we can figure as we go along."

Mildred shook her head with resignation. "Why do I get the feeling I've just been buffaloed?" she said. "This is every neighbor's barbecue I ever attended, I swear. As soon as people hear you're a doctor, they start asking you to look at their aches and rashes for nothing."

"Not for nothing," Krysty told Mildred. "Ryan's already paid, well in advance and well above the going rate."

"Yeah," Mildred agreed, looking back at their unconscious friend. "Yeah, I know he has."

THEY FOLLOWED THE corridors until they found the storeroom where their weapons had been placed. There were few people in the building, and it proved easy enough to avoid them or bluff their way through. Progress had proved to be an open and friendly place the last time the companions had visited, and there was no reason to suspect that anyone outside that council chamber would realize that they had a whole nest of vipers loose in their midst.

While Krysty and Mildred ushered Ryan toward the operating rooms in the lower level of the building, J.B., Doc, Jak and Ricky went to the storeroom to gather their weapons.

The room had been left unlocked and unguarded.

"Trusting souls, aren't they?" J.B. observed as he pulled open the door.

J.B. snatched up his satchel and his weapons, setting aside the blaster he had acquired from the Progress sec man. The others did likewise.

Once they were all rearmed, J.B. instructed the group on what they would do next. "Jak, I want you and Ricky to take Mildred's and Krysty's weapons back to them.

I'll keep hold of Ryan's," he said. "Doc, you and me are going to find out what we can about this setup."

Doc shook his head in sheer astonishment as Jak and Ricky departed. "You do know that you are asking the impossible from Mildred, do you not?" he said.

"The impossible's only the impossible until someone proves different," J.B. said. "Have a little faith, Doc. Millie won't let us down."

JAK AND RICKY dashed through the white-walled complex until they reached the lower level where the operating rooms were located. There were a few locals down there but, like the rest of the ville, it was underpopulated and had an empty and almost sterile feel to it.

Jak tried the nearest door, but as he did so he heard a hissed whisper call to him from along the corridor. It was Krysty, standing in the recess of a doorway. She wore a surgical mask tied around her neck, pulled down from her face, and when Ricky and Jak reached her she explained that Mildred was already prepping Ryan for surgery.

"I brought your blasters," Ricky said, handing Krysty her Smith & Wesson .38 along with Mildred's ZKR 551 target pistol.

Jak twitched nervously, spinning to face the far end of the white-walled corridor.

"Jak?" Krysty prompted.

"Trouble coming," Jak whispered. "Look."

At the far end of the corridor, four robed figures appeared, electrified batons strapped to their belts. It was immediately clear that they were the local equivalent of sec men and they seemed to be checking the corridor and the ones that bled off it, possibly searching for something.

"They're after us," Ricky said. "They must have found out what we did in the elevator."

"Stay back," Krysty whispered, her emerald eyes fixed on the sec men. Maybe—just maybe—they would pass without checking the operating room.

Everyone hunkered back into the recessed door, watching tensely as the four sec men trudged down the length of the corridor. Although they appeared casual, they were checking every room, trying the doors to confirm those that should be locked were locked, peeking in the reinforced windows that looked into the operating rooms behind. As soon as they saw the companions the jig would be up

Then, Ricky stepped out from the shadowy recess with a determined stride. He drew his blaster, the long-barreled Webley Mk VI, from its hip holster, before the sec men spotted him.

"Yeehaw! Come on, muchachos!" Ricky shouted, blasting a shot into the ceiling. "We're having a party!"

Even before the last words had exited his mouth, Ricky turned and ran down the corridor in the opposite direction from the sec men. A split second later, Jak slipped out from the cover of the shadows and chased after his friend.

"Plan?" Jak asked, sprinting after Ricky.

"Distract them," Ricky replied, "and give Mildred a chance to do the op."

Jak nodded, gesturing to a break in the white-walled corridor and urging Ricky to turn left. Behind them, the white-clad sec men took the bait, hurrying after Ricky and Jak, drawing their batons and calling for them to halt. Twelve inches in length, the white batons were held in hip slings, and they sparked with electricity as they were drawn.

Krysty watched the men whip past from her hiding place, and she breathed a heavy sigh of relief. Checking the corridor once more to confirm that no more sec men were coming, she ducked back into the operating room.

Mildred paused and looked up as Krysty walked in. Ryan laid spread out on the gurney, tied down by the two straps across his body with dressings over his face to frame the artificial eye. Mildred had a scalpel poised deathly close to Ryan's face.

"What is it?" she asked, the scalpel catching the overhead light. "I heard a shot."

Krysty wrinkled her nose at the strong smell of antiseptic that now dominated the room. "There were four sec men out there, but they've gone after Ricky and Jak."

"Will they be okay?" Mildred asked, retrieving her weapons from Krysty.

"Gaia, I hope so," Krysty said.

As she spoke, the doorknob to the operating room rattled and then the door swung open, revealing the fourth sec man—clean shaved with blond hair and long sideburns—holding one of the shock batons. The man looked surprised when he saw Krysty standing just a few feet from him, the surgical mask now drawn up over the bottom half of her face.

JAK AND RICKY raced down the next corridor, the footfalls of their pursuers loud to their ears. As they reached a T-junction, Jak peered back over his shoulder to judge how far away the sec men were. Three had followed but the fourth had to have turned back.

Dammit! Jak thought.

IN THE OPERATING room, Krysty and Mildred found themselves suddenly face-to-face with the blond-haired

sec man who had doubled back. The man's brows arched
in surprise as he saw Krysty's emerald eyes staring at
him from above the line of the surgical mask.

Krysty didn't hesitate. She drew her Smith & Wesson
.38 in a single move, firing from the hip and sending
a lead slug straight into the man's belly. The sec man
doubled over with the impact, clutching at his guts with
one hand as he stumbled backward, the baton sparking
like lightning in his other hand.

Raising her blaster, Krysty took a step toward him
and fired, sending a second bullet into his chest.

"Krysty!" Mildred bellowed. "We need to keep this
area real clean. I can't have blood flying around."

The sec man sank to the floor, dragging a tray of
metal implements down with him, but he was struggling to get up. Krysty fired again, delivering a
.38 bullet right between his eyes.

"Clear!" Krysty called back, nodding at her handiwork. For now, anyway, she mentally added.

At the surgical table, Mildred began her painstaking
work while Krysty found a cart and wedged it before
the door. No more surprises, she thought.

RICKY AND JAK frequently checked behind them to be
certain that their pursuers had not lost sight of them.
If those pursuers should lose them, they might head
back to the operating rooms where they would discover
Mildred performing her desperate operation to remove
Ryan's artificial eye.

Up ahead, the corridor came to a dead end, but Ricky
kept running, ignoring any of the bisecting corridors.

"Where go now?" Jak asked as they trotted toward
the waste bin at the end of the corridor.

"Do you want to know the secret of a good prank,

amigo?" Ricky asked cheerfully. "It's when you make your victim think he has a chance. Trust me." Ricky had played a lot of pranks on his family and friends back when he had been on Monster Island. Out here with Ryan's crew, such opportunities were infrequent and he clearly reveled in this chance to have some fun, ignoring the inherent dangers of the situation.

Fifteen feet away, the three sec men were running toward them, batons drawn, the crackle of electricity sparking in the air.

"Stop where you are," the lead sec man called, thrusting his baton out before him. A lance of electricity flew from the baton, arcing through the air in a lightning streak.

Jak ducked, and the blast missed his head by six inches, leaving a dark, smoldering patch on the blank wall behind him.

"Prank's over," Jak hissed, raising his Colt Python and blasting a bullet at the lead sec man.

The sec man seemed to watch the bullet as it raced toward him, drawing the baton across him with a sweep of his arm. A trail of blue-white static flickered in the air like stars on the night sky, and the bullet exploded as it touched them, melted shards clattering to the floor.

Ricky shook his head, grabbing Jak by the arm. "Prank's not over yet," he insisted, and he bolted to the right.

Jak followed, pulled along by Ricky's grasp. The youth had his escape route all figured out. As the sec men had advanced toward them, Ricky had spied the doorway in the side wall, just three steps ahead. In a swift movement he had the door open and was rushing inside, even as another crackle of electricity lit the corridor behind him.

They were in a storeroom, in reality little more than a cupboard.

Jak looked around, slamming the door behind him. "What now?" he asked.

"Window," Ricky said, gesturing to a small, boxy window on the far wall of the room.

Jak nodded as Ricky ran to the window and started working the catch. Located in the gap where two shelves met in the room's corner, the window was obscured and easy to miss. Jak had not been here before but Ricky clearly had. He had spent enough time in Progress to go off on his own and map the parts he visited.

As if reading his thoughts, Ricky turned back and smiled. "I came here a few times to get some privacy," he explained. "I hadn't really thought about it until I saw the corridor again. Lucky, huh?"

Jak nodded grimly, turning back to the door, his Colt Python poised in a two-handed grip. He looked for a lock, saw none, improvised by shoving a heavy box from one of the shelves so it landed before the door. Behind him, Ricky worked the catch on the window, forcing it open as wide as it would go.

The window was just wide enough for Ricky to squeeze through and, since the storeroom and operating room were in a semibasement, the window opened out at ground level.

As Ricky disappeared, something crashed against the door of the storeroom. Jak kicked out at a shelving unit, pushing his shoulder against it to start it rocking. Then he turned and wriggled his shoulders through the window as, behind him, the shelving unit toppled over, spreading its contents across the room.

The window had been tight for Ricky, but it wasn't as

bad for Jak. Behind him, the door crashed open, stopping abruptly as it struck the fallen box and the toppled shelving unit that now lay teetering on top of it. It left an open four-inch gap between door and frame. A sec man's face appeared in the gap, snarling when he realized his path was blocked. He pulled back.

Jak clambered through the tight gap of the window, wriggling. As his feet slipped out, the door behind him was shoved wider and the shelf screeched across the floor. The sec men were inside a moment later, slipping between the gap—now a little wider than a foot—and into the messed-up storeroom.

As Jak cleared the window, Ricky leaned down and poked his head through it, grinning as he peered inside.

"Too slow, lazy boys," he taunted. "You've got to move fast if you want to stay in this game. Let's go!"

He whipped back from the window as one of the electrified batons swung toward his head.

Scalpel in hand, Mildred leaned over Ryan, trying to relax. Her breathing was rushing, her heart drumming hard against her chest.

Ryan's eye was open, the artificial lens staring at Mildred, a cold, red light gleaming somewhere deep within the pupil.

Watching from the end of the gurney, Krysty held her breath as Mildred held the bottom of the eye down and pushed the scalpel blade slowly along that lower curve, making the first incision following the line of the eye. There was no effort to her movements, no force exerted. The scalpel blade was so sharp she didn't need to push to make it cut.

Ryan lay in silent oblivion, unaware of the operation.

JAK AND RICKY RAN, the younger lad confidently leading the way.

Through the window, across the pavement and into
the next building. This building was taller, roughly three
stories with a sloping roof in a perfect semicircular arc
and a line of windows very high up its otherwise blank
facade. Ricky scrambled toward a door located by the
north corner, jiggled the lock and slipped inside. Jak
followed, checking the empty, nighttime street behind
them for any sign of their pursuers.

"They won't be able to get through that window,"
Ricky assured him, "but they'll be able to see where
we went and they'll probably follow soon enough. By
then, we'll be long gone. Then we can double back and
meet with the others."

Jak nodded, not liking the plan.

The interior of the building was gloomy and it took
a few seconds for their eyes to adjust. While they did,
Jak's other senses were working to compensate—the
smell of oil and burning solder played in his nostrils,
the sound of metal scraping against metal. He was trying to recall the map he had made in his head when he
had explored Progress a week before, but coming out
through the storeroom window had got him all turned
around. Something nagged at him though, some old
danger sense.

"Where we?" he asked quietly, straining his eyes
in the gloom.

"Storage hangar," Ricky told him confidently.

They walked ahead, letting the door slam shut behind
them. The door echoed like a slamming coffin lid. The
hangar was dark and sounded lifeless, apart that was
from that eerie scraping of metal against metal. There

was another sound too, like chains clashing as though swaying in the wind; heavy chains.

They were on a walkway made of metal mesh, which would allow debris and liquid to be brushed through the holes and collected using a series of inclines underneath. The walkway led into the main body of the hangar, lit only by moonlight through the high windows.

"There's a door on the far side," Ricky explained, leading the way along the walkway at a jog. "Never went into this place until now, but it's easy to see the door from outside."

Jak peered down the walkway. It followed a straight path to a distant door identical to the one through which they had entered, maybe seventy feet ahead. As he peered at it, he saw something move across his field of vision, zipping through the darkness in a blur of shadow.

"What—?" Jak muttered.

Then the thing materialized from the gloom. It was a robot, nine feet tall with a human-style torso and arms and a set of bulky caterpillar tracks in place of its legs.

"What the heck is—?" Ricky began, bringing his blaster up to target the machine.

Beside him, Jak brought up his own blaster to target the robot. As he did so he heard noises coming from all around, things waking up in the darkness. A quick glance to his right confirmed his suspicion—there were more of them. Dozens. Maybe hundreds. And they were all just now coming to life.

Chapter Thirty-Seven

The sec men in the elevator had reanimated. Led by Roma, they gathered themselves, sending data about the escaped captives.

There was a gaping hole in Roma's gut where J.B. had blasted her. The hole went through her robe and showed her flesh and the circuitry beneath, glistening like some strange piece of jewelry—one that had been embedded beneath her flawless skin. Like the other residents of Progress, Roma was a simulacrum, a robot made in human form to integrate with the people around her.

She stood in the lobby of the council building, absorbing orders from a remote download as her sec team prepared themselves. "The fugitives are still loose," she explained. "Indications are that they have rearmed themselves and have split up. Two were spotted heading toward the factory quadrant. They must be located and deleted."

MOVING STEALTHILY, DOC and J.B. made their way to the single-story structure that housed the ancient military redoubt and the mat-trans they had arrived in. Few people were on the streets, but by sticking to the shadows and staying alert they managed to slip inside the redoubt without incident.

Lights flickered on as the two men entered, motion-sensors responding to their presence. The air smelled stale while the walls had been washed clean with some kind of antibacterial cleanser. It made for a nasty mix of acid scent and dust.

J.B. hurried through the bland corridor, making his way to the nearest workroom. Something flickered on his lapel as he entered, his rad counter picking up trace radioactivity nearby.

Standing inside the room were four desks with comps and desk lamps, behind which was a large, old-fashioned pin board that displayed a creased map of the local area beside a larger map of the United States of America with a copyright date of 1998.

J.B. stepped over to one of the desks, tried the comp and—when it whirred to life—drew up a chair and sat down.

"The power's working then," Doc observed.

J.B. nodded. "These old military bases ran on their own jennies," he said. "So long as nothing's been trashed they should still function the same way they did when they were shut down."

"A window into the past," Doc agreed. He took up a position at the doorway where he could watch the corridor while J.B. tapped out instructions on the computer keyboard. "Never thought I'd see the day I'd be grateful that Mildred showed me how to work one of these things."

"What are we looking for, J.B.?"

"Evidence," J.B. replied. "The council told us that they were following a plan that had been put in place before the nukecaust. I just can't believe that there was a plan to chill everyone to keep the U.S. safe. From what we've seen of the U.S.A. the survivors were the ones who'd rebuild."

"The council are the survivors," Doc suggested, "still manipulating things for the old order."

"Then let's see what that old order is," J.B. said, working the keys of the comp.

JAK AND RICKY stood in the vast, warehouselike room, staring out across the sea of metal bodies.

"Thinking this mistake," Jak told Ricky as the robotic things began to advance toward them. He had them pegged for military combat drones of some kind.

Behind them, a second group of drones came to life, bringing themselves erect as they powered up, striding down the walkway to block off the door through which the two youths had entered.

Then a dozen artificial voices spoke up as one, doubling as they came from speakers all around the room: "Unauthorized personnel. To be eliminated with extreme prejudice."

Jak turned to Ricky. "Run!" he shouted, before he took off toward the distant exit of the building.

Ricky followed, sprinting as fast as he could along the metal walkway that ran down the center of the room between twin banks of waking combat units.

IN THE OPERATING ROOM, Mildred worked the scalpel carefully around the edge of Ryan's artificial eye. Her hand was steady, her breathing slow and deep as she slipped into the almost-trancelike concentration level needed to execute this procedure.

Krysty had quietly stepped away from the gurney and was standing beside the only door to the room, just in case anyone tried to barge in past the heavy cart that she had dragged there when the operation had begun.

Sweat glistened on Mildred's forehead, above the line

of the surgical mask. She worked slowly, moving the scapel with absolute precision as she worked to loosen the eye. A spot of blood budded just below Ryan's eye where the blade had irritated an old scar, and Mildred swallowed hard as she watched that single speck swell larger. Carefully, she removed the scapel and waited, watching the bloody spot to see if it would continue to expand or if it would seal when she blotted it.

The tension in the air was palpable, like standing beneath a colossal weight, trying to balance it and continue walking.

Mildred waited.

INSIDE RYAN'S HEAD, the other voice was bickering with him.

You need to wake up to chill humans. You need to break out of this and chill everyone, otherwise they'll chill you, Ryan.

No one's getting chilled today, Ryan insisted, shouting the words in his mind.

Now, you know that's not true, boy. There's not been a day in your life since you left Front Royal that you haven't chilled someone. I know you. You're me. Don't kid a kidder.

I never chilled anyone who didn't deserve it, Ryan told the voice.

And you won't now either. You've spent all this time refining your skills and now you get to chill the mother lode, every last fireblasted human who ever got in your way. A full purging of the nation until it is finally safe and right again, the way it was before all this started, before they dropped the bombs and made a mess of everything.

Ryan thought about that as the voice continued to

goad him. That would make me what those people were who dropped the bombs, he argued. Just chilling people arbitrarily. No good can come from that.

All good comes from chilling. It's the only way to be sure that good can flourish.

Never! Ryan thought, recalling the image of Krysty by the river. "Whatever you are, you're not me. And you've lost.

"HERE IT IS," J.B. said, his eyes fixed on the stream of information running across the comp screen.

Doc eyed the corridor beyond them once before joining J.B. at the terminal.

"It's incomplete but it says here," J.B. read, "that the military had a fail-safe program in the event of a substantial—which is to say nuclear—attack."

"'To rebuild for humankind,'" Doc read, "'beginning with factories to manufacture robots to perform the necessary tasks in a world rendered temporarily uninhabitable and thus protect U.S. soil from invasion.'"

"I've heard it said that the nukecaust culled the population to 10 percent of what it had been," J.B. recalled. "Makes sense to repopulate using machines to get things started up again if the workforce just isn't there."

"But these machines have corrupted the program somehow," Doc concluded. "They should be working for the betterment of humankind, not to wipe us out the way they have been."

J.B. tabbed through the file, scanning over the document. "Some parts of the instructions are missing," he said, showing Doc where the data had disappeared, leaving strips of nonsense in its place.

"What would do that?" Doc wondered.

J.B. slapped the top of the comp terminal. "Mildred said that a system like this utilizes magnetism to function. Something could demagnetize it and wipe the data."

"Surely it would have been shielded from suchlike," Doc insisted.

"Big enough radiation leak in the redoubt's reactor could do it," J.B. proposed, and he automatically checked the Geiger counter on his lapel. "There's some radiation swirling around here, not a lot but still more than I would expect for this kind of place. Mebbe the end of something big."

"A radiation leak," Doc mused, "spoiling the data files and corrupting the good intentions of a generation of military men no longer here to correct it."

"Some of their plan survived," J.B. reminded him. "Which means we're sitting on a stockpile of tech designed for just one purpose—to eradicate 'the enemy.'"

"The enemy being the people of the Deathlands," Doc said gravely. "We have to stop this."

J.B. looked at Doc. "And do you have any bright ideas how we do that, Doc? I came back here to get Ryan some help for that eye—"

"Which was a sick part of this demented End Program," Doc cut in. "J.B., we must do something."

J.B. looked pensive. "Nothing we can do, Doc. It's gone too far."

THE FIRST BATCH of war drones loomed before Jak and Ricky as they ran through the vast room. Behind them, the door opened and the three remaining sec men came marching through, commanding the two companions to halt.

Ahead, the war drones' weapons cycled to life, heat blasters powering up to burn the intruders. They required no bullets, no reloading—concentrated heat was their weapon, generated in their metallic cores.

Ricky fired his Webley, sending a shot into the nearest war drone as it fired its first blast at him. Beside him, Jak dodged aside as a heat beam scored a red trail across the floor. Then Jak was in the air, spinning and leaping as two more drones sent beams of searing heat from their nozzlelike limbs.

Ricky fired again, drilling a bullet into the boxy mechanism that sat atop the war drone's "shoulders." The bullet clashed against the metal, kicking up a shower of sparks in the semidarkness. Unaffected, the drone shot back.

Jak ran for the next war drone. They were designed for distance work, he guessed, intended to travel shoulder-to-shoulder as they were now, eradicating all opposition. But close up they might be vulnerable.

Jak evaded another heat blast and clambered up the shooter at a dead run, rushing up the mechanical beast as if he was climbing a staircase. In an instant, Jak was atop the robot and he jammed his Colt Python against the thing's head. There was a series of plates there to protect the central processing unit, like the shell of a turtle. Jak yanked at one, but was unable to move it, so he simply rammed his blaster through the layers between plates until the barrel was as close as he could get to the drone's processing core. Then he fired, point-blank, cracking the "skull" unit and sending a slug into the thing's brain box.

Jak leaped off as the "brain" exploded in a burst of sparks, using the momentum of his point-blank blast to leap to the next nearest robot, landing atop its shoulders. The thing reacted, swiveling its torso as it tried to track its antagonist, heat beam blasting until it struck another war 'bot that erupted in a burst of flames.

Then Jak placed his blaster against the robot's processing unit, driving the barrel between the protective covers and sending a bullet into its "brain." The robot seemed to sag as soon as the bullet struck, stumbling aimlessly forward with its heat beam firing erratically.

On the deck, Ricky ran between two robots as their heat beams chased him. He was a small target, fast too, and many of the war drones were only now powering up to full functionality. As Ricky slipped between the robots, their heat beams crossed and then they were blasting each other, searing red circles appearing on their metallic torsos.

Ricky raced on as the two robots burst into flames while, behind him, the sec men continued to chase these two fearless intruders.

All around the warehouse, chaos reigned.

MILDRED MADE THE final incision that would grant access to the artificial eye. Then, using metal tongs, she clutched the eye top and bottom, gritting her teeth as she began to pull.

"Mildred…?" It was Ryan's voice, weak and muffled by the dressings Mildred had placed over his face. He was waking up. It gave her a shock.

"Ryan, don't move," Mildred said.

From across the room, Krysty hurried over and touched Ryan's hand. "Ryan, lover, it's me," she said. "Stay still. Stay really still."

Then Mildred began to pull, yanking at the eye with all her strength. For a moment it wouldn't come out, it was wedged so tightly in Ryan's eye socket.

"Come on, you tough bastard," Mildred spit. "Get out here already."

"Krysty? Mildred?" Ryan asked. "What's going on?"

"The eye's trying to change you," Krysty explained. "We're going to get it out."

IN HIS MIND, Ryan heard the other voice—the one that sounded just like him—laugh cruelly.

Chill them, it said. *This is the perfect opportunity. Chill them and end this nonsense. Your first casualties to the new world.*

MILDRED SWORE AS she fought to remove the eye. Suddenly it was free of the socket and clamped in the jaws of the tongs. But a great trail of circuitry wended back inside Ryan's skull, feeding him information along the tract of the optic nerve, still connected to him.

"Can't...get it," Mildred stated through gritted teeth.

"Can I help?" Krysty asked, watching her friend struggle to pull the eye loose. "Cut it mebbe?"

"Cutting it won't help," Mildred insisted. "Look at this—it's nanotechnology and it's reaching for Ryan's brain. Just cutting it won't stop that. We need to get it all out."

RYAN FELT HIS body tense, felt the pain of the eye being manipulated in his head even through the sedative. No, he told the voice. You're not giving the instructions.

I'm you, you idiot, his voice replied. *I'm the plan you've always been following. I'm the plan you'll always follow.*

ON THE GURNEY, Ryan's hand reached up and grabbed the eye from Mildred, pulling it from her grasp. Then he yanked, dragging the full length of the thing's artificial brain stem that was feeding information to his own brain out of his head.

"No, you're not!" Ryan snarled, tossing the rogue hunk of hardware to the floor.

The eye slopped against the floor in a smear of red, blood and fluid glistening across its surface. For a moment Ryan thought he could still see what the eye saw, watched himself on the gurney as he sat up and wiped the blood away from his face while Krysty and Mildred looked on in astonishment.

The artificial eye twitched for a moment, the long trail of optic nerve—seven inches in length and segmented like an earthworm with tiny metal barbs running its full length—wending like a snake's tail as it tried to move back to its victim.

Mildred's hand reached for the ZKR blaster she had replaced at her hip and shot the twitching eye to shrapnel. "Operation's over," she said. "And it was a total success."

Behind her, Krysty hugged Ryan as tightly as she could while his empty eye socket wept tears of blood.

Chapter Thirty-Eight

Ryan's head ached, and blood ran down his left cheek from the empty hole in his face. Still, he led the way, rearmed with the SIG Sauer in hand, Steyr Scout across his back and the panga strapped to his leg.

Mildred could not really explain why she trusted Ryan now, when just two days before he had tried to chill her. All she could say was that his demeanor was different—the way he carried himself, the way he spoke and acted. He was Ryan again, anyone who knew him could see that.

Krysty stuck close to Ryan, watching him with all the concern of a lover.

Ryan told them about the thing that had been in his head, trying to change him. "It spoke in my voice," he said, "but it said sick things, wanted me to chill."

"You didn't let it," Krysty said soothingly.

"I didn't have a choice," Ryan replied.

From the thing that had been in his head, Ryan could see what the Progress council's plan was. It was horribly direct and utterly efficient—to chill every human on U.S. soil so that it could be reclaimed.

"The council isn't human," Ryan said. "No one here is."

"How do you know?" Mildred asked as she checked Ryan's wound.

"They're like me," he told her grimly. "Like what I

almost became. Mebbe they started out as human but this thing—whatever it is—got them in its grasp and never let go."

"You're stronger than them, Ryan," Krysty said.

"No, I just have friends," he told her. "It's time we finished this."

The companions made their way down the corridors of the building, which were largely unpopulated. Whenever they saw anyone, Ryan would simply say "Machine" and the machine would be chilled. They were bureaucrats, functionaries—they offered no resistance. A trail of a half dozen bodies had been left in their wake by the time the companions exited the building.

Outside, Ryan stopped, looking at the council tower where it stood framed by the night sky. "We need to chill them," Ryan said, "or shut them down. Whatever it is you do to machines."

"Ryan?" The astonished voice came from close by, at the exit to the single-story building that housed the grand underground complex of the old redoubt.

Ryan turned and saw J.B. and Doc approaching, surprise etched on their features.

"My dear Ryan, you are alive!" Doc exclaimed, then corrected himself with embarrassment. "That is to say, you were already alive. I just did not expect—"

"It's good to see you too, Doc," Ryan said, cutting the man off.

Then Ryan turned to J.B. and a look passed between the old friends.

"Ryan," was all the Armorer said, but that was all that needed to be said.

"Ryan says we need to destroy these people," Mildred explained.

"Yeah." J.B. nodded. "We were thinking the same

thing. But we're outnumbered—real outnumbered. You have a plan?"

Ryan nodded slowly. "Chill the council. Once they lose their leaders the rest should lose direction."

"That's a mighty big 'should,'" J.B. said warily.

IN THE WAREHOUSE, the war drones had turned on one another and were carving up slices of the room while Ricky and Jak avoided the lancing heat beams. The sec crew was cut down in a matter of seconds, as the red beams zapped through the air.

Jak and Ricky remained low, crouching as they ran toward the far exit, smoke billowing all around them. Jak slammed against the door as another burst of heat burned the wall just two feet to his left. Ricky fired another round from his Webley at an approaching war machine.

Jak shoved at the door, forcing it open on its treads. As the door gave, the chill of the night air struck Jak and Ricky—so different from the stifling warmth of the room where the heat beams were zipping left and right.

They stepped out together, jamming the door closed behind them and running from the storage building. As they sprinted up the moonlit street, Jak spotted the rest of his companions talking in the shadows of the surgical center. He headed toward them, instructing Ricky to follow.

"Ryan, that you?" Jak asked as he sprinted across the empty street.

Ryan looked up, the red splash marring the left side of his face. "Jak. Ricky. I was starting to wonder where you two had gotten to."

"Is he...himself again?" Ricky asked, directing the question to Mildred.

"Large as life and twice as ugly," Mildred assured him.

Before Ryan could explain, Ricky had his arms folded around him in a hug. "I knew it," was all he said.

Across the street where Jak and Ricky had emerged, the door to the warehouse was glowing red as war drones sent heat blasts against it. A moment later, the door gave in a burst of red-hot shrapnel and the first of the towering war drones stepped out into the night air, torso swiveling as it sought the escaped intruders.

"I see you brought company," J.B. said. "Friend or foe?"

"Foe!" Jak and Ricky replied in unison.

"Then I guess it is time we made our exit," Doc announced with a flourish of his sword stick.

"Follow me," Ryan snarled, his lone eye fixing on the towering structure where the council waited. "I still have some unfinished business with these people."

With that, Ryan began striding across the street while the war drones struggled through the small door to the warehouse. J.B. eyed the war drones and pulled an explosive and detonator out of his satchel, which he tossed across the street, directly into the path of the towering machines. The companions turned as the explosive went off, ripping through three of the emerging machines and sending a shock wave through the warehouse.

"Well, they sure as hell know we're coming now," J.B. said.

THE LOBBY TO the council building was populated by Roma and the six sec men who had escorted the companions there when they arrived. Roma was working a self-repair program on her ruined torso while the sec men were working similar repairs, welding new pieces in place of their ruined chunks of body where the companions had attacked them. It was clear now that they were all robots or semi-robotic. Whatever humanity was left in their makeup was just so much flesh being carried by a machine.

Roma looked up as Ryan entered, balked as he thrust his SIG Sauer in her face.

"Ryan Cawdor, I didn't expe—"

Roma's face was obliterated by a 9 mm slug as Ryan pulled the trigger without a hint of emotion.

The sec men responded immediately, standing up and approaching the companions striding across the lobby.

Ryan glanced back to J.B. "Deal with them," he said before continuing toward the elevator. Krysty followed Ryan while J.B. and the others laid down covering fire, using the sparse furniture for cover and holding the sec men at bay. The lobby lit up with explosions and the flash of propellant.

THE COUNCIL CHAMBER was as dark as Ryan remembered, only this time he had no artificial night-vision to compensate. Hidden fans whirred and the air smelled recycled, as if it had circulated the room a thousand times before.

The council materialized as Ryan and Krysty stepped from the elevator, their dark, hooded shapes looming over the railing like specters.

"Ryan Cawdor," Emil said. "The prodigal son returns."

"I'm here to shut you down," Ryan told them, "and then we're leaving."

"Impossible," Emil replied calmly. "There's no escape from the ville unless we want you to escape. You and your friends are merely running yourselves ragged with no idea that we are watching your every move."

"You've lost people and equipment already," Krysty pointed out.

"Tools," Emil stated. "Those things can be replaced. Even now the next phase is beginning, when full production of the surgical team will begin in earnest."

Ryan frowned. "What surgical team?" he asked.

"You have already met the drones," the being Ryan knew as Una replied from her position on the shadowy council. "They are the surgeon's knife, there to cut out the infection of humankind."

Ryan reached for his panga. "Seems appropriate," he muttered.

"You would be better advised to surrender your will now," Emil told them both. "The alternative is more painful but will only achieve the same result."

"I don't surrender," Ryan said. "You must have missed that when you put your hunk of shit in my face." Knife in hand, Ryan ran at the tall wall of circuitry, pulling himself up.

IN THE LOWER LEVEL, J.B., Doc, Mildred, Jak and Ricky were containing the last of the sec men. They were cyborgs, just like the bikers the companions had fought with in Heartsville. Built things, made to fight. But, by tag-teaming, the companions managed to overwhelm the sec men and capture them the same way that the bikers had finally been stopped, using climbing ropes and other equipment that they carried to ensnare their enemies. It was more effective than trying to chill them, they knew—because an unliving thing was hard to chill.

Outside in the street, the hulking war drones were

emerging from another door in the warehouse area,
striding past the council chamber.

"Now, where do you think they're going?" J.B. wondered.

RYAN WAS ON TOP of the raised section of the room in a
flash, leaping to the balcony and grabbing for the encompassing robe of Emil. Ryan drew the panga back
in his free hand as the other members of the council
started to react.

"You owe me an eye," Ryan snarled as Emil's hood
fell back from his head.

When the hood fell back, Ryan saw that the man's
head was not really a head at all. The face was stretched
over a frame of metal piping, a headband of metal holding it in place. Behind the web frame was a blocky mechanism, with diodes flashing and a line of connected
circuits running upright in parallel lines, one next to
another. With the hood removed, the head didn't really look like a head at all—just a box of circuits with a
human face stretched over its facade.

Ryan blanched as he saw that, spun to face the other
councillors as they rounded on him. Each one was like
Emil, he saw now—each of them disguising their inhu-
manity by the loose hoods and robes they wore. They
did not even walk like humans, instead they trundled
like machines, bumping over the tiled floor like shopping carts.

In the moment that it took for Ryan to absorb what he
saw, he stopped, holding the panga ready to cut Emil's
eye from his face. "Are you—?" Ryan began. "Were
you ever—?"

"Human?" Emil asked, finishing the question. His
voice lacked that strange emotionless quality it had

had. Instead, he sounded strained and something else—scared. "Yes. But they took us, took our thoughts and made them their thoughts. They—you wait too long, plague thing."

Ryan spun, realizing he had been tricked. The other councillors were on him, descending like hyenas on a wounded antelope, grasping for him with inhuman metal hooks in place of hands.

"Foolish flesh man," Emil hissed. "Chill me and I will simply regenerate, take a new body, continue my good works in cleansing this once-safe nation of its enemies."

Ryan ignored him, striking backward with the panga, slicing the closest of the approaching figures across the chest. "Stay back!" Ryan shouted.

Had Emil tricked him or was it something else? Had he truly wanted to share the last of his humanity with Ryan in that single moment before the program took over once more? Ryan would never know. He was too busy fighting for his life. The councillors swarmed toward him, six inhuman grotesques, faces stretched over pipes and dials and circuitry.

But as the councillors overwhelmed Ryan, a revolver blasted in the darkness. Krysty had found an alternative way up and she balanced on the balcony, working the trigger of her Smith & Wesson and blasting the hooded figures as they grabbed for Ryan. They went down like dominoes, one after another. The machines had been designed for thinking, not for fighting—that was the role of the war drones and the robots that had been fashioned as sec men. Without their protection, the council had little chance against blasters and knives.

Una spoke as Krysty peppered her with bullets. "Destroy us, but you will never escape. The ville is in lockdown. You will be my next body, Red. I'll take your flesh and wear it like a dress."

Krysty drilled the last of her bullets into Una's brain box, sending her current thought programme to oblivion.

"Una is correct, Ryan Cawdor," Emil bragged as he watched the scene play out. "Destroy us here but all you do is destroy these shells. Our thoughts shall move on to the next vessel, whenever we choose. We have superseded the old flesh that humans wore, made it redundant and irrelevant. You cannot escape the ville, and tomorrow when we meet again we shall all be wearing new faces and you will bow down to the End Program, the solution to the mess that humankind made."

"No," Ryan said, thrusting his knife into Emil's fleshy face and driving it in all the way to the hilt. Emil's face sparked with electricity and his body vibrated as though having a fit as it shut down. "We'll reprogram."

OUTSIDE, THE VARIOUS Progress creations had amassed, grouping at the edges of the ville and across the far side of the dam to block escape. When Ryan and Krysty returned to street level in the elevator, J.B. explained the problem.

"We can't get out, Ryan," the Armorer said. "They've covered every exit."

"We still have the mat-trans," Doc reminded them.

"No, they've got that covered," Ricky said from his lookout post at the doors.

"And they'd follow us if we made a break for it," J.B. added.

"We're not going to run," Ryan told them all. "Not yet. We still have work to do."

Ryan stepped out into the street, his lone eye scan-

ning the crowd of mechanical things that waited at the
edge of the ville.

"Where are we going?" Ricky asked.

"They think we'll try to walk out of here but we
won't," Ryan told him. "You don't leave a pesthole like
this intact, Ricky. That just creates more problems for
you another day."

"Then what?"

Ryan stopped before the towering steps leading up to
the dam that powered the ville. "They'll go on forever
unless we stop them."

J.B. nodded. "I see what you mean," he said, a cunning smile crossing his lips.

In a couple of minutes, the companions were standing
at one end of the high dam wall that stretched across the
Klamath River and drew power from the current. The
dam fed everything in Progress. Across the wall, they
saw an army of mechanical beasts amassing, like the
war drones that Jak and Ricky had faced but number-
ing more than a thousand. Impossible odds.

"You're surrounded," an artificial voice called out
from the control room of the hydroelectric dam. "Lay
down your weapons, surrender the future." The companions could not tell if the voice came from a person
or just the speakers of a comp, but with what they knew
now that distinction didn't really matter here anyway.

The mechanicals on the far side of the bridgelike
structure of the dam began to trundle slowly toward the
companions. More of the mechanical figures waited in
the darkness of the track leading to the cliff paths and
out to freedom, and more still trudged down the main
thoroughfare of the ville, accompanied by the human-
like robots that had given Progress the illusion of being
a normal ville.

"Phew. Guess someone's been really busy with their construction kits," Mildred said as she eyed all those mechanical figures before them.

J.B. reached into his satchel for his stash of explosives. "It's time we deconstructed," he said, handing everyone a hurriedly preset explosive charge.

From the far end of the dam and all around the ville, mechanical figures approached the companions, certain that they had them trapped. Ryan drew the Steyr Scout from his back and began to blast the closest of them, rationing his shots to hold them at bay long enough for J.B. and the others to plant the charges. It felt good to use the scope again, just trusting his own eye to locate the targets.

The cyborgs observed emotionlessly as the companions dawdled at one end of the dam. They seemed unable to process quite what the flesh-men were doing—why did they not run from the ville now they knew they were in the enclave of an army that wanted to chill them?

"Primed," J.B. said as the group finished placing charges.

Ryan fired one last shot from his longblaster before slipping it over his back once more. "Good," he said. "I was out of ammo anyhow."

"Five seconds," J.B. warned, reaching for the edge of the dam. The churning, moonlit waters of the Klamath River looked less than inviting.

J.B., Doc, Mildred, Jak and Ricky all dived from the dam.

Krysty grabbed Ryan's hand. "When was the last time we went swimming, lover?" she asked.

"You know, I don't honestly remember," Ryan said as the first explosion hit.

Fiery blossoms ignited all around them, bursting to

life along the gray line of the dam. Ryan and Krysty jumped over the side as explosions began to rock it, leaping for the water as the stone strip erupted in a violent burst of fire. They leaped hand-in-hand, a gesture enviably human in its simplicity and closeness.

THE EXPLOSIONS PETERED out after five seconds and in their place an eerie silence seemed to usher through the valley. In the water below, Ricky stared at the dam in confusion as it loomed above him, dark smoke emanating from where the explosives had been packed.

"What's happening?" Ricky asked. "It's not…did we fail?"

"Be patient," J.B. replied, straining to keep afloat as the water threatened to drag him and his weaponry down.

Then they heard a mighty crack as the dam began to split, water pressing against the tiny fractures that the explosives had created. It took a few seconds before the splits showed, first one, then another, running up the surface of the dam like streaks of black lightning, wider and wider. Then the whole thing started to break apart as water rushed through those rents, pushing them wider apart and ripping through the dam.

Chunks of stone fell from the dam, tumbling into the river. The river itself raced onward, driving the rents wider, ripping through with all the unstoppable energy of a force of nature.

"Time to get to safety," Mildred shouted over the noise of the violent cascade.

As water bled over the side of the river and out into the streets of Progress, the companions started to swim.

Chapter Thirty-Nine

Everything metal sank. Robots, cyborgs and all the metal housings that they had relied upon disappeared to the bottom of the new lake that formed where the dam had been. The towers of Progress disappeared too, a few roofs peeking from the depths of the water but most were destroyed as the great wave struck them, knocking them down like tenpins.

Doc and Mildred found a chunk of wood that had been torn from a siding and, using it as a raft, gathered the companions up while the waters continued to whirl. Eventually, the cataclysm subsided and the water began to drop again, like a basin with its plug removed.

In the aftermath, Progress was just scrappy remains, but the low entrance to the redoubt remained. That was good news—the companions did not plan to stay in the area any longer than they needed to, and having access to the redoubt and its mat-trans chamber provided an ideal path to their next location, wherever that may be.

While the others gathered their belongings and scavenged for what food and supplies had survived the deluge, Ryan took in the last of the night air, peering out on the river whose banks had burst and receded all in the space of a few hours. He stood before the ruins of the hydroelectric dam, looking out at the carnage that lay in its shadow. His head ached deep in the bones where Mildred had removed the rogue hunk of tech, and the area around his missing eye felt more raw than it had in a long time, nagging at him the way a scar would nag when the temperature plummeted.

"How are you feeling now, lover?" Krysty asked, joining Ryan at the edge of the broken walkway looking out onto the Klamath River.

Ryan turned to her, seeing her beautiful face as if for the first time, marveling at the way her red hair framed that face like a fire. Krysty started, backing away just a half step before stopping herself. Her eyes were fixed on the empty socket that was Ryan's left eye, staring into the dark secrets held in the blackness there.

"I didn't mean to frighten you," Ryan said, turning away.

"You didn't," Krysty assured him, patting her arm with her own hand. "It was just...I hadn't expected..." Her words trailed off, and the sentence and its meaning were carried away on the night wind.

For a moment, Krysty and Ryan just stood there, watching the ever-changing water of the river as it hurried past them, washing away the wreckage of the ruined dam and the ville it had once fed; washing away the evil of a deranged plan to protect a long-gone nation.

"I've just remembered," Krysty said suddenly, breaking the silence between them. Ryan turned slyly and watched as she reached into the pocket of her shirt, the space over her heart. When her hand reappeared, it held a tangle of black material and cord—Ryan's eye patch, the one he had tried to discard right here at the river's edge. "I kept this as a keepsake of the man you were. You should have it back."

Ryan took the patch and looked at it with his remaining eye, judging its weight on his open palm.

"Aren't you going to put it back on?" Krysty pressed.

"Brings home how this is a step back," he said.

"No," Krysty said. "Never that. You wore this when I fell in love with you, and that's the man you'll always be—inside, where it counts."

Ryan looked at her and smiled. "Yeah, I guess so." As he spoke, Krysty took the eye patch back from him and stepped close, wrapping the cords around his head as she kissed him.

Ryan kissed her back, remembering for a moment the photographic image he had taken of her at this very spot, her hair catching in the wind, the river racing behind her. And even without the photograph, he could still see her in his mind's eye, beautiful as she always was, an image that he could call upon whenever he wanted to. There were other images too—of his son, Dean, and his father and mother, his friends and even his cruelhearted brother, who had tried to chill him. The pictures in his mind were the story of Ryan's life, and no tech could improve that or change that or take that away from him.

"We are everything our memories retain," Ryan said softly as Krysty pulled away from the lingering kiss, the black eye patch bound once again to his head.

"There's always space to make more memories," Krysty reminded him, taking his arm and pulling him away from the river.

Together, Ryan and Krysty walked back to the mat-trans where their companions were waiting. To make new memories, and one day find a new life—a life filled with hope.

* * * * *